Sacrifices of Joy:

Book Three of the Sienna St. James Series

Sacrifices of Joy:

Book Three of the Sienna St. James Series

Leslie J. Sherrod

www.urbanchristianonline.com

Urban Books, LLC
97 N18th Street
Wyandanch, NY 11798

Sacrifices of Joy: Book Three of the Sienna St. James Series Copyright © 2014 Leslie J. Sherrod

ISBN 13: 978-1-60162-721-6
ISBN 10: 1-60162-721-1

First Trade Paperback Printing May 2014
Printed in the United States of America

10 9 8 7 6 5 4 3 2 1

This is a work of fiction. Any references or similarities to actual events, real people, living or dead, or to real locales are intended to give the novel a sense of reality. Any similarity in other names, characters, places, and incidents is entirely coincidental.

Distributed by Kensington Corp.
Submit Wholesale Orders to:
Kensington Publishing Corp.
C/O Penguin Group (USA) Inc.
Attention: Order Processing
405 Murray Hill Parkway
East Rutherford, NJ 07073-2316
Phone: 1-800-526-0275
Fax: 1-800-227-9604

Sacrifices of Joy:

Book Three of the Sienna St. James Series

by

Leslie J. Sherrod

Once I was bitter and brokenhearted.

—Psalms 73:21

Acknowledgments

Whew! (Can I say that out loud?) It takes a lot of work to write novels—a lot of work, late nights, shortcut dinners, and support! I am grateful for having family, friends, readers, and others who provide me with the resources and support I've needed to keep writing. I am most thankful to God for being a constant source of inspiration and energy as I write for Him. My prayer has always been and will continue to be that He gets the most glory!

Special thanks to my husband and children who continually allow me space and time to write. I am forever grateful for Brian's artwork, Neyla's "big sister" helping hands, Nathan's encouragement, and Niara's hugs. I've needed everything you've provided. Also, thank you Mom and Dad, Jocelyn, Joanna, Daniel II, Ms. LaVerne, Jenae, and Marcus and the rest of the Datchers, Coles, and Sherrods for all of your love and support. I have an awesome extended family, including cousins, aunts, uncles, and more, who continue to stand with me in my writing dreams. Thank you.

Continued thanks to my church family. Your eagerness and encouragement help sustain me. Thanks to my friends Angela, Carla, and Charese for your pep talks, pep texts, and powerful prayers. I'm grateful for other authors who have given me support and true encouragement, including MaRita Teague, Yolonda Tonette Sanders, Tiffany L. Warren, and Victoria Christopher Murray. Thanks to my

Acknowledgments

coworkers, past and present, who've been supportive of my writing efforts. Really, there are many other names I could add here. Thanks to you all!

Here's a big thank-you to the inspiring Joylynn Ross and the Urban Christian family for ensuring that our stories make it to the marketplace. Thanks also to my agent, Sha-Shana Crichton, for all you do. I am grateful for all the promoters, reviewers, interviewers, bloggers, and bookstore managers who have allowed a platform for the Sienna St. James series to thrive.

Readers: This book would not exist if it were not for you. Thank you for supporting this series. I hope you enjoy reading about the exploits and adventures of Sienna St. James as much as I have been enjoying writing about her. Thank you!!!!

Chapter 1

1,067 days.

152 weeks.

25,612 hours.

92,203,200 seconds.

No matter which way you calculated it, that's how long it had been since I'd seen or spoken to Leon Sanderson.

He'd left on a Wednesday in May, three years ago next month, his truck piled high with all his earthly belongings, mostly clothes and kitchen gadgets. His long-lost niece sat smiling in the passenger seat, her infant daughter strapped down in the back. I'd cancelled my clients' appointments to be there to see him off and had baked some homemade chocolate chip cookies for them to take on the twenty-three hour drive to Houston.

Of course my cookies didn't taste as sweet as the ones he'd made for me during our two-year non-relationship.

The "non" part was my fault.

He'd wanted more, but I had not gotten myself together in time; hadn't gotten myself over the absence of RiChard.

RiChard.

Even now, the mere thought of my estranged, missing liar of a husband brought such a violent reaction to my body, I shuddered in my seat. The cold, hard plastic in which I sat at the moment fit more than me and my carry-on. It fit my mood.

"We'll be boarding for flight 109 to sunny San Diego in about fifteen minutes. Please have your boarding passes ready." The scratchy voice through the airport intercom did little to soothe my nerves.

I'd been dreading this day since I'd received the message last week from Roman. A bad, sick feeling lurked in the walls and corners of my stomach as I imagined anew the potential reasons behind his request.

What is Roman up to? He had just been home not long ago for spring break and the semester ended next month. I had not called back to ask my son any questions when he'd left a message for me last Friday, asking—no, begging—me to come out to see him today. And today only, he'd directed. Not before, not after. And to bring his mola blanket.

Nineteen years old, in college, and still a big baby.

I wanted to smile, but my nerves wouldn't let me. Too many other emotions whirled inside of me like chunky vegetables in a blender on pulse mode.

Sick to my stomach. That's what I felt. The sausage and egg sandwich I'd eaten on the way to the airport didn't help.

"You look like you're deep in thought." A man, a young white man, of about twenty-four or twenty-five years old studied me from the seat facing mine.

And you look like you need to mind your business, I wanted to say, but I put on a polite smile instead. I was off, I knew it. I was not in a mood for conversation. Looking away, I started digging through my purse and then pulled out my cell phone. I dialed my voice mail for the umpteenth time that morning and listened to Roman's message again. I felt the same wave of fear, worry, and nausea that had overtaken me the first time I'd heard it.

"Ma, I need you to come out here on Saturday."

It was a normal request, a casual demand.

But Roman's college was in San Diego and I lived on the East Coast in Baltimore. He'd stopped returning my calls during the fall semester and was supposed to be coming home for summer break in a matter of weeks. Why the urgent need for me to come out now? Why no explanation? And why had he been avoiding me?

1,067 days.

152 weeks.

Three years.

When I could not figure out anything else, I could calculate my sorrow. Leon's absence from my life was measurable.

He had not called.

I had not called him.

A flight to Houston began boarding at the next gate. My mind jumped into daydream mode as I imagined flying there instead of to San Diego; but my stomach twisted in knots. What if Leon wasn't even in Houston anymore? What if he was back in Baltimore? The thought horrified me, what it would mean; what was already meant?

The flight to San Diego was due to start boarding in half an hour. Maybe I had time to grab a soda to settle my stomach, settle my nerves; but I was flying solo and I did not feel like lugging my bag around or risk losing my seat by the gate window.

I needed the window to see what was going on around me.

I needed to know what was going on.

I listened to Roman's message on my voice mail one last time before shutting my phone off completely and squeezing my eyes shut. *Everything is okay,* I assured myself, fully aware of the reasons behind my fears.

I'd initially dropped out of college my freshman year to follow my first love, RiChard, around the world. My son, Roman, was finishing up his own freshman year with eager plans to study abroad in the fall, so I did not have to hold on to the worry that he was about to drop out like I had. And he'd given up the idea of searching for his father a few years ago, satisfied with the family connection he'd made with his half brother in California.

They were roommates at the same university.

I squeezed my eyes even tighter, as if that would shut out the searing pain that burned at the thought of Croix and the other three siblings who were evidence of RiChard's double life.

"I did not know you were still married. I did not know he had given you a son. I am so sorry. RiChard lied to all of us." The children's mother, Mbali, had blinked at me with beautiful, innocent eyes. Yes, RiChard had built a legacy of lies. He'd lied about his friend Kisu's death and the actions he'd taken to purportedly avenge it. He'd lied about his travels throughout the world over the course of Roman's life.

He'd lied and told me he loved me.

I never imagined that I'd ever hate someone, but there was no denying the feeling that came to me at the thought, the memories. The lies, the deception.

Hate.

As much as I wanted to push it away, as much as I wanted to cling to the love that's supposed to characterize a child of God, I knew that hate was the only thing pumping out of my heart, flowing through my veins, energizing my muscles, infiltrating my mind. Hatred of RiChard. Hatred of myself for allowing what he had done to me.

"Ma'am, are you okay?"

The voice startled me, brought me back. I opened my eyes and gave another assuring smile to the young man who sat across from me.

"I'm fine. Thanks. Just tired." That had become my answer over the past couple of years or so when anyone asked me what was wrong. Laz Tyson, the supposed new man in my life, had taken to asking me that question nearly every day. He didn't know that he was part of the problem.

One issue at at a time, I reminded myself, forcing my thoughts away from Laz and his never-ending drama and back to Roman and why he had me flying across the country with no explanation. *I never should have gotten myself tied to a diva.* That's what Laz was. A diva in a fedora hat.

The young man sitting across from me still stared. His eyes were a clear, bright shade of blue, like translucent crystals. His golden blond hair was short and slightly wavy, trimmed perfectly as if he had just gotten out of a barber's chair.

"Traveling to San Diego for business or pleasure?" His smile was gorgeous with deep double dimples. Hollywood. Vegas. There was charm, confidence, masculinity to his mannerisms. The quality of his short-sleeved light blue polo shirt and tan chinos spoke to old money, prep school, Wall Street. Wealth.

"I'm not sure yet." I exhaled. An honest answer. "What about you?"

He looked away, didn't answer. Deep thought flooded his face and took away his dimple.

I'd never dated a white man.

RiChard, my missing, estranged husband (*should I even call him that?*) had sometimes been mistaken as a well-tanned one. His mother was Italian, but his father was from the French Caribbean, making him the perfect blend of chocolate liqueur and vanilla bean. His thick black curls had nearly covered his peridot-green eyes. He'd had the longest possible eyelashes that I had ever seen on a man.

Roman favored his father, and at nineteen years old, I knew I'd be naïve to think he wasn't getting the attention of some California girl on his campus.

My face grimaced at the thought.

That was my baby, and I didn't want some fast-moving trick of a girl to get him off track from his international business degree and his plans to become the founder of a global conglomerate. That was his stated dream. And he was going to reach it.

I'd sacrificed too much for him not to. I'd worked my way from college dropout to a mental health clinic owner with a master's degree, all to take care of his behind.

And to make my life make sense to me.

"There you go, looking upset again." The man across from me smiled again. He looked like he was in his late twenties, not early, I decided.

Still way too young for me. 'Bout ten years too young. However, the intrigue of flirting with a stranger who I would never see again was enough of a distraction to keep my stomach from bending back into pretzel shapes.

"You like to study people." I smiled back. "Is that a hobby for you, or something you need to do to stay one step ahead of it all?" Okay, I was bad at flirting. Even when I tried to keep it light and easy, the therapist in me always found a way to pop out its psychoanalytical head. He caught on to the seriousness of my question. I could tell because his smile slightly dimmed.

Slightly.

"To say that I'm trying to stay a step ahead implies that we're all moving, and moving forward at that. That's a huge assumption." His voice was suddenly flat, monotone.

"You majored in philosophy at your Ivy League school." I took a chance.

"Theology." He narrowed his eyes. "And I went to a state college."

"Theology? A man of the cloth. I didn't see that coming." I raised an eyebrow, pretending to be interested.

"No. I'm no man of anyone's cloth. I'm an atheist. Not really an atheist. I don't believe in belief itself. Atheists believe that they are right."

A door was opening with him that I did not want to enter.

I just wanted to get on the plane to San Diego and find out why my son wanted me there a few weeks before the end of the semester. I'd wandered through mental mine-fields before and knew that I needed to step carefully to avoid explosion.

"The state school was against your parents' wishes," I pried gingerly. "They wanted you to go to some big-name university with a six-figure price tag and you did other-wise to prove a point to them, to yourself, to anyone who cared to pay attention." I was telling my sister's story, I knew—the upper-class version of it, anyway.

My sister, Yvette, was in a whole different league when it came to proving a point.

The man in the seat relaxed. He believed that I was on his side, or at least was trying to understand him, I reasoned.

"My life is a lot more complicated than that." His eyes bore through mine as he spoke.

I believed him. There was a level of complexity to the tone of his voice, to the blank stare of his blue eyes that told me that I had dug enough into this stranger's life, had sampled enough of his world to get that there were parts to this man's soul, stages of this man's history nobody would ever fully comprehend. I didn't like his flavor. His last statement would normally be the opening lines of someone who was just starting to tell their story, but I knew that he had no intention of telling me more about his complicated life.

I settled back into my seat, pulled my cell phone back out, fought the urge to turn it back on to listen to Roman's message one more time. There was nothing else for us to talk about, but apparently he thought differently.

"You're a therapist."

Did I have the word written on my forehead? Was there a sign on my person that let him know I was in the business of mental healing?

"I'm a social worker by training." I wanted to leave it at that, without explaining that yes, I was a clinical social worker with a private practice that had taken off unusually well following a shaky start in a chlorine-smelling, frayed carpet–looking, cheap-lease, and flickering-lights office building. I'd moved up to a bigger and better office space since and my current clinic offered tranquil views of woodlands and rolling hills in the Dulaney Valley area of Baltimore County.

But I had no interest in telling him all that.

"That's your center, isn't it?" He pointed to the tote bag leaning against my foot.

THE WHOLE SOUL CENTER, SIENNA ST. JAMES, LCSW-C, FOUNDER & CEO was written in gold letters on the maroon bag.

I guess I did have a sign on me.

"Yes, that's me." I gave a weak smile, trying to figure out how to straddle the ethical fine line between providing needed services and shooing away a potential new client who made me feel unusually uncomfortable.

"Do you have a card?" His smile was completely gone. His blue eyes, which before reminded me of precious gems, now felt and looked as cold and hard as ice crystals.

"Sure." I plastered on a smile big enough for the both of us and fished through my bag until I found one of the business cards I'd proudly designed myself. My artistic abilities had expanded into the graphic design realm and I was pretty darn good at it, if I said so myself. "Here." I extended the card toward him.

He did not budge or reach for it. "I did not say that I wanted your card. I just asked if you had one."

As I tried to figure out how to respond, he stood to his feet, glanced out the terminal window. He pulled out a cell phone, held it up like he was taking a picture. *A selfie?* I wondered as he appeared to have the lens pointed backward. I could see myself and my bags on the corner of his screen.

"It's a pretty nice day for a flight." He turned back toward me with a smile. Whatever iciness had been in his eyes moments earlier had thawed back into bright, sunny blue. "Have a nice trip." He turned to leave.

"Wait," I blurted. "They are about to start calling rows to board. You're not going?"

"Naw, not to San Diego." He shook his head, a distant look on his face. "I'm heading out to Chicago this morning." He pointed to a nearby gate. "I just wanted to sit next to the window over here for a moment. I like to know what's going on around me, same as you." He winked. He turned to leave, but then abruptly doubled back. "Actually, I do want your card. It might come in handy."

My stomach wrapped into tighter knots as he took the card from my fingertips and thrust it deep into his pockets.

"Do . . . do you have a card?" What was I supposed to say?

"You'll know my name soon enough." He walked away and settled into a seat at the opposite gate.

I was missing something about him. I felt it. Knew it.

My flight was halfway across the country over green and brown patches of farmland when the plane became a flurry of worried whispers and then full-blown chatter. Someone who had not shut off a cell phone as required had gotten word.

A bomb had exploded at Baltimore/Washington Airport.

That's all anyone knew. No further information was available.

A bomb.

A bomb!

I've learned through the years to trust my gut and, despite the lack of information and evidence otherwise, there was only one message my gut was telling me at the moment.

That man I talked to had something to do with the bombing, everything in me screamed.

And he had my business card in his pocket.

Chapter 2

I'd come face to face with a terrorist.

The thought ran over and under and through my mind as I prayed and hoped that it was not true. *Lord, please let my gut feelings be wrong just this once!* I could see those piercing eyes, feel the chill that had gone through me when he'd said that I would know his name soon enough. What was I supposed to do? All I had was a hunch, no more. I was moving, breathing, thinking on autopilot. A familiar voice jolted me back to awareness.

"Mom!" Roman half cried in horror, half shouted in glee as he tackled me just outside the baggage claim area at San Diego International Airport. "I couldn't get through to your cell and I didn't know your flight number or if you were near that explosion back in Baltimore. I heard about what happened. I'm glad you're okay."

The knots in my stomach had quadrupled. I felt dizzy, weak, and queasy in my intestines.

God, what is going to happen next? My entire body, inside and out, quivered.

"I know you're tired after all that waiting." He pointed back to the lines; everyone who'd flown in from Baltimore had to wait through to have their luggage and IDs rechecked, an extra precaution among many extra precautions that were in play at airports across the country.

Yet again, America was on lockdown.

And this time I had been close—too close—to the scene of destruction. I heard myself think of the threat toward my safety in the past tense, feeling, knowing, that the danger I felt was still very present.

Tired did not even begin to explain my emotional state.

I was not ready to ask if Roman knew if there had been any casualties.

Or if the perpetrator had been identified.

I shut my eyes, seeing again those icy blue ones that had pierced mine mere hours ago. I had no proof and no sane reason to think that young blond male had a role in it. We'd only talked for a few moments and the conversation had made me uncomfortable. Nothing about our exchange pointed to "terrorist," but everything in me screamed that I'd missed something.

"This way, Ma."

I tried to hide my shaking as I followed Roman to a short-term parking lot. He stopped and unlocked an older-model blue Mazda.

"So you went with the hatchback you told me about?" I collapsed into the front seat, trying to make life seem normal.

The immediate consequences of a terrorist attack: normalcy goes out the window. Roman played along.

"Yeah." He nodded. "It has a lot of miles on it, but the price was right. I'm saving up the rest of my money to send you and Ms. Ava on a Mediterranean cruise next year."

Ava Diggs. She was my mentor, my career coach and my former supervisor before she'd retired a few years back. I had not talked to her in a while. As much as she had been a cheerleader for me, I guess she'd also had an impact on my son's life as well.

Leon had an impact on him, too. I swallowed hard, fighting to stay afloat in the churning sea of emotions that were threatening to take me under.

"A cruise? Yeah, right." I managed to let out a small laugh. "You know full well that I would not expect or accept such a gift from you."

"You deserve it. Plus, you'll be turning forty."

"Don't remind me."

God, please don't let there be any victims. My mind was still at the airport in Baltimore, my heart in panic mode. *God, please be with everyone who is in the disaster zone right now!*

I felt like an agitator in a washing machine, spinning around in prayers, worry, and angst that my gut was right.

"Put your phone down, Ma." Roman did not look over at me as he drove, but he knew exactly what I was doing as I reached for my smart phone. I was ready to finally look at the news reports, ready to get the gory details, ready to feel the shared national pain.

Ready to confirm my horrific suspicions.

"Don't deal with it just yet, Ma. You can't change anything. You can't fix it. Let's just get through this evening, and then you can figure out how to heal the world."

I did not miss the bitter note in my son's tone.

I also did not fully understand it.

It took all I had in me, but I turned my phone off. He was right, I guess. I could not change anything that had happened. I would only sink into a sick despair when I got the details, which I would read and watch, and read and watch over again. And, though Roman didn't know my fears about my possible interaction with the suspect, my son would probably think I was overreacting, overreaching in my suspicions. Just hearing myself think that, *possible interaction with the suspect,* sounded ridiculous. Here I was a therapist, having grand delusions and panic attacks over a suspicion that was not even logical. I didn't even know what part of the airport had been targeted. I had suspicions about a stranger I met at a gate, and the explosion could have been anywhere at the airport: the baggage claim, a dining area, maybe even on a plane taxiing down a runway. I needed to take the suggestions I gave to my many clients, and exhale and relax.

After making sure my phone was completely off, I pushed it into the bottom of my purse. I tried to tell my shoulders to ease down, even if just for a few moments, but the swirling taste of bile in my mouth made it hard for my muscles to feel anything less than tense.

"So." I exhaled, determined to ignore all that I felt. "Why am I here? Why did you want me to come today? Where are we going and why do you need the mola blanket?"

When he didn't respond immediately and instead started licking his lips, I knew I was not going to like any of his answers. We drove for ten minutes in complete silence, and then I could take no more.

"Well?"

He'd stopped licking his lips.

"It's my sister's birthday. She is turning sixteen and having a party. I wanted you to come."

Really? His sister? This is why I came all the way to the West Coast? Just hearing him even acknowledge that he had a sister felt like a stab wound to my heart. It was hard enough knowing that he and his half brother Croix were roommates. I had helped Roman move into his dorm last fall before Croix arrived with his mother, Mbali, his sister, and twin little brothers.

I'd only met them all that one time at the airport when Roman ran away at age sixteen. He'd been determined to find RiChard but found the truth and them instead.

"You wanted me to come all the way out here for a . . . sweet sixteen party? I don't even remember her name,"

I lied, "and I doubt that she would want the other *other* woman who was also married to her father at her party."

Absolutely ridiculous.

There was much more I wanted to say, especially as I had changed my week around and flown out to the other side of the country at his request. And for a birthday party for a girl I barely knew?

And didn't really want to know?

I held my tongue, trying to understand Roman's reasoning.

"Mom." Roman's voice was barely audible. "What Dad did was real. He lied to all of us; he lied to them just like he lied to the two of us. Mbali, Croix, Abigail, Denzi, and Dillon are not liars. They are not responsible for what happened. They were betrayed just like we were. We all have to come together, Mom, so that we can all move forward. They are real, and they are a part of my life. They are my sister, my brothers, my blood."

His last line had all the markings of Mbali. I was sure I had read those exact words from her in a Christmas card she'd mailed to us two years ago. I didn't mail out any Christmas cards last year on account of the one she'd sent. It was easier to say I had not sent greetings to anyone than to feel like I had singled her out on purpose.

At heart, I knew Roman was right; but at heart, I also knew I was not ready.

"Mom, you have to do this." Roman's voice, still low, was firm.

"This isn't a good day. This isn't the right time." I shook my head.

"You're right. It isn't," he agreed as he parallel parked in front of a cupcake bakery. "Because of the terrorist attack, Abigail wanted to cancel the party, but her mother already booked and paid for the party room here. She scaled it back to a small event. It's only going to be us—family—and a couple of her closest friends. We're just going to sing 'Happy Birthday' and eat. That's it, Ma. You can handle this."

He hopped out of the car and headed to the colorfully canopied cupcakery entrance, leaving me alone for a moment to reflect on his words.

Over the past few years, I'd handled a lot. I'd helped a foster child who'd claimed to have a sister nobody said existed. I'd helped authorities find the perpetrator behind a series of unsolved murders. I'd lost and found my only child, survived an attack from an enraged drug addict in an abandoned house, talked my way out of certain death at an off-road creek at the hands of a desperate woman. I'd helped bring healing to broken relationships and answers to difficult questions, though I had often not been able to find those same things for myself.

You can handle this.

Sing 'Happy Birthday' to a sixteen-year-old. With RiChard's other family.

Address the horror I feel about a too-close-for-comfort terrorist attack. And make sense of my fears that I'd met the suspect.

Maybe I could handle it, but, honestly, I did not want to.

"Roman," I called after him just before he disappeared inside. I shook my head, gave a weak smile, shrugged my shoulders. "I . . . I'm going to find her a gift first."

He knew I had no intention of joining them and accepted with a slow, slight nod the excuse I'd given him to give all of them. He went inside.

I studied the busy street around me. I had to get away. Sit down. Breathe. Turn my phone back on. Find out the outcome of the tragedy back home. Laugh at myself for being paranoid about the suspect.

I realized my fear that I was right about the man back at the airport was what had really kept me up to this point from following the breaking news. Would the authorities be contacting me? *Should I be contacting them?* Leon would have helped me figure out what to do.

Too much for a Saturday afternoon.

I gave one last look at the cupcakery before heading down the street to an electronic store. Several people stared at flat-screen televisions displayed in the window.

It was time for me to find out if my gut had been right, though I was not sure what, if anything, I was supposed to do if it was.

Chapter 3

"She'd flown into town just to see me off to my prom." A teenage boy wept in front of the camera. "Here's a picture of me with my grandmother just yesterday." He held up a photo of himself dressed up in a dapper white tuxedo and standing next to a woman who reminded me of the late, great Lena Horne: bright smile, sophistication, and all.

Along with the sixty-one-year-old grandmother, there had been seventeen other casualties from the explosion at the airport. A man, a woman, and their eight-year-old son. The trio had been on their way to their private villa on a remote island in the Caribbean. A businessman from Tokyo. A newlywed couple returning from their honeymoon. Eight members of a college men's lacrosse team. Two flight attendants headed to their assigned gates. A custodian who friends and family members kept referring to as "Old Joe." Thirty-four other people were injured, ranging in age from nine to eighty-three, and they were in various conditions, from fair to critical, at area hospitals.

I forced myself to take deep breaths, to not collapse into the grief, anger, and shock that had become my usual mix of emotions when watching disaster coverage on television.

But another emotion, one that I had not had before when following such stories, swirled along with the others.

Dread.

The idea, the remote possibility that my suspicions were correct and that the man who I'd spoken with at the airport had something to do with this tragedy was enough to make me want to curl up, hide, and vomit. I had no firm reason to believe that he was, but his bizarre conversation and behavior, and the haunting memory of his last words, would not shake me:

"You'll know my name soon enough."

"Police have a suspect in custody but are not yet releasing any details of his identity or condition." A news reporter spoke solemnly into the camera. "A press conference will happen soon. That is all we are being told."

I still had to wait to find out if my fears were correct, although I still wasn't sure what I was supposed to do if they were.

Leon would have known.

It was a fleeting thought, a blurry vision of Leon in his police uniform. I wondered if he'd joined the force in Houston after he'd left Baltimore. When we first met him years ago, he worked at a community center as part of the Police Athletic League, serving as a mentor to many, a father figure to my son. Perhaps, he'd found a human services position in Houston working with other young people and had become consumed with helping them.

It was the only reason I could think of as to why he had not contacted at least Roman.

"Ma'am, we're about to close." The voice to my left startled me. An Asian man with long gray hair and a long gray beard to match brought me back to reality. The crowd that had gathered to watch the news coverage had dissipated and the flat-screen televisions were blinking off, one by one. "I'm leaving early today. Nobody's buying TVs, just watching them. I might as well do the same."

"Tragic. For the whole country, but especially for the families involved," were the only words I could get out.

The man nodded and mumbled some expletive about terrorists as he reentered his shop with a large set of jingling keys.

What now?

A café with outdoor seating was farther down the street. If I sat there, I would be able to see Roman come out of the cupcakery when the party ended, and I would have a chance to finally study the news on my phone. Now that I knew there were casualties, I needed to read all about them, see their pictures, learn more about their lives.

Let it all be real.

I knew from unfortunate practice that this was my healing routine when it came to such matters.

Giving honor to the lives and legacies of those lost.

I looked behind me to make sure that Roman was not already coming, and then turned toward the café, digging for my phone in my tote bag as I walked. I turned it on just before heading inside to order a quick bite, knowing that it would take a few moments for the news apps on my phone to fully upload. The food was just to have the right to sit at a table.

I had no appetite.

Chapter 4

LA BOHEMIA. I read the sign and stepped into the dimly lit café. All of my senses found a warm welcome. Orange beaded chandeliers dripped from the high ceilings, and bright-colored patterned tablecloths covered wooden tables. A white man with long blond and silver dreadlocks played a guitar from a small stage in the rear. The entire place smelled like Mediterranean and Indian spices, cinnamon, vanilla, and mint, a combination I assumed came from both the kitchen and the scented candles that dotted the otherwise rustic interior.

As the man strummed his guitar and sang a song about grief, love, and protest, I settled into a high-backed chair in the corner, away from the nine or ten patrons who nodded along to the music.

Roman could reach me by phone when he was ready, I decided, no need for me to sit outside. The vibe of the café felt safe to me. I needed a healing zone.

Without me asking for it, a brown girl with a pretty, red Angela Davis–sized curly 'fro set a small porcelain cup of hot tea and a plate of ginger-apricot scones in front of me.

"Welcome. This is on the house." She smiled. "Relax for a change," she directed as if she knew me, knew the stress, strain, and anguish that tormented my soul. Her name was Skyye, I read from her crocheted name badge. Although her skin was brown and her hair was a mass of spirals and coils, something about her features spoke to a multi-mixed lineage. I would not have been surprised if she told me that she was Jewish, Native American, Ethiopian, and Irish all in one.

As she stepped away, I dumped the entire cup of hot tea down my throat like it was a shot of liquor and immediately felt calm, loose, and tranquil.

And guilty.

My son had wanted me out here. Called me all the way from San Diego to join him and his siblings for a family event.

But they weren't family to me.

I hated RiChard and everything attached to him. Everything he did, everything he stood for was like daggers, dungeons, and death to me. Like the blast that happened in Baltimore, RiChard's crimes had innocent victims. My feelings toward Mbali and her children were not my fault.

How could I ever be healed from this pain?

Roman talked about moving forward, and I was glad that he had found a path to do so for himself. I needed to find my own way.

And I just didn't think a sweet sixteen party was it. Roman would simply have to understand.

The waitress set another teacup in front of me and I threw down a second shot of it, hoping the warm liquid that had hints of chamomile and lemon would wash away the growing pangs of guilt I felt.

I was disappointing my son.

A series of pings, dings, buzzes, and beeps sounded from deep inside my bag. My phone was fully on, updated, and informing me of various notifications. Before I reached for the lifeline that connected me to the rest of the world, I motioned for Skyye to come back to my table one more time.

"Do you sell anything here that a sixteen-year-old girl would like?" I had to at least make an attempt to assuage my guilt, placate my son. I had no idea what a café would offer other than food, but the ambiance of the place gave the impression that they wanted their customers to leave with more than a full stomach.

"I know just the thing." Skyye beamed and then disappeared behind a doorway covered with strands of orange beads.

I took a deep breath and took out my phone.

I'd missed six calls, five of them from Laz Tyson. There were two messages waiting, one from Laz and the other from a phone number I did not recognize, my visual voice mail app informed me. I didn't even recognize the area code of the second message. *Is that a Houston exchange?* I forced myself to breathe, and knew that I would be checking that message last.

What did it mean, this constant hope upon hope that Leon was somewhere thinking about me? That he would suddenly call me? It had been three years since we last talked. Three years of complete silence from him. What exactly was I hoping for?

He'd moved on.

And I'd given him the green light to do so. I had not moved fast enough to get the answers, the truth about RiChard.

I would come back to the message from the unknown caller. I listened to Laz's message first as planned.

"Sienna, please call me and tell me you are okay. I know you were flying out of BWI this morning and I haven't heard from you all day. I'm in DC covering the story with the help of one of my sources in Homeland Security. Please call me as soon as you get this message!"

Laz Tyson. An outspoken, controversial journalist who'd found his way back into the national spotlight following his coverage of my son's disappearance a few years ago. He was a member of my old church and, after Leon left for Houston, a frequent attendee of my mother's

Sunday dinners. Somewhere along the line, he started introducing me to his friends and colleagues as his girlfriend, a term I hated, but never corrected. For one, calling me his girlfriend made both my mother and Ava stop asking me painful questions about Leon, and, two, I don't think Laz would have heard my protests anyway.

Our "relationship" consisted mainly of him filling me in on his latest news stories; me showing him my latest art project, which he would critique; and us spending time at museums and cultural events on the increasingly fewer weekends he was actually in Baltimore.

It was a courtship of convenience more so than comfort. He needed a constant audience and I needed a continual noisemaker that could drown out the deep moaning of my heart.

Admittedly, I was kind of touched that he cared enough to leave me a message on a day of breaking news, the kind of day he lived for. But then again, I guess a man should at a minimum check to make sure that his "girlfriend" was alive following a terrorist attack that occurred at her last known location.

I dialed him right back. I had my own reasons to check in with him. With all of his DC connections, perhaps he had some knowledge about the suspect in custody. It was time to put my paranoia to rest.

He answered on the first ring. "Sienna?" he asked, sounding out of breath.

"Laz."

"Good, you're alive. I gotta go. The press conference is starting."

Silence. He'd hung up.

I could have gotten offended by the brevity of our conversation, but I accepted him for who he was and what had his focus. That's probably why we had made it together for so long. I didn't care that I didn't have his heart and he didn't notice that he didn't have mine.

I took a bite of the ginger-apricot scone. Warm, buttery, sweet, and spicy, it was just enough of a kick to help me do what I had to do next. I pulled up my CNN app. Laz's words had been few, but just enough to let me know that it was time to view the suspect. Finally. I felt faint, woozy. I took another bite of the scone to settle my stomach. The press conference was beginning; the breaking news alert on my phone buzzed.

"Here it is, the perfect gift."

"Huh?" My head swung up, confused.

"For a teenage girl? You asked?" The waitress, Skyye, was at my table, a huge smile on her face, and a masterfully crafted crocheted purse in her outstretched hand. Bright orange, it had a couple of crocheted flowers in a cheery shade of yellow attached to it with wooden buttons. The word "Joy" was woven into the front and the letters J and Y also served as elaborate swirling stems for the woven buds.

"That's beautiful. You made that?" I noticed anew her crocheted name tag. A few years ago, when I worked with a treatment foster care agency, I'd been forced to find something nice to say about a foster mother's faceless crocheted dolls. They were downright creepy. What Skyye had in her hand was the complete opposite. I was awed by the simple beauty of her complex craftsmanship.

"If you don't like this, I have other crocheted items you can view. Earrings, hats, maxi dresses, trinket boxes—but this is my favorite. I've been waiting to show it to the right person. It's—"

"Perfect. I'll get it. How much?" I interrupted, not just because I wanted to get to the news conference, but because I really did not need further convincing.

"I can't price it. Give me what you want, okay? I will wrap it for you. I have a pretty gift bag and tissue paper in the back that goes with it." She disappeared again.

Her presence was one of pureness, I realized as I sat at the table alone again. Strength, love, authenticity, and, yes, joy. Though I only knew her first name and her present occupation, the essence of her personality and character had shown through immediately.

I guess everyone has their own aura that can't be hidden. We call it first impressions, but what we really pick up when we meet someone is their distinct impact on the atmosphere. As I started tinkering with the buttons and notifications on my phone again, I thought of the man at the airport, understanding better now my suspicions.

I'd only been around him for a few minutes, but the aura he'd given off was that of an intense and secretive darkness.

What impact do I have on the atmosphere around me? A fleeting thought. I blocked it out as I imagined Roman and his siblings sitting in a cupcake bakery without me, left to wonder about who I really was, how I really felt. One's presence can carry an aura, but so too can one's absence, I concluded, thinking of RiChard, of Leon.

AUTHORITIES HAVE IDENTIFIED THE SUSPECT.

I clicked immediately on the headline that chirped on my phone and read the short article that followed.

Officials are reporting that one of the injured in the blast is also the instigator. A thirty-two-year-old biomedical engineer from the Northern Virginia area, Jamal Abdul, is being held at an undisclosed hospital in the DC corridor as he recovers from extensive injuries. We are told that he is in serious but stable condition in a medically induced coma and will face multiple charges upon his return to consciousness. Authorities are now holding him on undisclosed charges, and are also interviewing his wife and two young daughters, who were also at the airport at the time of the blast.

"Huh?" Something did not register with me as I tried to reconcile the man I'd met at my gate with the description of the suspect being held. I didn't get the feeling that the man I'd talked to was there with family.

PICTURE RELEASED.

The press conference was actively being held, I realized as another headline popped up on my phone. I clicked on it immediately and gasped at the picture of the man authorities were calling the sole suspect.

He was the color of polished bronze, wearing a charcoal gray suit in the file photo. I couldn't tell where the formal picture had been taken—other faces surrounding him had been blurred out—but he looked like he was having a good time wherever he was. A huge smile took up half of his face and his eyes nearly sparkled at the camera.

Wide nose, full lips, closely cropped hair.

A black man with an Islamic name.

"No, this can't be right." Everything in me felt unsettled. My heart, which had already been racing, picked up a few extra beats as I tried to make sense out of the photo and my gut feelings.

"Here you go." Skyye was back at the table, a calming presence in my current chaos. "I wrapped it up and put it in this gift bag," she announced with pride as she passed me a yellow paper bag adorned with a copper sunburst made out of rhinestones and glitter. "Here's my business card if you need any more gift ideas in the future, and here's a brochure with more info about our café, including upcoming events we're hosting."

She laid the card for Skyye is the Limit Crafts and the brochure for La Bohemia Café on the table and then headed toward the small crowd that was transfixed by the guitar player. He was playing a number that made me think of brightly colored flamenco dancers, though the words to his melody spoke to the sorrow, the tragedy that enveloped the nation. "This is a celebration of light," he sang into the microphone. "Light is always stronger than darkness. Life and light will always win."

I looked back down at my phone, wondering why I felt *more* disturbed after seeing the photo of the held suspect than I'd felt before I'd viewed it.

My gut was rarely wrong.

But the authorities know what they are doing. I shook my head at myself, remembering that I had to be logical in my thoughts, regardless of what my emotions shouted. I was just a woman at the airport, a passenger waiting for a plane, who had a brief conversation with a complete stranger who'd rubbed me the wrong way. The authorities of Homeland Security, the FBI, the CIA, the NSA, or whoever handled such matters had the expertise and the knowledge to know that they had the right man.

But the feeling in the pit of my stomach wasn't an emotion; it felt more like a knowing.

"Enough, Sienna," I whispered to myself. They had the man who did it. All I could do now was pray for the families, pray for the country, and be on the side of healing. What could I do otherwise?

As I reached for the off button on my phone and considered what I would have done if the picture of the suspect had been different, I thought of Leon.

There had been a second voice mail message, I recalled.

I pulled up the message from the unknown area code and held my breath as I pressed play.

"Hello, Sienna St. James."

It wasn't Leon. My heart deflated, but then nearly stopped as I listened to the rest of the message.

"I met you in the airport a couple of hours ago. I want to set up an appointment to talk with you about some matters that are important to me. I know you take great pride in calling yourself a therapist, and that as a therapist you will have to come up with some trivial diagnosis to bill my insurance company to justify the time of our meeting. Well, I am not interested in a diagnosis. I only want a conversation, and I will pay you the going rate of a conversation so that you will not have to submit any billing claims to my insurance company, but still have the necessary funds you require. I noticed on the printed travel itinerary that you had sticking out of your tote bag that you are returning to Baltimore Sunday evening. I will call you back at that time to schedule our conversation. I hope you are enjoying San Diego."

That man saw my travel itinerary? I recalled the snapshot he'd seemed to have taken with his phone when he'd stood by the window. My bags and I had been in the corner of his camera screen and I knew that it was easy to zoom in on digital images. How else would he have seen the tiny print of my travel itinerary in my bag?

It was a scary thought. My face on his phone. My card in his pocket. The chill that his eyes carried. Had he left the message before or after the blast, I wondered. And what would it mean either way?

My imagination was getting the best of me.

Delete? Save? My thumb hung over the two options on my phone as I debated what to do with his message. I wanted no part of this man. Didn't want him in my office. Didn't even want him in my voice mailbox. Did I have to call him back? Was I obligated to answer if he called again?

What area code was his phone calling from anyway?
740.

A quick Internet search on my smart phone revealed the number had roots in a large swath of Ohio.

I need to write this down, I decided, feeling a sudden compulsion to note any- and everything that this man said or did. I grabbed a pen from a side pocket of my purse and turned over the brochure that Skyye had left on the table so I could write on it.

I prepared to write, "740=southeastern and central Ohio," but my pen froze midsentence.

The back of the La Bohemia Café brochure featured an event calendar. On the evening of April 16, five days from now, the Monthly Lecture Series of La Bohemia Café had a special guest coming to talk about "The Political Meaning of Identity, War, and Revolution." It wasn't the name of the seminar that stopped me in my tracks. It was the presenter.

The speaker's name was Kisu Felokwakhe.

Chapter 5

For years, I could not recall his last name, but I had no doubts, no questions, no confusion when I saw it on the event list.

Felokwakhe.

RiChard and Kisu used to chuckle at my vain attempts to pronounce it, and let me settle with calling him Kisu "O" as that was the only syllable I could ever remember. They had been friends long before I met RiChard, having been roommates in a study abroad program they both attended in England as undergrads.

Kisu had been from the KwaZulu-Natal region of South Africa, and when he and RiChard returned to his home-land to preach a message of social justice and revolution in the waning days of apartheid, Kisu was attacked and killed.

At least that's what RiChard had said when he returned to Kisu's village with blood on his hands.

Blood, he'd said, that came from him avenging Kisu's death.

Blood that forever tainted my innocent view of Ri-Chard as I had given up my full college ride and my common sense to marry him and follow him around the world for his so-called mission.

Yes, I was bitter, but didn't I have the right to be, considering all the lies it turned out he was living?

I was there the day RiChard returned to Kisu's village and talked of killing men in retaliation for his best friend's murder. I watched in silence as Kisu's father gave RiChard the lion's head ring that would eventually become the symbol of RiChard's double life and his lies to me, to Roman; yes, even to Mbali, Kisu's "widowed fiancée," if that was such a phrase, whom RiChard would eventually marry without telling each of us the truth about each other.

Felokwakhe.

I remembered now that Kisu did not have a last name in the way the Western world dictated. In his community, names held special meaning, related to the circumstances of a child's birth, or prayers, hopes, wishes, or blessings. "Kisu" had not been a traditional name as such in his culture, but rather was the wish of his mother who had gotten the name from only who knows where. Kisu's father, the village chief, acquiesced to her demands, but, upon the admonition of one of his advisors who was supposedly keen to dreams and visions, uneasily gave Kisu an additional name, the traditional name of Felokwakhe. Kisu simply used Felokwakhe as his surname during his studies as he did not have any other name to use.

"One who dies for his own," RiChard had reminded the small village of Felokwakhe's meaning when he returned with blood on his hands. "The son, the warrior, the noble intellect has died for the cause of righteousness," RiChard asserted as the villagers came to terms with their grief over the loss of their prized son. Kisu was a martyr for the cause and the village was moved to action.

Unsettled and uncertain about what was going on, I moved back to the States, unknowingly pregnant with RiChard's first child, Roman.

Years would pass before I would learn that Kisu was not dead.

When Roman was fourteen, I received a package in the mail, supposedly of RiChard's ashes; but instead the lion's head ring was inside. A whirlwind search for answers revealed that Kisu was behind the delivery.

I'd had many questions, but I had never gotten all the answers. As a result, I'd lost chances at love and healing, and, I conceded, the loss of my son's respect along the way.

No more.

Kisu Felokwakhe was going to be at the La Bohemia Café in five days. I was going to be there too.

I did not know what that meant for my work week, my scheduled appointments, my return to Baltimore *that man from the airport*—but this was one seminar I was not going to miss.

I'd spent years learning lessons about myself, failing lessons on love, reliving lessons on moving forward. Here was a final exam on finding answers, and this test I would not fail, come hell or high water.

Something told me I was in for both.

Chapter 6

Mom, are you coming?

Roman's text buzzed me back to the moment. I'd been in San Diego less than two hours. From the airport, to Roman's car, to this café hosted by the sunny Skyye, I had not covered much physical ground; and yet my life felt like it had moved to a whole other internal location over the past ninety-seven minutes.

I'll be there soon, I texted right back, though I was uncertain whether I would but knew I had to. I looked at the gift bag Skyye had left on the table. She had not given me a price, leaving it up to my discretion.

What kind of naïve, trusting young girl is this? I balked inside, wondering how Skyye could entrust her favorite creation, crafted from the diligent labor of her own hands, into the good graces of a complete stranger.

"I've been waiting to show it to the right person," she'd said. What made her think I was the one? I realized then that her trust wasn't so much in me, but in her intuition. As I took out my wallet, and started counting bills, I could not help but ponder how much we all operate on gut feelings and instinct.

And my gut feeling is that the authorities have the wrong suspect in custody.

I quickly shook away the nagging notion, reminding myself that as a responsible adult and trained mental health professional, logical thought outweighed irrational emotions. *Right?* I guess what it came down to was figuring out what guided your gut feelings, and knowing where your intuition had its roots.

I took out two twenties and laid them on the table, but as I picked up the gift bag and thought about the extra care, trust, and diligence that went into both the purse and the packaging, I added two more twenties, then one more.

One hundred dollars.

Who knew getting a bag of joy would cost me so much?

I shook my head as I stuffed the brochure and business card into my purse and headed to the front door.

"Roman?" I raised an eyebrow at the sight of my son sitting in his car, which was parked right outside the café. The windows were down and I spoke through them until I plopped down into the car myself. "What are you doing here? Have you been waiting long? What time is it? Is the party over?" I checked my watch as he started the engine.

"I saw you go in there and figured I'd just wait for you out here." He pulled off and then turned onto a major boulevard, heading in the direction of his college. A deep heaviness clouded his face. My guilt, which I had successfully assuaged earlier, returned full force.

"I . . . I'm sorry, Roman. I did get your sister a present. Oh, and the mola blanket, I brought it like you asked. It's in the duffel bag you put in the trunk. Were you planning on giving that blanket to her?"

"No worries, Ma."

I got the sense that he was avoiding eye contact with me.

"Roman, we can go back. I have her present and we have the blanket. Turn around. Let's go back. I'm sorry." Why hadn't I been a big girl in the first place? What was wrong with me? I did not really want to see them, but I also did not want to see my son like this, either.

"No worries, Ma," he said again. I didn't miss that his voice was slightly louder.

"Roman, is the party over? You didn't have to leave early because of me. Did you tell them I was out getting a present?"

"No."

"Well, what did you say?"

"Nothing. It wasn't necessary."

"I don't understand." I shook my head, trying to make sense of his words.

"Ma, Abigail didn't want us there, you or me."

"Huh? I'm confused. You said—"

"I said that it would be good for us to all come together, so that we could all move forward."

"Roman—"

"Ms. Mbali told me about the party and she was glad when I came in just now. But Abigail wasn't. They were about to start arguing, and I didn't want that, so I left and waited for you."

"And your brother Croix?"

"Croix hasn't been my roommate since last semester. It just . . . Things haven't worked out. Nothing has been going right."

"Roman, I had no idea all of this was going on. Why didn't you tell me?"

"I tried, Ma." He looked me straight in the eyes as he waited for a light to turn green. When it did, he looked away and kept driving. "Every time I tried to bring it up, you said you didn't want to talk about Dad's lies, so I honored your wishes. I didn't tell you about the party because I knew you would not have come. I guess, in the end, you probably shouldn't have. I'm sorry for messing up your weekend."

Look what RiChard has done to us. All of us. The rage in me turned up another notch as I studied the obvious slump in Roman's posture, the defeat in his eyes, the pain inside of him that I could not fix. All my son ever wanted was a complete family, and nobody had ever been able to give him that.

Not even me.

And it was all because of one man who hadn't shown his face to either one of us in nearly two decades.

How could one person's absence cause that much hurt and pain?

The rage was a slow, steady boil.

"Roman, I wish you had talked to somebody. Anybody. You shouldn't be carrying all this around by yourself."

"I talked to Leon a couple of times."

The rage turned to ice. I froze. Every thought, feeling, motion inside of me came to a standstill. I think even my heart paused for a moment, struggling to remember how to beat.

"You . . . Leon . . . uh . . ."

"It was some time ago. Thanksgiving. Christmas. Something like that. He's moved on, Ma. And you need to too."

He turned into a student parking lot near his dorm. I had reservations at a hotel nearby. From the silence that ensued, it appeared that neither one of us wanted to keep talking.

"Roman, is there anything else you had planned for us today or tomorrow?" I asked as he searched the lot for an open space.

He shook his head no.

"Did you want to go out to eat?"

He shook his head again. "Honestly, I have a project due Monday. I should be working on it as we speak."

"Take me back to the airport," I blurted. "It's been a crazy day, and I think I need to go back home."

He didn't object and I didn't reconsider. What else did San Diego hold for me at the moment? I would be back in a few days anyway, I reasoned, though I didn't tell Roman that.

It had been a long, crazy, twisted, terror-filled day. Telling him that I'd found Kisu seemed like it would only add to the uncertainty, add to the pain.

We were both silent as he drove me back to San Diego International Airport.

"Thanks for coming, Ma." He kissed my cheek just before I got out of his car. "I love you."

"I love you too, Roman, and I'm proud of the man you have grown to be."

We smiled at each other and then we both turned to our separate paths.

As I entered the airport, I checked my phone for available flights home. BWI Thurgood Marshall Airport was closed, all flights cancelled due to the ongoing investigation. I'd have to fly into National or Dulles in DC.

Laz was in DC, I recalled. Maybe he could pick me up from the airport since my car was in the express lot at BWI.

It was time to move on.

Chapter 7

Five Fascinating Facts About Me

I looked at the e-mail header and wondered what to do. The sender of the e-mail was named Everybody Anybody and the e-mail address started with 123ABC.

Was this spam that had somehow made it into my inbox? A virus that was waiting to be unleashed? I stared at the new message notification blinking on my phone and wondered if I should just send it directly to my trash folder.

I was on a layover in St. Louis, waiting for my next flight, which would take me to DC. I'd turn on my phone to send Laz a text with my flight information so he could pick me up, when I'd noticed the new e-mail. It was late, I was tired, and now I had to make sense of this foolishness on my phone.

It had to be spam, I reasoned, knowing that the only reason I was giving the e-mail a second thought was because of the voice mail message on my phone from earlier.

That man—I didn't even know his name—had me spooked and I couldn't stand it.

"Again, ladies and gentlemen, babies and children, we apologize for the lengthy delay, but we will finally begin boarding in just a few moments. Please have your boarding passes ready." A male flight attendant who was way too energetic for three in the morning boomed over a loudspeaker.

"Oh, what the heck." I decided to go ahead and open it. I didn't want to spend the entire flight obsessing over what was probably random junk mail. *Or it could be a virus*. I swallowed as the e-mail uploaded. I waited for a moment to see if my phone screen would suddenly go haywire. When it didn't, I read through the entire numbered list that comprised the message.

1. I brush my teeth for seventeen seconds.
2. I ate grilled chicken for dinner tonight.
3. I hate papier-mâché.
4. My favorite color is ochre, not because I like the way it looks, but because I like the way it sounds.
5. I have had twelve pets in my lifetime, but I cannot stand animals.

Random nonsense. I read through the e-mail one last time before shutting off my phone for good. I didn't get it, didn't know who sent it and, at the moment, I was too tired to care. Maybe after I had some solid sleep, maybe after I'd had a chance to process the disasters of the past twenty-four hours, maybe after I'd studied the e-mail a few more times, I would know exactly what I was supposed to do with it. That was the only reason I didn't delete it. Sometimes with a clear mind comes clear direction.

Clarity is all I wanted.

I touched down in DC just before 6:30 a.m. Sunday morning. The time zone differences, lack of comfortable sleep, and landing in a city that still was not home had me disoriented with a migraine brewing. I'd sent Laz a text hours earlier asking him to pick me up, but I hadn't even bothered to see if he'd responded.

A terrorist attack had happened in our corner of the world, and his job as an investigative reporter for a major network in Baltimore would mean that he was all over the scene. This was the type of news story Laz lived for on his way to getting his dream job as a correspondent on a national network.

He was close.

Many across the nation already recognized him for his unbridled commentary and willingness to take both physical and verbal risks. A live on-air rant about Hurricane Katrina at the beginning of his career secured his image.

I was on my own, I was sure of it.

I picked up a map for the local Metro, which had a stop at the airport, to see how to get to Union Station. Though I lived just an hour away from DC, I was not all that familiar with the nation's capital; but I knew that the MARC train, a commuter rail that stopped at Union Station, traveled from there to my hometown, with a stop, I thought, at BWI where my car was parked.

"I can't even think straight to figure this out." I sighed to myself, trying to make sense out of the colors and routes and times and destinations on the map. "I'm stranded."

I picked up my things and headed toward the exit. An app on my phone calculated a near one-hundred dollar cab fare from Reagan National Airport to BWI, assuming I could even get to the lot where my car was. The investigation was still active. "And I just gave that girl one hundred dollars for a crocheted purse." I sighed and shook my head, too exhausted to figure out what else to do. I could take a cab, if all else failed, but I really didn't want to keep throwing around money like that.

I considered contacting my mother, my father, or even my sister Yvette, but I knew that all three of them would be in varying stages of getting ready for Sunday morning worship. Aside from interrupting their routines, I did not feel like hearing my mother's nags about my decreasing church attendance.

Actually, I'd stopped going all together, but managed to catch enough of Pastor McKinney's Web casts to join along in the spiritual discussions over my mom's Sunday dinners.

Hard to believe that Yvette had more to say about Jesus than I did these days.

"There she is."

The voice outside the terminal exit caught me off-guard. I turned to the left and saw him. Head tilted to one side, his signature fedora slanted the opposite direction, Laz stood leaning against his gleaming white Benz. The passenger door was open.

"Come on, now, Ms. St. James." He flashed an easy smile. "You know they'll be telling me to move my car in a moment."

I smiled back at him and resisted the urge to pat my hair back into place. I was certain I looked as exhausted and worn as I felt, and no amount of fooling with my tresses would change that. I was a newly natural girl, and my hair had been styled in an elaborate up-do of flat twists and spirals, all of which had become mashed on the headrests of planes and automobiles.

"You came," was all I could say as he put my bags in his trunk. We both sat down in the spotless beige smooth leather interior. Today his car smelled like spicy vanilla.

"Of course I came. You needed me to come get you." His satellite radio was on. Jazz. The classic kind. Count Basie, Billie Holiday, Duke Ellington, Ella Fitzgerald. This was Laz's Sunday morning station of choice. "Why would you think I wouldn't come for you?" His smile stayed easy as he looked at me from the corners of his eyes.

"Breaking news story? Terrorist attack?" I bit my tongue to keep from sharing my irrational fear that I'd talked to the perpetrator. A suspect was already in custody, I reminded myself.

"Exactly." Laz nodded as he weaved his way through the traffic leaving the airport. "There was a terrorist attack and you were much too close to it. When I got your text, I dropped everything to make sure that I was here to get you. I'm sure you're frazzled."

"Frazzled doesn't even begin to describe how I feel right now." I bit my lip, looked up at the flawless blue sky through the partially open sunroof. Hard to believe such horrors could happen under perfect springtime skies. "What's the catch?" I demanded, turning my attention back to him.

"Say what?"

"The catch? You said you dropped everything to come get me. That goes against everything I know about you, Laz. There's a catch somewhere in this deal."

"Okay, you got me." He let out a slow chuckle. "There's always a catch; but don't worry. You'll like this catch."

I rolled my eyes. Didn't this man know I was too tired to be playing games? My exhaustion and nerves were reaching a point of delirium.

"Calm down, Sienna. Really, that's the catch. I'm going to need for you to relax and let me pamper you. You've been through a lot over the past day, and the fact that you came back from your trip earlier than expected tells me that there's more you're not telling me. So my catch is simple. I booked a suite for you at the Ritz-Carlton where you'll be able to rest while I go back to work. At noon you have an appointment at the spa for an organic facial and an eighty-minute Swedish massage. And then at six, no matter what happens in the news, regardless of what story I'm working on, we have reservations for dinner at a little restaurant I recently discovered in Georgetown."

"Laz, I—"

"Nope," Laz interrupted before I could get out any other words. "You asked for the catch and that's it. You cannot protest or tell me any other plans. You are not allowed to think about the explosion, your work week, your car back in Baltimore, your crazy clients, or whatever happened just now back in California. Your catch is that you have to do as I say and let me make this day special for you."

"I don't like the word 'crazy.' My clients—"

"Sienna, I'm not playing with you, girl." He turned up the music and drowned out whatever else I was going to say with a lively, off-beat trumpet and percussion duet. Within minutes, we were in front of the luxury hotel.

"Take care of her." He nodded at a doorman who opened my door and reached for my bags in the trunk, which Laz had popped open. "Here, Sienna." He passed me a small white envelope. "The room key is inside. The suite number is written on the back. Go get some sleep. Don't miss your day spa appointment, and meet me right here at five-thirty." He winked at me and I turned to get out.

"Wait," he commanded. I turned to face him again and he leaned in toward me. He paused and then leaned even closer and planted a soft kiss on my cheek. His sharply trimmed goatee scratched against my face and his breath was warm in my ear. "I'm glad you're okay, Ms. St. James."

I smiled but my emotions were a mixed bag. Weariness, guilt, fear, anguish, and confusion stunted any other feeling that may have tried to break through.

He pulled off the moment I was out of the car. I exhaled and entered the lobby.

Chapter 8

The opulent suite he'd booked had a living room, formal dining room, one and a half bathrooms complete with limestone and slate, a soaking tub and a bidet, French doors, a separate office space, and a view of DC that would make you smack your momma.

And yet, I did not notice any of that as I marched straight to the bed and collapsed into it. I did not stop to admire the massive flower arrangement he'd left on a side table. I did not bother to open the box of chocolates or read the greeting card that was propped up next to it in the living room.

I completely disregarded the three large manila envelopes that lay next to each other on the bed. Fatigue kept me from caring that each envelope had a sticky note on it that read "No Peeking." I tossed all three to the floor and each landed with varying thuds.

During the three and half hours that I slept, my phone rang twice; it buzzed that there was new breaking news, beeped that I had a new voice mail message, and dinged that new e-mails waited in my inbox.

I ignored it all.

Even when I did get up, I left my phone alone, determined to clear my head and block out any thoughts that disturbed me. In the half hour I had before my day spa appointment, I headed to the boutique hotel's fitness center. One thing about trying to keep up with Laz over these past few years, I'd changed my exercise habits and had managed to maintain a weight and muscle tone I was proud of.

By all appearances, I had it all: healthy body; successful therapy business; a relationship with an ambitious, well-paid professional; a son in college.

Inside, I felt like the falling sand in an hourglass: slow, steady loss, plunging downward into a narrow, dark hole, with just a matter of time left before my attempts at looking whole were fully exposed and all that would be left to do was flip over and flip out.

I pedaled with a vengeance on an exercise bike and then collapsed into a stupor when it was my turn on the massage table. However, by the time five-thirty rolled around, the kinks that had been kneaded out of my shoulders, back, and neck had been replaced by new knots.

I'd successfully avoided the news on television and the notifications on my phone, which I'd left in the suite in a futile attempt to stay relaxed; yet the noise in my head was louder than ever.

Laz was late.

I waited outside for him where he'd directed, dressed in a long black and white floral sundress with matching beaded jewelry. Since I had not known why Roman wanted me in San Diego, I'd packed an outfit in my carry-on that could handle any social setting, from the casual to the dressy. My multipurpose dress seemed to fit the bill for the evening. As the minutes ticked from 5:30 to 5:45 and then 5:52, I moved from standing by the entrance to sitting in the lobby.

A woman sitting near me was watching live news coverage on her computer tablet. I had no choice but to listen in.

"Authorities are offering few details about the suspect in the bombing at BWI, but an official at the hospital where he is being treated has confirmed with our network

that Jamal Abdul remains in a medically induced coma.
The official, who did not want to be identified, further
states that the suspect was conscious for only a short
period of time upon arrival at the medical center. He was
escorted there by members of Homeland Security, the
FBI, and the National Security Administration.

"Another official close to the investigation states that
Abdul, when he was conscious, vehemently denied being
part of the attack, stating that he was traveling with his
family to visit relatives in Chicago. Initial reports indicate
that the blast came from a piece of luggage belonging
to the suspect, and an additional official confirms that
video surveillance captured the entire sequence of events
leading up to and following the explosion.

"Authorities are confident that they have the right
suspect in custody and are not looking for any additional
suspects, stating that evidence supports the notion that
Jamal Abdul acted alone. A possible motive has not yet
been identified and questions remain about the nature of
the explosive device used and how Abdul was able to get
it past airport security and checkpoints."

My heart began racing again as the hairs on my arms
came to attention. Everything about the report made me
queasy. Everything felt wrong.

These are trained government officials. They have
proof. They have evidence. They have the right man in
custody. I fixed my mind on the facts and tried to squash
yet again the nagging fear that all was not what it seemed.

"So sad." The woman with the tablet noticed me listening in. She wore a pale pink business suit with a single
strand of pearls, and her blond hair was secured in a tidy
bun. "I'm glad they at least got the bastard."

I tried to say "yeah" but the word got lodged in my
throat.

"These nutcases need to go back to their desert sand piles, or, in this case, the jungles where they come from," she continued. "Seems like they are letting anyone into the country these days, and they need to simply stick to having real Americans in our land to reduce these types of terror risks."

"Uh . . ." I wasn't sure how to respond to that. Did the suspect they had in custody come from another country? I completely understood the anger, but I wasn't sure what she defined as "real Americans" and how she differentiated between fake and authentic.

"No offense to you." She looked at me sympathetically, confirming my suspicions. "You look like you're a shining star in your community. Beautiful, proud black women such as yourself give me hope that everybody is capable of assimilating to the American way." She smiled at me like we were friends, confidantes, almost equals.

"Excuse me," I managed to squeak out as I stood and walked away. The range of my emotions had widened, and not toward the happy end of the feelings spectrum.

Laz, dinner, or not, I headed back to the suite.

As I walked to the elevator, I realized what bothered me more than the confusing exchange I'd just had with the woman in the lobby.

The news reporter had stated that the suspect said he was about to fly out to Chicago at the time of the blast, the same place that mystery man had said he was headed. *Was Jamal Abdul and his family at the same gate as that man?* I strained to remember if I had seen that polished bronze face with the huge smile sitting or standing across the aisle. Perhaps if the media showed pictures of his wife and children I would recall seeing them there.

Knowing that the suspect had been on his way to Chicago gave me a strange comfort. Maybe my gut feelings were right. Maybe the sense that I really had looked at or talked to the perpetrator was correct, I just hadn't realized it at the time. I remember feeling like I'd missed something as I boarded the plane; maybe I'd seen Jamal Abdul in passing and realized on a subconscious level that something was awry.

This new line of thought did not fully jibe with what I was feeling, but I was determined to be logical in my approach. Truth was, there were probably several flights headed to Chicago. I still did not know where exactly in the airport the explosion had occurred. I needed to see more news coverage. And I needed to make what I felt fit in with the facts, not let a loose, unfounded instinct keep my stomach in knots.

It was 6:02. If Laz truly had reservations for dinner at six, we weren't making it tonight. I wasn't upset about it; I actually felt relieved. I wanted to do nothing more than make my way back to Baltimore and get ready for the week ahead.

I had clients waiting for me in the morning and a return trip to San Diego to plan. Not to mention, the nameless man from the airport had left a message indicating that he would contact me again. Irrational bad feelings about him or not, I needed to get myself together emotionally and physically to deal with it all.

And spiritually, a small voice inside of me said.

I exhaled as I got off the elevator and headed back to the suite.

"Father, I don't know what I'm feeling right now, or why, but please help. Help us all, Lord Jesus."

It was the first prayer I'd prayed out loud in a long, long time.

I hoped it was enough.

Chapter 9

I entered the suite and was startled to find the lights dimmed and Luther playing. Spicy vanilla filled my nostrils and lit candles of all shapes and sizes filled the entry room. I walked into the dining room and saw that the table had been set with dinner for two: tossed salad, buttered rolls, and chicken cordon bleu. Bubbly liquid-filled champagne flutes were at both settings, and a chocolate quesadilla adorned with real flower petals and fresh strawberries and raspberries served as an ornate centerpiece.

"I wondered how long it would take for you to come back here. I'm surprised you didn't call me."

Laz.

He was leaning against the wall by the dining room's buffet table, wearing only a sleeveless white tank, brown khakis, and leather bedroom slippers. His fedora hat twirled playfully around his fingers.

Oh, no! Does this man think . . . ?

"Calm down, Sienna." Laz chuckled and walked toward the table. "It's just dinner. Nothing more. I've done nothing but respect your very high standards, avoid your barbed wires, and backed off of your brick walls, even though we're in a supposed relationship."

Something about the way he said "supposed" unnerved me, but I said nothing and instead sat down in the chair he pulled out for me.

Luther Vandross melted into Brian McKnight. My feelings were getting more complicated by the second.

"You . . . fixed all this?" I inhaled slowly. The smell of herbs and butter, cheese and chocolate, vanilla and cologne swirled around in my nose, an uneasy complement to the mix of emotions that whirled inside of me.

"No, of course not. No time." Laz sniffed his drink. "I picked all this up from a restaurant down the street. I did set the table, though. I hope that suffices for the lady." He smiled at me and his pearly whites looked devilish in the glow of candlelight.

"It's nice. Thank you." I prayed a silent blessing for the food, took a bite, and looked away.

"So you're still not relaxed?" Laz asked between munches. "I got you the best room available, sent you to the spa, gave you a four-star dinner, and you still look like you are about to crack and collapse. What is it, Sienna?"

"I'm fine, Laz." I took a sip of the bubbly and almost choked. The Baptist roots of my upbringing kept me from being completely comfortable with drinking, though on occasion I tried to look like I could handle it. At the moment, a part of me wanted to find the whole bottle and chug it down, choking, tears, and all. "How was your day?" I wanted to change the subject. "I'm sure you've had your share of excitement."

"Yes, I have, but we'll get to that in a moment. First, please tell me how you're doing. I can't imagine how you're feeling being that close to a terrorist attack. You missed it by what, thirty, forty minutes? Is that what's eating at you?"

I hesitated, but then put my fork down and decided to put it all on the table. "I met a man at the airport yesterday morning who gave me the heebie-jeebies. He was on his way to Chicago too, like the man they're holding, Jamal Abdul."

Laz stuffed a large bite of salad into his mouth and then used a cloth napkin to wipe a trail of vinaigrette dressing off his lips.

He looked bored.

"So you're worried that the man may have been hurt in the blast." He reached for his champagne flute.

"No, I think he did it."

Laz looked at me from over the top of his glass before setting it back down. "You do know that they have who they think did it in custody. The man you just named, Jamal Abdul."

"I know, Laz, but something is not sitting right with me. I can't put my finger on it but I feel like they have the wrong person. You've known me long enough to know that my gut is normally right. I wish I felt differently. Heck, I've been trying to feel differently, but this feeling won't go away. That man I talked to"—I shook my head—"he knows something, he did something. I'm sure of it."

There. It was out, and now that it was, I didn't feel as crazy as I had when I tried to keep it in.

Laz didn't look convinced. He took another bite of his salad and followed it with a piece of the chicken cordon bleu. "What was his name?"

"I don't know."

"Where was he from?"

"I don't know."

"What did you talk about?"

"I don't remember." I shut my eyes and opened them again. "Look, he said, 'You'll know my name soon,' or something like that. He was . . . creepy."

Laz put his fork down. "And yet the bomb has gone off and he has not put his name out there for you or anyone else in the public to know."

"And he said he didn't believe in God. Or, he didn't believe in believing. His words were really bizarre."

"Sienna, I think this has been a traumatic experience for you and, like anybody else would, you're trying to make sense of what happened. You're trying to find a way to make it better, to be the superhero who saves the day. But it happened. There's nothing you could have done to stop it. You did nothing wrong. It was horrible. You survived. Now, we have to heal and move on."

"Laz, this is eating at me." I looked down and picked at my plate. "I gave him my card and he called and left a message saying that he wanted to have a conversation with me. Plus, I got a crazy e-mail at three in the morning, and I wholeheartedly believe that it came from him."

"What did it say?"

"Uh, the sender was 'Everybody Anybody,' or something like that, and had five fun facts about him, or whoever sent it. It said that he didn't like animals or papier-mâché. That he brushed his teeth for a long time and, well, I don't remember. It was weird."

"And possibly random spam, right?"

"I guess. Let me get my phone and I'll show you. I left it in the nightstand drawer."

"I know where your phone is. It was ringing and dinging like crazy. I shut it off and put it in my pocket. And I'm going to hold on to it for a little longer. You need a break. You really need a break. I'm trying my best to give you one."

"I know, thanks. I'm just trying to make sense out of it all." I shook my head, opened my mouth to say something else, considered demanding my phone back, but fell quiet instead.

"Hmm . . . Tell you what, Ms. St. James." Laz's easy smile returned. "I'll let my source at Homeland Security know that you were at BWI right before the explosion and that you met a man who made you feel uncomfortable. If there is a need for further investigation, they will make that call. How's that?"

I bit my lip, nodded. "Thank you. I appreciate it. I'm not trying to come off as delusional. I've just learned to trust my gut, and my gut is telling me something is wrong, that there's more to the picture."

"Sienna, it sounds like you met someone who might need mental health treatment. You are a trained clinician, so you're going to pick up on such things. He has your card and will contact you for an appointment. It's a win-win situation. He needs services and you are a darn good therapist."

"Not that good." A tear that I didn't know was in my eye splattered down my cheek and landed on my plate.

"What are you talking about? You have a practice that has grown exponentially over the past three years to the point that you're hiring other therapists to work for you. You've been recognized with awards from local organizations and getting grants from government contracts to expand your clientele. Even Ava said she was proud of you, her protégée, and she is a legend in the world of social work, at least that's what you've told me. You must be doing something right, babe."

"Yes, I'm a therapist, and I help all these people. But somewhere along the way, I haven't been able to help myself." I paused, thinking of the dizzying array of emotions that had been jostling me around as of late. "Or my son. He doesn't even talk to me about the things that affect him most. Or maybe I just haven't listened. I listen to and help everyone else, but my own household, my own heart is in pieces. The trip to San Diego yesterday was a disaster."

I could not hold back any more tears. I hated looking, feeling, sounding like a weak, sobbing woman who needed to be rescued, but a dam broke inside me that I could not repair. For the first time since I'd heard about the terrorist attack, for the first time since I'd gotten

Roman's call last week to come out to San Diego, maybe even for the first since I'd learned about Mbali and her children from RiChard's double life and lies, I cried.

No.

I wept, snotted, moaned, blubbered, and bawled.

More than anyone else in my life, including Ava, my mother, even Leon, Laz knew the facts about my history with RiChard; but he didn't know my feelings.

He'd never asked.

From our first meeting several years ago, he'd always called me a strong woman, and I, for whatever reason, had done my best to maintain that image in front of him.

Today was a fail.

Sitting across from me, twiddling his hat between his fingers, he stared at me as I sobbed, his expression unreadable as I no longer tried to hide the oppressive emotions that had finally caught up with me. Then he stood and came by my side, took my hand, pulled me to my feet.

"Come here, Sienna." He led me to the separate office space that was part of the luxurious suite. "It's time to get to the business of why we're here. I did all this today for a reason."

He opened the doors of the study and in between whimpers I saw three large manila envelopes spread out over an oversized desk. They were the same three envelopes that had been on the suite's bed when I first came in the room that morning, the envelopes I'd knocked to the floor without a second look. This time, however, the sticky notes that read "No Peeking" had been removed and replaced with the numbers 1, 2, and 3.

"Enough with the tears, Sienna. I've got answers to all your problems." He waved a hand over the envelopes. "In order." He smiled. "I need you to open each one."

Chapter 10

I looked from Laz to the envelopes, not sure where this was going, but determined to push back my tears.

It was obvious he wasn't for all that.

The envelope marked 1 was the thickest. I picked it up and slowly undid the clasp. Laz put on a dress shirt, sports coat, pushed up the sleeves; sat down in the accompanying desk chair, leaned back, and held his hands together, a slight smile on his face.

"Well?" he asked as I pulled out a collection of papers.

"What is this?" I flipped through them, noting certificates, programs from award banquets, business portfolios, and what looked like copied pages of high school and college yearbooks and old grade school photos. I held up one picture of a bucktoothed, large eyeglasses–wearing Laz dressed in a one-piece jumper patterned with frogs. He looked all of five or six years old. "Um, you intentionally wanted me to see this photo? What is this about?"

Laz chuckled. "I'm aiming for a few new positions in life, and when you go to an interview, you bring your résumé, right?"

"Please tell me this is not what you bring to job interviews."

"No, of course not." He laughed along with me, but then slightly sobered. "Sienna, there is a new position I am applying for and I'm putting it all out on the table. What you have in your hand is me in an envelope. I want you to fully know who I am, where I've come from, what I have accomplished. I want you to have visible evidence of my successes, my failures, my embarrassments, and my superiority above everything that has ever tried to keep me down."

I studied some of the awards and chuckled at a few additional photos before looking back at him. "So I have you in an envelope. What am I supposed to do now, mail you off, wait for another delivery?"

"Aren't you tired of waiting for deliveries?"

I narrowed my eyes, inhaled, wondered where he was going with all of this.

"I remember," he continued, "you telling me that at your old place, you used to keep out a lot of knickknacks from around the world, artifacts that were shipped to you from RiChard as he was traveling the world and neglecting you and your son. I can almost picture you waiting for the delivery truck to come back around to remind you that you were still relevant. To him."

I was completely silent now. Though Laz was the only person with whom I'd really had any discussion about RiChard, it still pained me to bring up the subject, to hear that man's name. And those artifacts . . . The only facts that had come out of those deliveries, I'd learned, were that they were just overstock items from his small store on the West Coast, a store he'd used to support Mbali and their four children, all the while lying to us all.

"For reasons you probably could not even explain to yourself," Laz continued, his voice barely above a whisper, "you've spent the last near twenty years calling yourself Mrs. St. James, even though there's been no Mr. St. James present. I've never pressed you, and I didn't ask you, but I'm assuming you avoided finalizing a divorce because you were too busy finishing school, raising your son, and growing your business."

He took the papers from my hand and spread them out on the desk in front of me. "This is me." He picked up the second envelope and passed it to me. It was remarkably thinner than the first.

"Sienna, envelope number two is the envelope that represents you. You can do the same thing as I did and fill this up with pages that represent your life. You are capable of doing that yourself, and I'm sure that you would put in old report cards, your degrees, some family photos, the license for your practice. There is one paper, however, that you don't have that needs to be added to those pages. A divorce decree. The good news is that I did the legwork for you. I researched the best attorneys and got the initial needed forms."

He took the second envelope from my hands and pulled out the papers inside. "These are the documents you need to fill out to finally end the RiChard chapter of your life. There is more that needs to be done, but this is where you can begin. I've done what I can, but you need to do the rest, if you are willing. And I'm not sure why you wouldn't be."

I picked up the forms, one by one, and tried to make sense of what I read, what I saw. What I felt. Why had I never done this? Laz was right. I didn't have an answer. My hands, my legs shook. I was numb, speechless. Still shaking.

"Last envelope, Sienna."

Laz took the forms from me, placed them to the side, and then passed me the envelope labeled 3. He sat down in the desk chair again, his smile returning.

My hands shook even more as I tried to focus on opening the next clasp. I pulled out the single sheet of paper that waited inside.

"A . . . job offer?"

His smile grew even wider as he moved from the desk chair and sat on the edge of the desk, closer to me.

"What we've been waiting for." Laz's tone was sober though his eyes glistened. "I was offered my own nightly news show with a national audience. This is as big as it gets, Sienna. I still have to iron out the format, but they are giving me a lot of say about its structure. All I do know at this point is that it's going to be taped live nightly at the network's headquarters in Atlanta. We're Georgia bound and going prime time, baby!"

"Georgia? We?"

"I told you that I'm trying to move up to new positions. The job in Atlanta is only part of what I'm after. Sienna, you have my credentials, my background, my life's résumé in that first envelope. I'm submitting my application to you to be the man in your life. Permanently. I want you to come live with me in Atlanta. I want you to marry me."

My jaw dropped. My eyes widened. *Did my ears hear right? Is this man asking me to marry him?*

"Sienna, yesterday was a game changer for me." He wrapped both of my hands in his. "You could have been at that gate when it exploded, and I don't know how I would have handled that kind of news. Every time I called you yesterday and you didn't answer, I sunk into a lower depth of despair. I'm sorry that it took a terrorist attack to make me realize how much I treasure you, but I do. And the day you finalize your divorce, we can make 'us' official. You will be my wife and I won't ever have to fear that you will leave this planet without knowing how much I care about you."

His hands left mine and held my cheeks as he planted a kiss first on my forehead and then softly on my lips.

I was too numb to think, to feel, to speak; but as his words sunk in, my questions began, and not just about his proposal.

"Laz, I don't know that I want to pick up my life and move it to Atlanta."

"It's a new chapter for both of us, together. From my estimation, the whole divorce process should take about six months. Six months from now you'll be divorced from your past and married to your future. Six months gives you time to figure out what you want to do with your therapy practice, whether you want to close it down and start new in Atlanta, or find a different type of social work job down there, or maybe stop working altogether and focus on your art. I will be making more than enough for the both of us."

Wait, did this man just casually tell me what to do with my practice? I'd spent years putting myself through college, going through the licensing process, establishing and growing my clinic, and he had the nerve to tell me to drop everything and follow him to a different state for him to pursue *his* dreams?

Whatever had frozen in me thawed.

"Uh, Laz, do you think you are being a little presumptuous with your plans for not just you, but me?"

"Not at all. Sienna, I've known what you needed from the first time I met you, and I'm about to give you the world."

"And in six months, I'm supposed to drop everything I know and have in the town I've lived in my entire life and turn my back on a career that I have been building, so that I can focus solely on you and yours?"

"Social work is not your dream job."

"Excuse me?" I could feel my nostrils flaring.

"Social work and therapy was your response to Ri-Chard. You thought he was someone who was all about making the world a better place, but when he failed you, you made it your mission to show him that you could do it better by taking on a career that is all about service. But he never came back around to see what you accomplished without him. You need to let it and him go. Start your own life, Sienna, with me."

"Have you lost your mind?" I sounded like my mother, but didn't care. Every now and then I had to summon that Isabel Davis attitude and tell it like it was. "How dare you? You think that I have wrapped my whole life, career, and reason for being around a man I haven't seen in nearly two decades? Are you serious?"

Laz, the journalist who never backed down from a fight, who made a reputation for not holding his tongue with anyone, simply shrugged at me. "If I'm wrong, then tell me why you never took the time to tear the knot with him. Why are you still walking around with his name, even now, three years after finding out he lied to you in every way imaginable? Why did *I* have to research your divorce options?"

"I kept my name because I wanted my son and I to have the same last name. I wanted Roman to have a sense of continuity, of family, and that is what I chose to offer him. I did not pursue a divorce because it was too emotionally exhausting and I was too busy putting my efforts on what mattered most to me: my son and, yes, my work. Don't pretend like you know anything about my intentions, my decisions, my sacrifices, or what I have had to go through!" I threw my hands up in the air. "I cannot believe, Lazarus Tyson, that you have the audacity to not ask me what I want, but stand there and tell me what it is you want me to do. This can't be a proposal. You didn't ask me anything. You haven't even offered a ring!"

"I was getting to that." Laz's smile returned. He strolled over to a cabinet in the study, pulled open one of its solid wood doors, and took out a familiar bag: the bright yellow bag with the rhinestone and glitter sunburst.

The bag Skyye had given me back in San Diego.

Only now her carefully wrapped present, the crocheted purse I'd wanted to give to Roman's sister, was not inside, I noted, as Laz handed the bag to me. Instead there was a tiny velvet black box with a huge red satin bow tied around it. Laz sat back down in the desk chair, took off the slippers he'd been wearing and put on some shoes. His smile never left as he grabbed his fedora from the desktop where he'd laid it last and began twirling it around his fingers again. "Are you going to open it or not?"

A sound somewhere between a groan and a sigh escaped from between my lips. "You could go out and get a dinner and do all these wonderful things for me today, but you couldn't get your own gift bag? What did you do with my joy?" I'd meant to say "joy bag" but I was struggling again to get my words out. I was not trying to have a tantrum, but there were no words to explain the mixture of emotions colliding inside of me.

The past twenty-four hours had taken their toll.

"Open the box," Laz demanded.

I shook my head no and pulled the ribbon off and lifted the top anyway. A vintage platinum ring was inside, with no stones set in its prongs, no jewels in its empty ridged sides.

"I want you to get the lion's head ring and disassemble it," Laz announced, referring to the ring that had been passed from Kisu's father to RiChard's bloody hands, that had shown up in a package to me years ago in an urn that was supposed to be filled with RiChard's ashes but wasn't, that almost cost Roman his safety and me my sanity—the ring that had been the link that Mbali had found that exposed all of RiChard's lies.

"We're going to take the rubies, sapphires, and diamonds from the lion's head ring," Laz continued, "and give those jewels a new home in the ring setting you have in your hand. I respect your past, Sienna, how it's shaped you, affected you, changed you forever. Now, I am offering you a chance to take that past, acknowledge it, and start over, make it work for you in a layout of your choice.

That is what I'm offering to you. I'm not just asking you to be my wife. I'm giving you a chance to live your life."

"I am living my life! And this is your idea of a proposal? Telling me what I need to do with my life to line it up with yours?"

"This is us, Sienna. You pull, I push. I give, you take. And at the end is a fat check from my dream job in Atlanta." He cocked his head to one side and put his hat back on. "Don't feel like you have to figure it all out right now. Aside from the fact that this has been a ridiculous weekend, I have to get back to work. I don't have time this evening to wait for you to process all your feelings. I'm going for the night, Sienna. I'll send a taxi or something for you in a couple of hours so you can pick up your car at BWI. Go eat the chocolate quesadilla and enjoy your downtime."

"Laz, you are the most arrogant man I have ever met."

"And yet, I'm all the man you'll ever need." He winked as he walked toward the door of the suite. "I mean, really, who else could take care of you better than me?"

I saw the apprehension flash in his eyes the moment he realized what he'd asked. He knew I saw it, too.

We both knew there was another.

Leon.

The two had been cordial to each other the weeks leading up to Leon's move to Houston; but the day Leon left, Laz seemed to exhale and never hold his breath again.

Until just now.

"I don't need anyone taking care of me. Good night, Laz." I smirked and closed the door behind him, determined to win my power back.

I had a lot to think about, consider, mull over, and decide.

I needed to pray.

I needed to use that soaking tub.

And I needed no interruptions.

That last need would be met, I realized as I nibbled on a piece of the quesadilla.

Laz still had my phone.

That man from the airport had a left a message stating that he would be calling me Sunday evening, now, to schedule a "conversation." The fact that I would not be able to get a potential phone call from him calmed and frightened me all at once.

Chapter 11

As always, over the top.

At exactly eight-fifteen, I received a call from the front desk to inform me that my limo was waiting. I gathered my belongings, including the envelopes and the gift bag with the ring, and left the rest of the suite's mess for Laz to address. I headed downstairs in a hurry, anxious to get back home, ready to put this crazy weekend behind me.

I'd been near a terrorist attack, run from family drama on the West Coast, been somewhat proposed to, and had my entire life, existence, and purpose challenged by a man who truly got on my nerves, but treated me to a day spa.

I could not imagine what else waited in the coming week, though my gut told me more absurdity was on the radar.

Plus, I had to plan my trip back to San Diego. Though I'd successfully avoided thinking about it, I still had the brochure from the La Bohemia Café in my purse.

Kisu Felokwakhe. 7:30 p.m. Thursday.

In light of Laz's offers, I needed definitive answers about RiChard's whereabouts, all the more reason for me to speak with Kisu. Perhaps he would be able to help shed some light on the unending mystery that was RiChard. Unbeknownst to Laz, I had in the past looked up what needed to be done to divorce an absent spouse. A divorce by publication. Since I did not know where RiChard was, I would have to show the courts proof that I looked for him as best as I could, and could not find him. Then, the decree would have to be announced in a newspaper and other widely published outlets for a specified time period with no response from him to make the divorce final.

That's if I even went forward with it.

Why wouldn't I? Laz was right. I could not fully answer my own question. Aside from the energy it would require, and my efforts to stay focused on my son and my job, a part of me, I realized, had secretly wondered if it was okay to pursue a divorce. Though I had every reason to do so, would I be breaking some moral or spiritual law or code to end a marriage made before God, even though by any reasonable estimation it never really existed?

I felt so far from God, and had been feeling a growing distance for years now. It hurt to think in the spiritual and I did not know why.

"Ms. St. James? I can help you with your bags." A man with gelled black hair and a three-piece black suit met me at the entrance and helped me with my luggage. Laz had booked a white stretch limo for the forty-five minute or so drive to the Baltimore/Washington International Thurgood Marshall Airport where my car waited.

"Thanks." I nodded as the chauffeur opened the door. I stepped inside nonchalantly, as if driving around in a limo was my usual routine. The interior was dark and cool with a flat-screen television, light refreshments, and more flowers and chocolate. On one of the seats lay a sheet of paper with the words, "This is how your life will be with me—LT," and next to the note were my cell phone and my "joy bag."

I picked up the bag, traced the letters, and wondered why I felt so empty of the very thing the bag purported.

It was time to rejoin my life and the world around me, I thought as I put down the bag and reached for my phone. As I turned it on, I thought of how much of my day, interactions, and schedule hinged on my smart phone.

We were fully en route to BWI as my phone came to life with its usual buzzes, dings, and other notifications. Laz had not been kidding about all the action on my phone. Just in the past few hours, Roman had called and texted me several times to make sure that I had returned home safely. I'd missed several other phone calls as well, mostly family and friends who hadn't known that I'd been traveling that weekend, but who had learned of my plans from Roman and were checking on me too. I recognized all of the phone numbers and waiting voice mail messages except for one, and the one I didn't recognize was a Baltimore-based phone number.

Good. I exhaled, remembering the phone number with the Ohio-based area code.

Maybe I would never hear from that man again.

Since all of my voice mail messages were local and mostly familiar, I decided I would check them later after I got home.

A quick scan of my e-mails gave me further relief. Nothing unusual or unexpected. A couple of clients had e-mailed to schedule appointments as the terrorist attack had unleashed new anxieties, fears, sadness, and worry. Ava had forwarded information about a seminar she thought would interest me; and then there were the normal e-mails of store circulars, sales, and specials from mailing lists I'd forgotten I'd signed up for. My junk mail folder was filled with just that—junk. I was now certain that the bizarre e-mail I'd gotten in the wee hours of the morning was a random spam message that didn't get filtered out by my server.

All of this silly worrying. I wanted to laugh at and kick myself. *The therapist needs a therapist.*

I was thinking about my conversation with Laz and how I failed the very lessons I taught my clients about relationships, communication, and self-assessment, when the limo reached the main road that led to BWI.

The road was blocked and all manner of official vehicles and uniformed personnel milled around. The flashing lights of countless emergency vehicles lit up the night sky, cast shadows, and revealed the intense investigation going on at the scene. One of the officers approached the limo with a flashlight and stopped at the driver's window. After a few moments passed, the chauffeur sounded through an intercom.

"Ms. St. James, most of the airport is closed. There's only one runway in operation with limited flight service, and all vehicles are being checked before entering the loop. Did you confirm that your flight is still scheduled?"

"I'm not flying anywhere. My return flight here was cancelled and I came in through National. I'm just trying to get to my car, which is parked in the express lot."

A few more moments passed and then the chauffeur spoke again. "Okay, pass up your parking ticket that has what number space your car is parked in. Also, pass up your car key. They will get it for you and bring it down here."

I'd clipped my parking ticket to my original flight itinerary. I pulled it out and passed it up to the chauffeur through the privacy partition. The limo pulled onto the side of the road under the direction and careful watch of a police officer. As the seconds turned into minutes, I decided to turn the flat-screen television on to catch up on the news.

Just think, this will be Laz at the anchor desk soon, I thought as I flipped through several national networks on the satellite TV. I stopped at a station offering a live report.

"Those who know Jamal Abdul are expressing shock and disbelief at the allegations that he singlehandedly performed this atrocious act of terror. Born and raised in Prince George's County, Maryland, he was valedictorian of his high school class and graduated from college with a 4.0 GPA. He holds two master's degrees, one in biochemistry and the other in mechanical engineering, and he was currently pursuing a doctorate in biomedical engineering. He had been working with his employer on a government contract developing new and advanced prostheses for wounded soldiers. Staff and patients at the Walter Reed Medical Center in Bethesda, Maryland, where he is said to have volunteered on a regular basis, have expressed disbelief and disgust regarding his alleged involvement in the explosions."

As the reporter spoke, a montage of pictures of the suspect filled the screen, including graduation photos, a work ID, and snapshots of him embracing disabled veterans. The reporter continued.

"Jamal was raised alone by his mother, Thelma Johnson, who currently works as an office manager in Largo, Maryland. His father, Abdullah Abdul, whose relatives say has not been in Jamal's life since he was three years old, is a Sudanese immigrant who works as a school bus driver in Portland, Maine. Jamal has been married for seven years to his wife Keisha, a kindergarten teacher, and the couple have two daughters: Hailey, age five, and Chloe, age three. Here is what Jamal's sixth-grade science teacher, Esther Mansley, has to say about him."

The camera focused on an older woman wearing what looked like her Sunday best: large, shiny costume jewelry, bright red blush on her cheeks, black patent leather purse, and all.

"Oh, it's on?" She turned to the reporter. "This is live?" She quickly looked back at the camera, and her face became awash with tears. "Yes, Jamal was in my sixth-grade science class. He was quiet, studious, and never got into any trouble. I cannot imagine what happened to make him become so dangerous, evil, and radicalized. He had us all fooled!" She frowned at the camera and then turned back to the reporter. "How'd I do?" she whispered.

I didn't miss the reporter's slight roll of the eyes and half step away from the lady. "This is Regina Anderson reporting live from Largo, Maryland. Back to you in the studio, Alan."

"That's enough about the suspect for now. Let us focus again on the victims of this horrible tragedy," the man named Alan remarked from behind a large anchor desk. "Here are their names and faces once more."

As the photos began rolling across the screen—bright smiles, family photos, school portraits, all races, ages, colors, and creeds—I tried to swallow down the huge lump that formed in my throat. And the flutter of fear that jumped from my stomach to my esophagus. *What if they have it wrong? What if it wasn't Jamal?* I could not stop the questions from forming, but quickly reminded myself that Laz promised to mention my fears to his source at Homeland Security.

I typed a text to remind him and to calm my nerves. Don't forget to tell your person about the man I met. I pressed send, hoping, expecting to feel better.

I didn't.

"Ms. St. James?" The chauffeur's voice startled me back to the moment. A uniformed officer stood next to the driver's side window again. "They need to see your ID."

"Sure." After fishing for it in the deep depths of my purse, I passed it through the partition. The small window slammed shut after I'd done so.

"What's taking so long?" I mumbled to myself before my attention turned back to honoring the dead and injured whose faces still flashed on the TV screen.

They'd gone through all eighteen victims who'd passed, and half of the list of the thirty-four injured, when I realized that almost half an hour had ticked by since we first pulled up to the checkpoint. I was still waiting for my car. I knocked on the privacy partition and it opened with a slow, noisy squeal.

"Has anyone said what's taking so long?" It was nearly 10:00 p.m. I wanted to be home.

"I . . . I'm not supposed to say, but . . ." He spoke softly and looked over at a group of four uniforms before turning back to me and speaking in an even lower voice. "I don't think they can find your car. They wanted your ID to confirm your travel plans to see if you really flew out of here like you said. They're being extra cautious, you know, in light of what happened here yesterday." He looked back at the officers. One of them broke from the group and started walking toward the window. The chauffeur slammed the privacy partition shut, and I went back to digging through my purse.

"They can't find my car? What kind of foolishness is this?" I groaned as I searched for the printout of my flight confirmation from yesterday morning. "Here it is," I shook my head as the officer bypassed the driver's window and instead opened the door to where I was sitting.

"Ms. St. James?" His voice was all business. "Please get out of the car."

I snapped off the television and exited slowly, trying to figure out what was going on. I just wanted to get to and in my car and go home. The officer shined a flashlight up and down me and then took out a pen and paper he used to take notes.

"What is the make and model of your car?"

"I drive a black Honda Accord."

"What is the license plate number?"

I belted out the number and letter combination, but quickly added, "My car is parked in that numbered space written on the parking ticket I gave to the first officer."

"There's no car parked in that space, ma'am." He eyed me. "You just flew out of this airport yesterday?"

"Yes." I unfolded the paper that held my flight confirmation number and handed it to him. "I visited my son in San Diego, but the trip didn't go so well. I came back last night, but landed in DC since BWI was closed at the time. A friend of mine booked this limo so I could come pick up my car and go home. Are you sure you checked the right parking space?"

The officer, who had been reading over my handout, looked up at my question, but didn't answer. "Wait here," he commanded and walked away.

My cell phone started ringing inside the limo. I decided against getting back inside to answer it. I wanted and needed my car! Several moments passed, and then the officer returned.

"Okay, Ms. St. James. Everything you said checks out. I'm not sure what to tell you about your car. It appears to have been stolen. It is likely that in the panic that ensued yesterday, someone may have gotten into it and driven away."

"I have a very sophisticated anti-theft package."

"Even still, the best I can tell you is to file a report for a stolen car. Perhaps the limo driver can take you home, or to one of the car rental places around here so that you can get home yourself. I'm sorry. There's nothing more I can tell you. You're going to have to leave now."

"Wait," I said as he began walking away. "Can't you make a report for me? And wouldn't there be video surveillance that could help determine if someone stole my car?"

The officer paused. "In light of the lives lost yesterday, looking at video coverage and searching for your car will be taking a back seat to the overall investigation at this time. As a federal officer, I suggest you contact your local authorities to address this matter after we leave. Understood?"

"I understand." *But I want to scream!* I stayed cool, calm, and collected despite the Grand Canyon geyser–sized wail that was going off inside of me.

He handed me back my license, keys, and papers and I got back into the limo.

"Can you drop me off at one of those car rental places we passed?" I buzzed into the intercom.

"Sure thing," the chauffeur replied.

The limo started and I settled back into my seat.

A little over an hour later, I pulled up to my townhome in Rosedale. The car I'd rented, the last available compact car the rental company had on its lot, cut off with a loud sputter. Sleep weighed down on my eyes and on the rest of my body and helped me decide not to do a darn thing else but go to bed. I'd deal with the police report tomorrow. The e-mails and voice mail messages would have to wait. Thankfully, I'd had enough sense before I'd left for my trip to San Diego to clear out my Monday morning schedule. No clients to see until one tomorrow afternoon.

Nothing else to do but go to bed and sleep late into Monday morning.

Well, my mother always told me that God knows what you need when you need it. God knew that I needed my sanity to function, because it was His grace that kept me from checking my e-mails once more before I went to sleep.

If I'd read the e-mail that came into my inbox in the midnight hour, I probably would have lost my mind.

Chapter 12

Five Fascinating Facts About You

I blinked and stared and blinked again at the headline of the e-mail. It was ten o'clock on Monday morning and I had finally pulled myself up out of my bed. I'd had a full cup of coffee, a hot shower, unpacked, and was ready to finally go through my messages and prepare for my day.

If I acted like life was normal, then maybe it would be, I told myself as I fought back thoughts about Roman, Mbali, Kisu, RiChard, terror, Leon, and Laz. Each thought represented a different circumstance, a different issue in my life, but the underlying feelings were the same.

Exhaustion, anxiety, sadness, and confusion.

And now this, I swallowed, debating whether I wanted to open the e-mail that had come at 12:13 a.m., or delete it for fear of what could be in it.

"I'm being silly." I shook my head at myself as I sat at my kitchen table. A plate of cold eggs and half-eaten sausage links sat to the side of my laptop. I'd been staring at the e-mail headline for over twenty minutes. The plan was to check my e-mails on my computer and then go through my phone messages, but this second message from Everybody Anybody had thrown my plans for a loop.

I clicked the e-mail open.

1. You enjoy eating red velvet cupcakes.
2. Your mother works as a top administrator for the Baltimore City Public School System.

3. You celebrated your son's eighteenth birthday last year by taking him on a Harbor Cruise.

4. Your favorite color is purple.

5. You enjoy creating artwork and frequenting museums and galleries.

"Is this some kind of sick joke?" I whispered to a nameless messenger. My heart felt like it was skipping right out of my chest as I read each line again. Everything on the list was true. But how? Who? I stood up, then immediately felt dizzy and sat back down. "God, what is going on?" I rubbed my cheeks so intensely my skin began to feel warm and raw. Prickly heat formed on my brows, my hairline, and over my top lip. I picked up my phone and dialed Laz and started talking the moment he picked up.

"Laz! This is serious. I got another crazy e-mail. I think it's from the same man. Did you tell your source yet? I don't know what I'm supposed to do. I'm scared. I think he's stalking me."

"Sienna, whoa, whoa. Calm down." Laz was eating something crunchy. He paused to swallow and then munched again on whatever was his meal. "One thing at a time. I'm sure there is a reasonable explanation for whatever is going on. Read me the e-mail."

I started at the beginning and felt my fears rise anew as I spoke each line out loud.

"Yeah, that's a little weird, but, honestly, Sienna, all of that information could be learned from your Facebook or Twitter accounts. Don't you have a red velvet cupcake as one of your profile pictures somewhere?"

"Okay, that makes sense, but who sent this, and how did he get my e-mail address?" I heard myself say "he."

"Don't you have your e-mail address on your Web site for your practice?" Laz sounded bored. "Look, it's probably from one of your clients acting like a goofball, or maybe even your sister messing with you. Shoot, how do you know it's not from me? Maybe I could just be trying to show you that I pay attention to the little details of your life."

"But it's not from you."

"No, but the point I'm trying to make is that your mind seems set on instant extreme scenarios. Calm down. Look at this rationally. Somebody looked you up online and sent you a message. There was no threat or request or even a stated purpose. They have a suspect in custody, and even if they didn't, I seriously doubt that Homeland Security would come running because someone e-mailed you that you like the color purple." Laz took another bite of whatever he was eating. I tried to process his words.

"And, Sienna, if by some random chance these e-mails are coming from the man you met yesterday, just help him. He might be a little unbalanced, but that doesn't mean he's a terrorist. He's not sending you e-mails talking about body parts and death. You're a therapist. You're the right person for the job. You can give him the help that he needs."

"Oh, so now you are applauding my career choices."

"I never said you weren't good at what you do. I just said that I'm not convinced it's what you want to do."

"Laz—"

"Look, we're not going to get into that right now. For whatever it's worth, I really think those e-mails are from someone you know playing a game with you. You know how these dumb games and trends get passed around the Internet. Shoot, I'll probably have a 'Five Fascinating Things About Me' e-mail in my inbox before the week is over. I wouldn't worry that someone is stalking you. It's been a tough weekend. You're paranoid. Relax, Sienna." He chewed again.

"What are you eating?"

"A red velvet cupcake."

"That's not even close to funny."

"Just kidding, Sienna, but I do need to go." As was his custom of late, he hung up to announce the end of the call. No good-bye, nothing.

Maybe I *was* overreacting.

It hadn't just been a tough weekend. It was traumatic. I knew from my professional training that enduring trauma could make one feel hypersensitive and jumpy, on constant alert, and fearful that something bad was about to happen.

I talked myself through a progressive muscle relaxation exercise, something I did with my clients who felt overly anxious or stressed or who were diagnosed with PTSD. I did feel better when I finished.

"Relax, Sienna. Think logically," I told myself. *Pray,* a quiet voice within me whispered. I reached again for my phone instead. Not that I didn't want to pray, but thinking about my relationship with God seemed to stir up my nerves again. I felt too far away. He felt too far away. And acknowledging that out loud to Him and to me felt uncomforting.

Calm enough to go through my messages, I sent text messages to Roman, my mother, and my sister, Yvette, to let them know I was home and okay. I'd make actual calls later. I sent an e-mail to Ava Diggs to thank her for the link about the upcoming conference. I still was not sure what to do about my car, who to call, what to say. Perhaps I could look up the non-emergency phone number for a police station near BWI. I checked the time. I had to leave soon to meet with my first client of the day. I could look up a contact number when I had a break this afternoon, I decided. Finally, I tackled the last voice mail message, the one from the Baltimore-based phone number I didn't recognize.

I could feel my heart pick up a few extra beats as the message began. "Calm down, Sienna, be logical." And then I smiled. The message was from my pharmacist, reminding me to pick up a prescription.

Pills for my recurring migraines.

I shut my eyes and exhaled, and then laughed at myself. I'd become an expert at working myself up unnecessarily. I shook my head. Was I on the edge of a breakdown?

A text buzzed on my phone.

Glad you made it home safely, Mom. I'm sorry about the weekend. I love you. I WILL talk to you soon. Love, Roman

The message warmed me, made me smile, and gave me enough of a reason to get up from the table and move forward like it was an ordinary Monday and not the start to a terrible week. As I plodded about my house, getting ready for my full afternoon schedule of appointments, I stopped at the joy bag I had tossed on my sofa in exhaustion last night.

I picked it up, ran my fingers over the yarn that spelled out "joy," rubbed the buttons in the centers of the flowers, squeezed the whole thing to my chest. Perhaps I would mail the bag to Abigail anyway. I still had the Christmas card from Mbali with their address.

Yes, that's what I would do. Today. Before I headed into work.

This would be my peace offering in a war we hadn't asked for, in a fight none of us had started. Mbali, Abigail, Croix, none of them were my enemies. RiChard wasn't even my enemy, I realized.

My feelings about him threatened more than anything to rob me of my peace, to kill my joy. Maybe the reason I had not been able to move forward was because I had let pain paralyze me and leave me in a place of ineffective-ness.

Terrorist attack, Laz's deals, nothing could unsettle me if I had peace within myself, I decided.

Yes, this would be my peace offering. I was going to fight for my happiness so I could have a clear head to handle the rest of my life. No, I hadn't prayed, but I felt like God was talking to me anyway. That's how good He was to this daughter. Even when I wasn't together, He was.

I felt good about the day, about my life, even about my ability to finally think through Laz's propositions.

I felt real good, that is, until I stepped outside.

Chapter 13

"Huh?" My eyes grew wide as I stepped out onto my front steps. I blinked, rubbed them, and tried to make sense out of what I saw. Was I dreaming? Or maybe the weekend had been just a terrible nightmare and I had awakened to an ordinary Monday.

My car, my black Honda Accord, was parked out front.

It wasn't in my usual space. The compact car I'd rented was parked where I'd put it last night. The Accord was on the other side of the lot, in one of the spaces earmarked for visitors of the fairly new townhome community.

"Where did it come from? What? Who?" I knew I looked like a crazy woman talking to myself on my front steps, but I felt like one at the moment. Had my car been there all night? It was possible. I'd come home in the darkness and, in my exhaustion, I'd gone straight inside. I would not have noticed the car parked across from my house.

I pulled out my phone and dialed 911.

"What is your emergency?" an operator immediately responded.

"Um . . ." I had not thought this out. "My car was stolen. But now it appears to have been returned. I am not sure what is going on."

"Do you need the police, firefighters, or an ambulance?" The female operator seemed unfazed by my confusion.

"I don't know. I mean, I need the police."

"Ma'am, are you in current danger? Is someone threatening you? Is your person or property at risk?"

"No. Maybe. I don't know. Can you just send someone here?" I gave her my address.

"Police are on their way. Call back if anything changes while you are waiting."

Seven minutes later, a police cruiser pulled up behind my rental car. As the officer got out of his car, I had a quick vision of Leon. How many times had he come to my house dressed in that same uniform? To talk, to share a meal, to bring one of his home-baked desserts, to take out Roman . . .

How did I lose him and why?

"Miss, you have an emergency?" A broad, brawny, overly tanned man with hairy arms approached.

I pointed to my Honda. "My car was stolen from BWI airport."

The officer followed my finger and raised an eyebrow. "That car? The one you're pointing to? That's the vehicle you want to report stolen? From the airport?"

"No, I mean, it *was* stolen. I went to get it from the parking lot at BWI last night, but it was missing. I was going to file a report today, but when I came out, it was parked right there."

The officer looked from me to the car and back. "So, you want me to . . ."

"Find out what happened. Who took it? Who brought it back? What's going on?"

"Miss, your car is back; that is, if it was really ever missing." He looked at me like I was a nutcase. "You're saying that it was parked at BWI. Perhaps a concerned friend or family member brought it back for you in light of the tragedy that occurred there to help reduce the obvious strain you are under."

I ignored his last comment and the look on his face. "So there is nothing you can do? I just want to know what happened."

"There is no stolen vehicle report to file because the location of your car is not unknown. Unless there is something wrong with your car, there is nothing more I can do. Is it damaged? Does it start okay?

He walked with me over to it. I circled it, inspecting for any marks or bruises, and then got in.

Nothing was awry, missing, or out of the ordinary. Except that it had magically appeared in front of my house overnight. Even the fast food breakfast sandwich wrapper I had tossed on the passenger seat still sat where it had landed yesterday morning. I put the key in the ignition and it started with its usual smooth purr. I cut it back off.

"Everything okay?" The officer looked antsy to get to a real emergency to save the day.

"I . . . I guess." I got out of the car and shook my head, feeling like a fool.

"Take care, ma'am." He fished through his pockets. "And if you ever need to talk to someone, here's a number to call." He passed me a card for a mental health crisis hotline. I recognized it immediately because it was the same card I gave to some of my clients.

I wanted to tell him that I was not having a mental meltdown. I was in my right mind and not teetering on the edge of an emotional collapse.

I wanted to tell him all of that, but I was beginning to question it myself.

"Thanks," was all I said as I accepted the card and then I watched him pull away. I looked at the card and then slipped it into my workbag next to a pile of brochures detailing mental health resources. I kept them handy to pass along to clients.

Once again, I'd overreacted. There's always a logical explanation for everything. Maybe the officer was right. As unlikely as it seemed, perhaps Laz had told Yvette or my mom that he was taking care of me, and one of the two had picked up my car to save me the hassle of trying to figure out how to get it back home. I'd given the extra key to my mom when I'd bought my car earlier in the year. I'd call to confirm and thank them later.

But how would they have known where my car was parked? And why bring it back in the middle of the night without telling me?

Admittedly, nothing about this version of possible events made sense, but I was determined not to jump to extreme conclusions. I didn't need to call anyone else right then. I would keep my crazy to myself, now feeling embarrassed about the entire exchange with the police officer.

And I also needed to start my workday. Something in my life had to be normal. I'd go to the post office another time, I decided, throwing the joy bag in the back seat. Abigail and company were not expecting anything from me anyway.

Perhaps regaining peace in my life was not going to be as easy as putting a package in the mail.

I knew that. I was simply desperate for a normalcy that continued to evade me.

Chapter 14

"There you are." My executive assistant/receptionist/office manager Darci Dudley smiled as I entered my office suite. "You have some new messages, some old messages, and a bunch of other odds and ends I'm taking care of."

"Thanks, Darci. I don't know what I'd do without you." I grinned, feeling more confident that the day was finally heading in the right, and mundane, direction.

In the three years since I'd opened The Whole Soul Center, the practice had grown from a small single office space with a miniature waiting room in Rosedale in which I sat in by myself, to a four-office suite complete with a full-sized front desk and chart room. I'd hired three other therapists who worked varying hours to keep the clinic open from early morning to late evening, occasional Saturday mornings, too. The arrangement worked well for me; I was able to build more visibility for my center and the financial payoff was more than what I'd anticipated.

Darci was a young woman in her mid-twenties who was working her way through college to become a nurse. A single mother to three-year-old twins, I understood her plight and allowed her to make the job's days and hours fit her schedule when I first offered her the position. Somehow, she managed to maintain full-time hours at my office while continuing her studies. This brunette, green-eyed beauty had been a godsend since she'd responded to my job listing on Craigslist last year. Her authenticity and eagerness to help proved that not everyone in this country was hung up on race and cultural differences. From the suburban soccer moms to the foster children to the court-mandated parolees who made up my clinic's diverse clientele, Darci, at the front desk, genuinely accepted and welcomed all of the people who came through the door.

"Hope you had a great weekend!" Darci, ever the optimist, grinned at me as she shuffled through some papers on her desk.

"Yes." I smiled back, not wanting to disappoint. "Any changes in the schedule today?" Darci had access to my online calendar, but I had not checked it prior to entering the office.

"Nothing major. The usual," she chirped. "Your one o'clock called to say she is running late. Your two o'clock, Mrs. Groves, called and said that she will be bringing her husband along for her appointment. Your three o'clock cancelled, and I am waiting to hear back from the administrator from juvenile justice to confirm your meeting with him at four-thirty."

"Great, sounds like a regular Monday." I knew Darci would have no idea how significant just saying that was to me.

And, indeed, the afternoon plugged on at its usual pace. After checking in with a couple of the other therapists who were present, I began my forty-five-minute sessions with my clients. I helped a thirty-three-year-old new client explore the alcoholism that defined her family tree; I sat supportively and quietly as another client bravely confronted her husband about his philandering ways. I caught up on paperwork and work-related e-mails during the hour of my cancellation. I was waiting to get word about the late afternoon meeting when Darci knocked on my door.

"I hope you don't mind, but I just squeezed in an intake for you. I don't think Mr. Jackson from DJJ is coming so you have a new client waiting in the waiting room. He's a walk-in." Darci knew that I was open to walk-ins as my schedule permitted. My practice had benefitted from being an open door to newcomers in crisis. Just the same, something in me immediately felt uncomfortable, and not just because Darci had come in person to tell me about this intake. She usually merely buzzed me from the front desk.

"Is everything okay? You don't normally come back to tell me there's a newbie in the waiting room."

"I know," Darci looked serious for a moment, and then she let out a mischievous giggle. "I'm trying to stay professional, and coming back here was the only way I could save face. Sienna, forgive me for saying so, and I'm not trying to be inappropriate, but this man is seriously hot. It's a good thing I'm not a therapist because I'd be in danger of breaking all kinds of ethical rules and regulations. Okay, I'm going back to my desk before you fire me. My game face is back on." She dropped the grin and managed to take on the expression of a severe schoolteacher.

"I'll be right out," I called after her, the pit in my stomach inexplicably widening.

No, there was an explanation.

I bet it's him. I shut my eyes, seeing those icy blue ones that had bored into mine Saturday morning. He was out there waiting for me, I was sure of it. My nerves were on high alert. *Calm down, Sienna,* I told myself, taking two deep breaths and tightening and relaxing my shoulder muscles. I had to remain grounded and logical. Too many times over the past couple of days I had jumped into a panic for no good reason and to no good result.

I got up from my desk and walked toward the waiting room.

"There she is," Darci said to someone out of my view as I approached the waiting room filled with plants, paintings, and soft music. "Ms. St. James is coming to get you right now," she continued, poised and proper, but with an unmistakable sparkle in her eyes.

"Hello, welcome to The Whole Soul Center." I smiled and forced myself not to scream or freeze as I rounded the corner.

It was him.

Chapter 15

Muscle tee. Torn skinny jeans. Unbuttoned light denim shirt. Navy blue canvas shoes.

He looked like a poster boy for a fashion magazine. Today his blond waves were lightly tousled atop his head. He smiled up at me when I entered the room, a small smile, a pensive smile. A harmless smile. Uncertainty filled his eyes, none of the ice, none of the steeliness I must have imagined when we first met.

If he has mental health problems, then help him. You are a therapist.

Laz's words brought a burst of calm and confidence as I extended a hand to the man. He gripped my hand in a dry, firm shake.

"You sought me out." I smiled. "Come on back."

Without a word, he stood and followed me back to my office. I had a large corner room with floor-to-ceiling windows on two walls. The rolling hills and pastoral views of Northern Baltimore County were my backdrop.

"Have a seat," I offered, waving a hand at the large leather couch that faced my armchair. He sat down and I took my seat. Both my armchair and my desk were closer to the door than where my clients sat, a first lesson learned in graduate school.

"Before we begin, I need to let you know that whatever we talk about in here is confidential, unless you are having suicidal or homicidal thoughts, or you disclose a child, past or present, who has been abused or neglected.

These exclusions to privacy are to keep everyone, including yourself, safe. More details about our policies are in the welcome packet I will give you at the end of our session today. If you have questions at any time, please ask." It was my customary spiel that I said to each client at intake.

He nodded and his smile widened, showing off perfectly aligned white teeth. Darci was right. He had movie star good looks. Why had I been so unnerved by this man again?

But good looks meant nothing.

"Okay," I continued. "Let's get started." I grabbed a blank intake packet, an ink pen, and notepad.

His smile suddenly weakened some.

"You don't like me taking notes." I said what he had not voiced.

"You can take notes," he spoke softly, his smile now fully gone.

"Let me just get some basic information from you, have you fill out some forms, and then I will put the pen and paper away. How's that?"

"You didn't get my message?"

The e-mails! "Uh . . ." I tried to think of what to say.

"I left a phone message for you Saturday." He studied me as he spoke. "I said that I can pay you myself. You don't have to worry about any insurance billing paperwork."

"Oh, yes, that." *He's not talking about the e-mails. Exhale, Sienna.* "I did get your message." I managed a weak smile as I continued. "You stated that you wanted to simply meet to have, what was it? Conversations. No insurance forms. No diagnoses. Just talking. We can do that, but I still need to get some basic information from you."

He raised an eyebrow. I quickly continued.

"Like, your name? Your age? Your address? Your contact info? That sort of info helps if we are going to talk."

"What does a name tell you?" He crossed a leg over a knee and sat back more comfortably on the sofa.

"Well, it lets me, and the rest of the world, know how you want to be identified, for one."

He stared at me intently for a moment, then cocked his head to one side. "The Non-Exister."

"Excuse me?" I tried to avoid blinking my eyes, but my eyelashes fluttered anyway.

"You asked how I want you and the rest of the world to identify me, and that is who I am. The Non-Exister." The man continued to stare at me intently.

"I need your name," I asserted.

"No, you said you needed to identify me."

"So, you don't have a name that you answer to?"

"I have a name. It just doesn't match my identity. And you asked for my identity."

I looked down at my notepad and considered whether I needed to take notes. *A personality disorder? Schizophrenia?* I was determined to stay a step ahead. A working diagnostic impression, even if I didn't write it down, would give me a frame in which to base therapeutic treatment. Was therapy what he even wanted?

"Okay, let's start this again. Hello, my name is Sienna St. James. I am a therapist and the founder of The Whole Soul Center. And your name is?"

"Little blessed one," he responded immediately.

We both sat in silence and stared at each other.

"You asked for my name and I gave it to you." He spoke again. "Now you have both my name and my identity. What else do you need to know so we can have our conversation?"

I narrowed my eyes and studied him as intently as he studied me. "You said on Saturday that I would 'know your name soon enough.' What did you mean by that if you aren't even willing to tell me who you are?"

"You know who I am."

A chill went through me, but I had to stay composed. I could not let this man sense that he was getting to me. I shuffled through the papers in my hand but didn't break my gaze. "I have no idea who you are."

"I just told you my name. I just revealed to you my identity. What else do you need to know?"

"Okay, how old are you?"

"Infinity."

I let out a loud sigh. "Okay, Mr. Little Blessed One who doesn't exist."

He smiled at my title of him and his blue eyes twinkled.

"I need you at a minimum to sign a consent form if you want treatment."

His smile stopped and his eyes turned icy. "We are not here for treatment. We are here for a conversation." His voice was flat.

He said he didn't want treatment, so I had every right to dismiss him from my office, escort him out of my clinic. But clearly the man was delusional. I had an ethical obligation to at least assess him for safety and ensure that he was not suicidal or homicidal.

Or worse.

I shook the thought away as I regrouped, and reframed my approach.

"Okay, we'll do things your way." I put my pad, packet, and pen down. "Let's talk." Then I said nothing, waiting to see where he wanted to take the conversation. Ten minutes of uncomfortable, complete silence passed as he sat looking at me, and I looked at him. Then I looked at my wall clock.

"Looks like you're not wanting to talk just yet. I'm here to listen when you're ready. I'm going to finish working on something. Let me know if and when you are ready to talk." This was what I usually said to belligerent teenagers who were pushed into my office by exasperated moms and dads. I stayed true to my word and walked over to my desk and began typing up a report I'd been working on for weeks. My intention was to check in every few moments with a gentle reassurance that I was open to listening. I'd had some clients in the past who'd sat in silence for two or three entire sessions before the floodgates opened. The silence did not bother me.

After another five minutes passed, I looked over at him and smiled. "Again, I will listen to you whenever you are ready to talk. No rush, no worries."

He kept his eyes on me. His smile was gone and his expression was unreadable. I turned back to my desk.

Another five minutes of silence passed. Finally:

"So this is how you have a conversation?" The irritation in his voice was unmistakable, though his face remained unreadable.

I stopped typing, spun my desk chair around to face him, but stayed silent.

When another minute or two passed and nothing else was said, he got up from his seat and headed toward the door. "I'll be back tomorrow to see if you are ready to talk, but I'm not paying you until we have a conversation." He shoved my office door opened and marched down the hallway.

I wanted to tell him that I didn't want his money anyway, that I did not have time in my schedule to see him tomorrow, that I wanted him to leave and never come back.

But this man obviously needed some kind of psychiatric help, and one of the first rules I held to as a clinician was to meet the client where he or she was.

He was out of my office and out of the clinic front door before I had a chance to respond.

"Darci." I turned to my right-hand helper the moment the door closed behind him. "Did he tell you his name?"

"No, I didn't ask." She was focused on her computer screen. "I just gave him the usual face sheet we give all newcomers." She pointed to one of the waiting room chairs. "Looks like he left it over there. Also, he said something about talking to you personally regarding his payment arrangements. Let me know what kind of co-pay you need me to collect from him next time. Is he going to call to schedule his next appointment?"

I missed all she said, focusing only on a paper-packed clipboard that sat in an empty seat next to where the man had been waiting. He hadn't written down a single word on any of the pages of the registration packet.

But he had drawn a picture.

A window.

Using black ink, a detailed picture of a window with striped curtains filled the corner of the top sheet. He'd also drawn a cat perched on its wide sill.

Odd, but worth keeping, I decided, and I slipped the sheet of paper into a folder along with a note about his "name" and "identity."

"Do you want me to file that?" Darci looked up from her work and pointed to the folder in my hand.

"No, I'm holding on to this one."

"Mmmm. Sounds juicy." Darci giggled. "I'm just kidding. I'm a professional. Just a lonely, semi-desperate professional." She giggled, but then quickly sobered at my silence. "A professional who has enough sense to not get involved with a client," she added.

No, especially not this one! I wanted to scream. My head hurt as the beginning of a migraine rapped on the top of my skull. It was nearly five p.m. Though I'd only worked half a day, I felt like I'd just finished a twelve-hour shift. "I'm going home now, Darci, but I'll be in early tomorrow."

When I left the building ten minutes later, I felt off-kilter, unbalanced. Very few clients I'd worked with left me with that feeling. In fact, one of the last times I felt like this was when I'd engaged in a couple's counseling session a few years ago with a man and woman who had more secrets, dead bodies, and high crimes in their past than I cared to know. Got kidnapped and nearly killed because of it, because of them.

That had been the beginning of the end.

Right after dealing with their drama, I'd found out the truth about RiChard, lost Leon for good, and Roman started looking up colleges in San Diego.

Too much to think about on a Monday evening.

I knew as I started the engine of my lost and found Accord where I was heading next. Though I knew I'd face a lecture about my waning church attendance, I also knew I'd get a hot meal with few questions about what was really bothering me.

My mother wasn't into details and sob stories. She just wanted to make sure I was living right.

Chapter 16

"Jerk chicken. Fried plantains. Curried sweet potato soup." My mother, Isabel Davis, lifted the lids to each pot on her stove and let me inhale the mouthwatering scented steam. "Your father said he was in a Caribbean mood tonight. I hope that means he is finally giving thought to taking me on that cruise I've been hinting about."

My mother didn't give hints. Only commands. I chuckled to myself.

True to expectations, she'd had no questions for me when I showed up at her front door. As soon as I was in her living room, she'd pushed me to the kitchen, clanging through pots and pans, showing me herbs, rubs, and spices, and explaining her approach to that night's dinner. Her questions about my spiritual life would come later, I knew, but at the moment she was making sure my soul and stomach were fed.

"Taste this." She stuck a spoon of the soup into my mouth before I could object.

"It's good." I nodded. "Really good." It was.

"Go set the table. Yvette's coming over too."

I was almost forty years old and my little sister was thirty-seven; and yet, my mother still treated both of us like we were her little girls.

Too tired, weary, and frazzled to challenge her, I quietly obliged.

"These terrorists are something," she huffed.

The silverware in my hands clattered onto her hardwood floor. "Sorry, Mom," I mumbled as she gave me a sideways glance before tending to the jerk chicken.

Why was I so jumpy?

I knew why, but I had no rational reason to believe what screamed inside of me.

I don't believe in belief itself. That man had said those words to me during our first conversation. A perplexing statement, an unsettling proclamation, but not necessarily the words of a cold-hearted terrorist.

A suspect was already in custody, I reminded myself.

"I'm sorry, Sienna." My mother studied me as she stirred her pot of soup one final time. "I forgot that you were at the airport just before it happened. Roman called here in a panic worrying about you. Your father and I didn't even know you were flying out to San Diego. Was it a good trip?"

That would be the most she would ask me about RiChard and his other family.

"Good enough."

That would be the most I would answer.

The television boomed in the basement and my father sat watching it from his favorite armchair. Coverage of the attack at BWI continued. I curled up on their old leather loveseat that faced the same.

"Anything new, Dad?"

"I don't believe this brother." My father shook his head. A longtime truck driver for a bakery in Little Italy, he still had on his work uniform. He must have come into the house, marched straight to the basement, and plopped right down in front of CNN. "He had it all," my father continued, "nice family, great job, lots of money, and a future with even more good things in store. Then he blows it all up, literally, and for what?"

For what? The question echoed in me and something clicked. In all my doubts, confusion, gut feelings, and anxiety, I'd never stopped to ask the question why.

Tragedies of this magnitude rarely ever have a defined reason or explanation, but motives and intentions are usually exposed. I'd assumed, as I was sure the rest of the nation had, that with a name like Jamal Abdul, the motive was one based in religious radicalism. Had something else come to light?

"Are there any reports about . . . the suspect's motives for the attack?" I asked slowly, not sure why the potential answer worried me. My father's eyes were glued to the television set.

"Nope. That's what we're all trying to figure out." He spoke like he was part of the investigation team.

"Does it have anything to do with his beliefs?" I didn't know how else to ask.

My father looked at me for the first time since I'd come into his lair. "Well, considering that his fellow church members at First Unity Baptist Church have been weeping on television about how good a teens ministry leader he was, I'm not sure that's the case, but who knows? We make a lot of assumptions about people these days."

He turned back to the TV, opened a can of soda before continuing. "They say he had recently reconnected with his father, who happens to be an imam in his community, and that he was planning a trip with him to Sudan to visit family members. Not sure what that tells us, but that's what some of these television networks are focusing on."

I thought about the woman in the hotel yesterday and the sweeping allegations we all tend to make based on color, ethnicity, and creed. And I felt shame. Can it really be that simple, to peg people into categories without knowing their story, without knowing more than surface facts we pick and choose to discover about their lives?

Can we really make assumptions about others without knowing their true relationship status with The Way, The Truth, and The Life?

"I'm going back upstairs, Dad." I sighed. "Sounds like Mom is putting the food on the table."

He dismissed me with a grunt, his eyes still glued to the television.

"Dad?" I paused on the steps. "Do you think they have the right person in custody?" I had to ask to quiet the battle within me.

"Of course." He didn't hesitate. "They have the best resources, intelligence, and knowledge to not waste time on the wrong guy. They just have to figure out the why and the how, that's all."

The why and the how. I knew right then that until those questions were firmly answered, my doubts were not going to go away.

As far as I was concerned, there was still the possibility, albeit small, that the man I'd met in the airport, and who had sat in my office today speaking gibberish, could be behind the attack.

Listen to what you are telling yourself, Sienna. Gibberish. The man had not been capable of making sense. Of course he wasn't capable of pulling off one of the few terrorists attacks on this country since 9/11. And what would be his why and how? He was nothing more than a client who had severe delusions and psychiatric needs, I told myself again and again. I was a therapist, and I was going to help him.

But why was convincing myself that he was harmless this much of a fight?

I sat down at the table with my parents: my father's usual quiet accented by a somberness I knew came from him trying to make sense of the explosion; my mother abuzz with all things Caribbean and dropping more not-so-subtle hints about her cruise dreams; and me trying to pretend, as always, that I was okay.

And then my sister showed up at the door with a bigger smirk on her face than usual. I knew right then my act was going to come to a quick close.

Chapter 17

"We set a date," she announced as she waved the gaudy, probably fake engagement ring she'd been wearing on her left hand for the past two years.

Her latest "boo," as she called him, had stuck around longer than most and seemed intent on binding himself to Yvette's chaotic life. I had nothing against Demari. Indeed, the fact that he held a job and had his own apartment put him head and shoulders above the usual riffraff my sister tended to gravitate to. He even seemed to be the one who'd gotten Yvette more active in church over the past couple of years. However, he was attracted to my sister and all the craziness her life entailed, including the constant drama wrought by her five children and their fathers, the ones who were still alive. His attraction to her alone made him suspicious.

"May third," she voiced triumphantly as she sat down at the table, but then looked at me with slight concern.

Does she think I'm jealous of her? I noticed that both my parents were eyeing me as well. Though no one questioned me about my love life anymore, I'd noticed that both my parents and my sister seemed to step lightly around me when the subject of relationships and marriage arose.

None of them had ever really asked me about RiChard.

Or exactly what had happened with Leon.

"We're not doing anything really big," Yvette stated almost apologetically as she piled her plate high with plantains. "Pastor McKinney agreed to marry us after communion service next First Sunday."

"That's in three weeks." My father raised an eyebrow. "Why the rush? Are you pregnant again?" Each word he said was louder than the next.

"Of course not." She laughed. "Demari and I committed to celibacy last year and we've been true to our promise. We were out at the movies on Saturday when word came about the terrorist attack. We got to talking about it and the brevity of life and decided it didn't make sense to wait anymore. God gave us each other. Might as well make 'us' official."

Brevity? Since when did Yvette use words like brevity?

I wasn't jealous that Yvette had found her equal. The part of me that cared was happy for her, though another part of me was hurt for her. It would be just a matter of time before things turned sour between them. Heartbreak was inevitable.

I listened to my line of thinking and realized I needed to do a reality check. Just because my romantic experiences had turned south didn't mean that hers would too, although I'd made better life choices, had a better education, lived in a better neighborhood, and *my* son wasn't in jail.

Listen to me! I heard the checklist of my supposed superiority going off in my mind, as if I deserved better since I'd lived better. But didn't I deserve better than Yvette? This waging war within me made me feel uncomfortable. And ashamed. Since when had I become so judgmental?

And bitter.

God is no respecter of persons. His mercy covers a multitude of sins. We're saved by His grace, not our own merits. Faith, not works, is the key that unlocks His generous promises toward us. A sermon I'd listened to online flashed through my head. Instead of comfort, the message made me feel concern. I realized something about myself in that moment. Despite my successes, somewhere on my life's path, I was failing.

And failing badly.

One look at the joy on my sister's face told me that loud and clear.

"Congratulations, Yvette," I heard myself say. I think I even smiled. Whatever act I put on appeared to work. I noted a collective exhale at the table. Yvette had tears in her eyes.

"Thank you, sis." She reached across the table and squeezed my hand. "It means a lot coming from you. And don't worry, who knows what will happen with you and . . . Laz."

Laz!

What did it mean that I had not had a single thought about him or even considered that he had proposed to me just yesterday? What did it mean that I had no pressing desire to share with my family his proposal and his offered opportunity to move with him to Atlanta? It hadn't crossed my mind even after Yvette mentioned how her wedding date was motivated by the terrorist attack. Laz had quoted the same motivation during his proposal, or whatever that was he offered last night.

I kept the smile on my face but stood up from the table. "Dinner was really good, Mom, but I need to start heading back across town."

I needed to call Laz, and not even about the proposal, I realized. Remembering him made me recall that he was supposed to talk to his source about my fears that they had the wrong suspect.

I really am not thinking straight. I shook my head. That sounded ridiculous even to me.

"I'll talk with you later, everyone." My parents and sister were engrossed in details about wedding plans and barely acknowledged my departure.

I was fine with that.

I didn't want any questions, comments, or stares.

"So, have you considered my proposal?" Laz answered on the first ring. I'd waited until I was home to call. Nothing like handling difficult conversations from the comfort of your favorite lounger with a heavy comforter wrapped tightly around you.

"I'm not ready to talk about that."

"Okay, what's up?" The syrup left his voice and we were all business.

"Did you talk to your person?"

"Huh?"

"Your source in Homeland Security?"

There was a pause. Then, "Yes."

"Okay?"

"Okay."

"No, Laz, I mean, what happened? What did he say? What did you say?" *That I have a nutcase of a friend who thinks you have done a completely wrong investigation and she has singlehandedly figured out who is the real bombing suspect.* I shut my eyes, realizing that I had never fully thought through what Laz would say about me or my claims.

"Well, I said that I have a friend who was at the airport just before the explosion, and that this friend had a conversation with someone who made them feel uncomfortable and that this friend wondered if any additional people or witnesses needed to be interviewed."

"And?"

"You can put your mind at ease, Sienna. The government is not looking for any additional suspects. As you
can imagine, they have pretty solid evidence that this
Jamal Abdul they have in custody is the one who most
likely planted the bomb."

"Most likely?"

"Yes, most likely, Sienna. This is America, remember?
Everyone has a right to proclaim their innocence. There's
no guilt until a jury or judge says so."

"Of course," I acquiesced. "I guess you think I'm crazy,
huh?" I tried to let out a small chuckle but my windpipe
felt like it was being squeezed shut.

"You're not crazy. Traumatized. Worried. Terrorized,
really. That's why I am trying to help you. Let this one go,
Sienna. It's okay to do that now."

"I talked to him today. That man came to my office for
a session."

There was another pause. "And?"

"And he was clearly delusional."

"Delusional. Psychotic. Neurotic. I told you, Sienna,
you met a man who needs mental health treatment.
Because of the circumstances and because of where you
were, you're trying to make it all fit together, when, really,
your therapist antenna was just effectively at work identifying someone who is in significant need of treatment.
He is not your average Joe. He probably does not fit the
profile of your usual client, but that doesn't mean that
he's a terrorist, Sienna."

"Right."

"Sienna." Laz sighed. "I need you to spend your energy
and thoughts on figuring out what you want. With me. My
proposal is still on the table. I know that this has been a
tough weekend for you, but start thinking about my offer
so we can talk. Okay?"

"Right," I said again. "I will. One thing, though. What exactly did your contact say? I am letting it go. I just need to hear the exact response to my concern."

Laz groaned. "If you must know, Sienna, the exact response I got from my source was, and I quote, 'Even in the most horrific of tragedies, there are always people who try to gain interviews and end up on TV for their fifteen minutes of fame. Your friend sounds like one of those people.' End quote. Please, Sienna, let it go. You're going to have me looking bad. I cannot be ridiculed at this moment in my career."

"Oh, I'm sorry, Laz. Not just for you, but I am representing myself as a professional. I can't be seen as a camera-obsessed loon." That was not what I felt or wanted. I just wanted peace.

"All right, Sienna, good night. Get some rest. I will be calling you tomorrow and the next day and the day after that until you tell me what I want to hear. I will not be taking no for an answer." He chuckled.

"Of course you wouldn't." I joined his laugh, wondering at heart why he put up with me. Wondering if I was in the process of running him off like I'd done Leon. "Good night." I disconnected the call first before I could wonder anything else.

Peace.

That's all I wanted.

Maybe some joy. Love would be nice.

For the moment, I settled for sleep.

Chapter 18

"A million stars above and a million stars below. Neither the sky nor the sea can contain the brilliance of our love or the pureness of our mission."

We were on a kayak tour at midnight on the calm waters of a bioluminescent bay. The warm, salty water shimmered with an eerie fluorescent blue beneath our coordinated but quiet paddles. Like a dance team in perfect sync, we moved our oars as one beyond a lagoon filled with mangrove trees and into the open bay. Billions of microscopic organisms that had the same chemistry as fireflies made the water magical under the moonlit sky.

The moment had felt perfect. I believed that I was on the side of right.

I was supposed to be in a dorm room, at the college in rural Pennsylvania where I'd earned a free ride. Full tuition, books, room, and board. My parents were so proud. My sister, age sixteen, was already pregnant with her first child and actively dropping out of school. At eighteen years old and a full-time college student, I was my parents' joy and hope; there was no secret about it.

And yet there I was, on a bio bay in Puerto Rico, on a spontaneous trip with a man who was a graduate student at the school.

RiChard St. James.

I hadn't packed a bag, asked where we were going; just got into the car with him when he'd said, "Let's go to the airport. I want you to see the world we're fighting for."

I'd been awed by his messages of social justice as he preached revolution and decisive action on the college's marble steps. I'd been a sponge at the lectures that he gave as a teacher's assistant and at symposiums that he'd organized and held in the school's student union.

And I had believed and held on to every word he told me that night on the bay.

"We are lights in this world, Sienna, and just like these little dinoflagellates in this bay shine brightest when together, our lights will shine brightest if we work as a team. I brought you here, Sienna, so that you could see the magic that could be possible if we join forces. I think . . . I think we should get married and travel the world together to bring change to it right now."

I considered that moment often and imagined that the light of the stars above and the glow of the water below reflected in my eyes as I looked up at him. He must have seen the worship of him in my eyes and figured that was reason enough to marry. I thought about that night often and still couldn't figure out why he asked me to be his wife; and why I went against all that screamed within me, and said yes.

What a fool I was.

Never again.

I woke up around four o'clock in the morning. Sweat made my hair stick to the sides of my face and my nightshirt stick to my chest. I was out of breath, as if I had been fighting in my sleep.

"You became a social worker to prove something to RiChard," I could hear Laz say. No, I had become a social worker because I genuinely cared about others and wanted to take real steps to help. RiChard's way was flawed. His motives weren't right.

Mine were.

And so were my gut feelings.

I'd talked myself into believing that I was on the right path, marrying him, following him blindly into the world unknown. I'd covered my ears to the gongs that had sounded within me, the warning bells that clanged and tolled like a solemn alarm. When I sat at my parents' Thanksgiving table five days after telling RiChard yes, telling them I was leaving school to marry him and travel the world, I'd ignored the part of me that agreed with the horror I saw in my mother's eyes, the defeat that showed clearly on my father's face. When I said my vows at the Baltimore County Courthouse just a few days later, I'd said them over a primal scream of fear and uncertainty that I drowned out with the promises of love.

He'd put a bone on my finger as a ring. It was a piece of a vertebrate that came from some rodent in South America that he said was the tradition of some tribe I had never heard of. It was a bone; but I thought it was love.

I sacrificed myself for his cause, and in the end, I was truly the one who got burned.

Never again.

My gut feelings had tried to warn me, to keep me from going astray, but I hadn't listened. Was intuition the Spirit of God that spoke to us and gave direction when clarity was needed? Verses about the heart that my old Sunday school teacher had made me memorize as a child flashed through my mind.

The heart is deceitful above all things, and desperately wicked: who can know it?

and

A man's heart deviseth his way: but the Lord directeth his steps.

There was a difference between following your heart, which could be misguided by its own desires, and following the gentle nudging of Christ, I decided.

"I feel too far away to know the difference right now," I half prayed, half said to myself out loud. There was a Bible in my nightstand drawer. I could take it out and read it, but where would I begin? I grew up in the church, knew a lot of scriptures, but I could not figure out where to begin again. Sweat continued to coat me. I tossed off my comforter and sat up on the edge of my bed.

My initial gut feelings about RiChard had been right, I admitted to myself. And now my gut feelings were telling me there was more to that man from the airport. That didn't mean he was a terrorist, I conceded, but something about him, everything about him, was off, wrong. He most likely had nothing to do with the explosion or an evil-filled plot; but a rescue, an understanding, a deliverance of some nature, were needed in the worst way.

That was what my gut clearly told me, and I was going to act.

A sense of urgency got me out of my bed and led me to the folder of notes that I'd brought home. No name, no age, no contact information, just an illustration in black ink of a window with a cat on its sill, and a name and identity that didn't make sense.

Wait, I did have a phone number. I recalled that he had left me a voice mail message from a phone number with an Ohio area code. I reached for my phone and scrolled through its log. When I found the number, I wrote it down.

Was that where he was from? Did he have a local address here in Baltimore? Did he have family nearby? He'd said he was going to Chicago on Saturday. Did he go and come back? Did he never leave? What business did he have there? Family? Work? Did he even have a job?

I didn't know the answers but I wrote these questions down and every other one I could think of in a notepad I kept on my nightstand. It was supposed to be a journal, but grocery lists, random thoughts, phone numbers, and other mundane notes filled its pages.

So much for deep thoughts.

"Conversation." I wrote the word down and underlined it, realizing that I had never asked him what he meant. One of the first rules in therapy was not to make assumptions about meanings people held. He wanted to call our sessions "conversations" and not treatment. I needed clarity of what he meant by that.

I filled my notepad up with more questions. Though it was only about five in the morning, I felt invigorated with a sense of purpose and focus. I was going to figure out this man's problem and help him. He was a mystery for me to solve; and if there was even more danger surrounding him . . . I let the thought go, determined to stay rational. Shoot, if he really was a terrorist, I would not feel at all comfortable being in the same room with him, I realized, and not once had I felt like my life was threatened around him.

But that didn't mean anything, I knew. I thought I had known RiChard.

"Little Blessed One." I looked at my notes, read what he'd given as his name. With no other idea of what to do with that one, I turned to my handy sidekick: Google. I typed the phrase and added the word name into the search engine on my phone. I gasped when I saw the first line of results.

The meaning of Bennett is little blessed one.

Bennett.

That could be a first name or a last, but everything in me agreed that this man's name in some kind of way was Bennett: little blessed one.

Chapter 19

Name and identity.

I thought about those two concepts as I pulled into my office parking lot an hour early. I kept several clinical books in my office and I wanted to review them for ideas of how to work with this man.

He'd said he was coming back today, and I wanted to be ready.

Name and identity.

Those words meant two different things to him. He took them seriously, literally, and I had to figure out how and why. I had to start there because that is where he'd started.

My office suite was on the second floor of a small three-story office park. It had its own entrance from the outside and a professionally designed sign that hung in the large glass window. Actually, I had been the "professional" who'd designed it, loving the fact that I could merge my two best talents, counseling and art, together. Several other small businesses made up the complex, including a dry cleaner, a tiny and exclusive exercise studio, a hair salon, and a day spa. A family-owned café anchored the building with outdoor seating and benches.

I skipped the elevator and opted for the stairs, digging through my purse to find the keys. It was too early for even Darci to be there, so I was on my own. Still digging through my purse as I exited the stairwell, I paid little attention to my surroundings or to the scene at my doorway, which was three doors down from the stairs.

When I finally had my keys in hand and looked up, I froze in place.

The man, Bennett Something or Something Bennett, sat cross-legged on the floor in front of my door. Today he wore a light blue dress shirt with the sleeves rolled up, a dark blue striped tie, and jeans. My heart skipped a beat as I tried to figure out whether I should keep walking toward him or turn around and go back down the steps. There was no one else in my office suite, and the idea of being alone with him in there unnerved me.

Of course I could not turn around; he was looking at me and knew I'd seen him. Thinking on my feet, I put on a smile and hurried my pace toward him.

"You're here early. I was about to grab a quick bite from the café downstairs." My words came out as I thought them.

"I'll come with you." He spoke and stood before my fast thinking could keep up.

"Um, okay." I kept the smile on my face and turned back toward the steps. I heard his footsteps behind me.

Looked like we would be having breakfast together.

The café served fruit, muffins, and bagels as well as simple hot entrees during morning hours. I settled for a fresh strawberry-banana smoothie, knowing that my stomach was too knotted to try to eat a full meal. I sat down at a table in a quiet corner as he ordered, wondering how to best approach the situation.

The man asked for only a glass of water and then he approached me.

"Are you ready to talk?" he asked as if we were colleagues or old friends, and not therapist and client. Then again, he had said that he wasn't seeking treatment.

But keeping our "conversation" in treatment mode was my only goal.

"What exactly are we going to be talking about . . . Mr. Bennett?"

He froze, narrowed his eyes, and then slowly sat down.

Upper hand. Checkmate. I wanted to give myself a high five.

But his sudden growing smile gave me pause.

He'd wanted me to look him up. He'd counted on me calling him Bennett. Maybe it was some kind of trick and not even his real name. Or maybe it was his name and he was trying to hide his surprise that I'd figured it out.

I didn't know what to think.

"I see you've done some research. I'm impressed. That happened faster than I expected."

"So, your name is Bennett?" I took a chance.

He shrugged. "Maybe it is, maybe it isn't; that's beside the point."

"What is the point?" I pried.

"You took time to look it up. You're my new hero."

"Hero? That's a pretty big title for someone who is just trying to confirm your given name." I kept myself from cocking my head to the side to avoid coming off as too psychoanalytical.

We were having a conversation.

I could not let him think this was treatment.

"Hero." The man's voice was flat again. "Someone who rises above the rest. Someone who shows strength of character by being selfless."

"Are you writing a dictionary?" I asked.

He laughed, but didn't answer.

"How is trying to figure out your name being selfless?" I was determined to get some kind of answer from him.

"What did you use to look up what you believe to be my name?"

He was not answering any of my questions, but he was talking. That was enough for now.

"The Internet," I obliged. "I entered 'little blessed one' online and got the name 'Bennett.'"

"Exactly." He picked up his glass, took a sip of the water, never broke eye contact with me, put the glass back down. Whatever trace of his previous smile or laugh was gone. "If you believe Darwin, you would agree that humans are continually evolving."

Are we talking about evolution, the Internet, or his name? I stopped smiling so as not to look simple, naïve, or confused. "So you are . . . heavily into Darwinism."

"Absolutely not. Evolution implies that there is a beginning, and if there is a beginning, then there is a Creator; otherwise, there is nothing but infinity."

"Infinity. That is the age you said you are." I nodded, as if I fully understood our "conversation."

"And of course that is not accurate." He nodded back. "Because then that would require existence, a beginning, and an end."

"Right, because your identity is the non-exister. Okay." I pushed my smoothie glass away. "We need to have a reality check here. You are talking about a lot of unrelated things that, honestly, are not making sense to me. I simply asked you why you called me your hero and now you are talking about evolution and infinity."

"Exactly." He smiled, his blue eyes seeming to suddenly sparkle with excitement. "If humans are evolving, then the technology and inventions we currently have would be the best that could be offered for mankind in this moment. And what is the best that we offer? I would argue the Internet, more than anything else, because everything else is where? On the Internet."

"Okay, I am trying to follow you."

"What is the purpose of the Internet, Ms. Sienna St. James?"

"Uh, to be a gateway for information."

"No, I asked what is the purpose?"

"You got me." I sat back in my seat. "I don't know what you perceive is the purpose of the Internet outside of being a modern-day encyclopedia of information."

"It's not about facts and details and data. When people talk about the Internet, they talk about social media."

I didn't say anything, just let him talk.

"Yes, there are Web sites for information and businesses, and even dictionaries and encyclopedias, but what are the most successful sites? What Web pages get the most visits? I'll tell you: e-mails. Chat rooms. Instant messages. Facebook. Twitter. YouTube. Social media."

"So, you're saying that the purpose of the Internet is for people to connect with each other?"

"Absolutely not."

Was that anger in his eyes?

"The purpose is vain glory. Self-indulgence. Exhibitionism." The man leaned in as he spoke. "Human beings have a need to tell their stories and have the crazy notion that others actually want to hear them. Every day, the world over, people take snapshots and write down random thoughts of mundane moments, monumental milestones, and everything in between, and then post them on social media accounts. They wait for someone to click 'like' or retweet or post a comment or reply, and then get devastated if nobody notices, and then angry if everybody does.

"If we are evolving," he continued, "then we are turning into self-absorbed creatures whose entire existence is based on waiting for others to applaud every second of our lives, regardless of significance. But of course, I don't believe in evolution. Just existence, and the world as it exists is nothing more than a globe full of itself. Ms. St. James, when you took a moment to use the Internet to figure out my name, you fought against human nature.

You didn't use the Web to succumb to a moment of exhibitionism. You used it as an altruistic act to learn more about me. Therefore, in your act of selflessness, you became a hero."

What? Huh? I felt my eyes blinking as I tried to keep up and attempted to stay a step ahead.

"Don't heroes save people? You forgot that aspect in your definition earlier." *Should I even bother with reality testing?* The man had said he didn't want treatment so what good would any of this talking do? He hadn't said anything remotely suicidal or homicidal, so maybe it was safe just to leave him alone and let well enough be. *He most likely had nothing to do with the explosion or an evil-filled plot, but a rescue, an understanding, a deliverance of some nature, were needed in the worst way.* My thoughts from the early morning hours resurfaced. Rescue. Deliverance. And here he was talking about heroism.

Perhaps this wasn't all just coincidence.

"You're right, Ms. St. James. Heroes do save people, and that's what you have done, are doing, and will do. Your heroism is fascinating to me."

Fascinating.

The word jumped out and startled me and I knew exactly why. The two e-mails from the sender Everybody Anybody or whoever it was had had that word in each of its headers.

It's just a coincidence, Sienna. I told myself to calm down. *"Fascinating" is a common word. His word choice meant nothing. I'm just being overly sensitive and analytical.* Even if it was in an e-mail sent over the Internet, the very thing he'd just spent time talking about, explaining his view that the world was self-absorbed, wanting to share every mundane fact about ourselves . . . *Five Fascinating Things About Me. Five Fascinating Things About You.*

Was it all really a coincidence? I had to talk to Laz about this again, I knew.

The man finished his cup of water. My fruit smoothie was nothing more than a tall glass of melting slush.

"I've enjoyed our conversation today." He set his glass down with a loud thud. "I'll be back tomorrow so we can continue." Without another word, he got up and left.

I watched as he crossed the parking lot to a yellow Jeep. It had tags from West Virginia. I jotted down the license plate number before he pulled off the lot.

Then I grabbed my things and hightailed it out of there.

Chapter 20

I dialed Laz's number as I ran back up the staircase, but hung up just before his phone started ringing. What was I supposed to say to him? That I'd figured out that strange man's name may or may not be Bennett and that he used the word "fascinating" so he must be an Internet stalker, or worse, a terrorist?

Even I heard the foolishness in those claims.

The front door of my suite was unlocked.

"There you are." Darci's sing-song greeting met me as soon as I came in. She was emptying wastebaskets, tidying up the waiting room magazines, preparing for a full day of clients.

"Look at you." I smiled. "Are you working today or do you have other plans?" I raised an eyebrow at the clingy, yellow wrap dress she wore, black high heels, and yellow and black jewelry.

"Nope, no other plans. Just thought I'd spruce myself up for a change. It's amazing what you can find when you actually go through your closet."

Her smile was bigger than usual. She seemed bright, glowing, and not only because she wore a sunbeam-shade dress.

Had she heard that man say he was coming back today? I thought about how her eyes had lit up when she'd announced his presence yesterday. Was her outfit in any way related to him? It was a wild thought, but even thinking it made me uneasy.

No, Darci! Don't get caught up with him, no matter how gorgeous you think he is. I screamed this in my head, but knew I'd have to say it out loud if there was any hint of my suspicions being true. But there was no need to embarrass her and make myself look like an idiot, I decided.

When and why had I become so paranoid? I guess I suffered from my own delusions, I concluded.

"Your son called." Darci was back at her desk. "He wants you to call him back as soon as possible."

Roman.

With all the craziness that defined my life these days, my son was the one constant, the one person who made sense.

And yet I had failed him by never fully seeking complete answers about his father and by rejecting the idea of a relationship with the siblings he called family.

"Thanks, Darci." I hurried to my office and shut the door behind me.

The need to talk to someone "normal" was nearly overwhelming me. I tried to shake off the convoluted feelings that Bennett, or whatever his name was, left me, and dialed my son. He picked up on the second ring.

"Hi, Mom."

"Hi, Roman. How are you?" My heart always melted when I heard my son's voice on the phone, like it did the first time I'd held him in my arms. He was the only positive to RiChard's negative.

"I'm fine. Just wanted to check on you."

"I'm fine, Roman." There was a long pause. "What's wrong?"

"I don't think I'm coming back here next school year."

"Wait. What? Why?" I heard the gasp in my voice and questioned it. Weren't these the words I'd been longing to hear come from his mouth?

"I can't deal with it anymore. I'm too far away from my family."

I'd said the same thing when he first applied, ignoring his assertions that he had family, brothers and a sister, with whom he wanted to connect.

"Roman, you can't . . ." My voice faded as I searched for the right words to say. "You can't let whatever is happening between you and . . . them keep you from finishing your degree out there. Keep your eyes on the bigger picture. Didn't you say your program is nationally ranked?" I felt dizzy as my mouth said the complete opposite of what I felt like saying.

"It's not working. I don't want to be here. They don't . . . feel like family. I just want to come home. For good."

I did not know what was happening. I hadn't been there for him, to listen, to understand the way that I should have been (and I was a therapist!) so I knew I had to get this right. I didn't want my son giving up on the relationships that meant so much to him. As much ambivalence as I felt about Mbali and her children, I knew it was right for Roman to keep fighting for the family connections he dreamed of having.

"Listen, I'm coming back out there on Thursday. Don't make any firm decisions right now. Let's talk some more then, and I will support you in your efforts to fix whatever is going on with you and your brothers and sister. Don't run across the country away from them; otherwise, it will never be resolved and you'll have those relationships hanging over your head like a weight."

"Mom, I'm a grown man. I don't need you flying back out here to rescue me."

Rescue.

The word jumped out at me and I remembered the uneasiness I'd felt moments early.

"It's not a rescue, Roman. I already had plans. Something I need to do."

In the several seconds of silence that ensued, I could almost hear his brain struggling to figure out what I was up to. He gave up trying and didn't bother trying to ask me questions, seemingly knowing that I would have already given him answers if that was my intent.

"Mom, you have never wanted a relationship with them yourself and you never really wanted me to come out here in the first place. Why the sudden change of heart?"

"Because this isn't about me; it's about you. I don't want you making the same mistakes I did and end up spending a lifetime overshadowed by loose ends from broken relationships." I let the words settle before continuing. "We'll talk more on Thursday. Maybe we can have that dinner we missed on Saturday. Or better yet, lunch." Kisu's seminar was in the evening. I didn't want to take any chances of having to explain to Roman where I was going.

He was in the situation he was in now because I hadn't found out the answers I'd needed for both of us years ago.

No more loose ends.

But no telling him about it until those ends were tied. I didn't want to prolong the pain, for either him or me, any longer.

We hung up after a bit of small talk about his projects and exams. I resumed my workday, floating through individual and family therapy sessions; catching up on notes; thinking about family, love, and relationships. I'd made a living out of helping people sort through complex feelings, communication failures, and the choices that affected them all.

By seven-thirty that evening, I'd helped a woman talk through the bitterness she felt over an abusive ex, listened to a teenage girl plead with her mother to stop ignoring her crying, and guided a grieving widower through a healing exercise to address his deep feelings of loss. I helped them and many more clients, both scheduled and walk-ins, before I headed home. I finally took care of the rental car return and then I collapsed onto my bed.

And I'd also made a decision about Laz.

Four hours, thirty-three minutes.

16,380 seconds.

I was calculating time again, my old standby, a safe constant.

That's how long it had been since I'd made up my mind about Laz. Now I just had to tell him.

Curled up on my bed with my comforter wrapped tight around me, I'd turned on the eleven o'clock news, knowing that in the midst of the harrowing stories about the terror attack and its aftermath, Laz would come on at some point. Though there'd be no telling exactly where he'd be when the live shot came, it was guaranteed that he'd find some new angle, some unexposed facet of the story on which to report.

Laz looked for and reported controversy.

His story came on at 11:07, early in the broadcast. He must have good information. I turned up the volume and waited for him to start speaking.

And waited to see if, when I saw him on the screen, my heart would confirm what my head had decided.

"Even as authorities are trying to better understand how the suspect, Jamal Abdul, was able to plan and initiate the attack, many are just trying to understand the suspect. From close family members to longtime friends to neighbors, coworkers, and former little league coaches, those who crossed paths with Abdul are grappling with what made the suspect turn on his own country and wreak havoc, injury, and death to his fellow citizens." Laz looked in the camera solemnly, his hat fixed straight on his head.

"Investigators are looking at potential ties through his father that may connect him to radical groups. Those who know him best are looking back over the days, weeks, and years they've spent with him, trying to see if and how they missed any warning signs of this current disaster."

"Jamal used to come to our center and play board and card games with us." A taped interview began playing and an elderly man sitting at a table spoke as several other seniors surrounded him, nodding their heads and looking forlorn. "Spades, pinochle, checkers; he even helped run some bingo nights."

"His wife would bring pound cake and lemonade to share with us, and his two young children were a real hoot," a woman wearing a crooked wig chimed in. "We are shocked, flabbergasted, and in total disbelief. There has to be some kind of mistake. I just can't believe it."

The screenshot dissolved into a collection of photographs of the suspect at various community and charitable events. One picture showed him in a white tuxedo at what looked like a fundraising ball for cancer research. In another snapshot, he wore denim overalls and stood alongside several youths in an urban community garden. As the pictures continued, Laz's voice rejoined the report.

"While those who know Jamal Abdul are trying to come to terms with the allegations against him, the rest of the country, indeed the world, is seeking an explanation for how a monster could be hiding inside someone who appeared to be a hero to many. This is Laz, live from another ground zero, if you will, at BWI. Back to you, George."

Hero.

The word cut through me, grabbed my attention, and made me forget what it was that I'd been looking for when I'd first turned on the nightly news. I sat there for a few minutes, unaware of the remaining broadcast as

I reflected on the conversation I'd had with the Bennett man earlier that morning.

And then I laughed at myself for being so darn paranoid, working myself into a tizzy over the word "hero." *Or am I?*

As soon as the news went off, I dialed Laz. When I can't shake nagging feelings, I have to do something about it until it's clear to let them go.

As much as I wanted to deny it, the nagging feeling in my gut that I had missed something, that we all had missed something, still ate away at me.

"Hey, pending fiancée," he greeted me on the fifth ring.

"Hi, Laz, I have a question."

"I was hoping you had an answer."

"I do, but I can't get into that yet." I heard his sigh, but I kept talking anyway. "I saw your report on the eleven o'clock news. Where did all those pictures of the suspect come from?" I held my breath, not sure why it felt so important to me to know how the station had obtained the photos.

"You mean the photos of Jamal Abdul seeming to save the world before he went and turned it upside down? My crew and I found them online."

"On Facebook? On Twitter?" I exhaled, then inhaled sharply again.

"Yeah, but not on his accounts. They were photos posted on different people's pages, organizational Web sites, that sort of thing. It doesn't appear that he had any social media accounts beside his professional networking ones."

"Oh," I replied, wondering what I was supposed to think or do about that new bit of information.

"Why do you ask?" Laz asked, then paused. "Wait, does this have anything to do with that man you're worried about?"

"No. Well, yes. It looks like I'll be treating him on a regular basis. We met this morning and had a really bizarre conversation about the Internet and social media sites and eternity and existence and, well, it was weird. He had a lot of opinions about Facebook and that sort of thing."

"So, you are thinking that because this man talked about Facebook and some pictures of the suspect pre– terror attack came from Facebook, the man you spoke with should be questioned?"

"No, that's silly. That's not what I'm saying. I don't know what I am saying."

"You need to be saying that you've agreed to become my wife." He chuckled. "I've got to go in a moment, Sienna. You said you had an answer for me. Can you tell me something, please?"

"Let's meet for dinner tomorrow night. We'll talk then." I didn't think answering a wedding proposition was an appropriate topic for a hurried phone call.

Laz groaned but agreed. "Okay, I'll give you a call sometime tomorrow when I'm free. We'll figure out where to meet and when. I'm gone, Sienna."

He disconnected and I was left alone again to wade through the murkiness of my own thoughts and imaginations.

A billion people use Facebook. A quadrillion pictures are posted online every day. Why was I worried about the peculiar ruminations of a man possibly named Bennett?

Chapter 21

Wednesday morning.

I'd set my phone alarm early so that I could get a quick workout in before dawn. After doing some crunches and riding the exercise bike I kept in my spare bedroom, and getting showered and dressed, I sat down at the kitchen table to plan my day. I had a lot to accomplish and little direction except for my questionable instincts and my weary heart.

And you have me.

It was a still small voice that spoke to my consciousness, one that I rarely heard these days. I glanced over at a worn Bible I kept near my kitchen table on a rack by the pantry. It had been my grandmother's. And like her, it felt like a distant, but warm memory of better times, love, and soul food.

When was the last time that I had picked up that Bible, any Bible? I strained to remember. There was a time in my life when I'd read scriptures for daily nourishment. Like breakfast, lunch, or dinner, I would sit down in the armchair in the living room of my old house—the one I lived in before I'd learned the truth about RiChard—and study passages, meditate on the meanings, and digest the truths that I knew were changing my life, giving me direction.

I truly could not remember when I'd stopped having my daily spiritual meals. I would read and listen and pray, sometimes cry, then smile, hum or sing.

And worship.

What was that really about anyway? I mean, it had been so long since I'd really taken time to talk to God, to genuinely thank Him, to contemplate His character and the safety of my life in Him, that the idea of worship felt distant, foreign.

Nearly out of my reach.

As I sat in my kitchen, staring at my grandmother's Bible on the shelf near my cookbooks, I recalled late nights years ago when I'd pondered verses and prayed intense prayers. *This must be what a relationship that's grown cold feels like.* Blazing fires of love and total infatuation had somehow been reduced to mere glowing embers, a roaring waterfall into a hollow drip, a melodious string symphony into a single out-of-tune violin.

What had changed?

It wasn't God. *The same yesterday, today, and tomorrow,* a Bible verse about God stated.

That only left one party at fault in our two-party relationship.

Me.

I'd stopped going to church regularly nearly three years ago, but I knew that was not the root issue, just a superficial symptom. Not going to church was like avoiding a favorite café at lunchtime because you knew an old flame would be there. This wasn't about me missing church. This was about me missing *Him.*

I'd stopped spending regular time in the Word, praying, waiting, reading, listening, ages ago. I mean, ages.

I shut my eyes, but refused to let the tears that burned the back of my eyelids fall. Everything in me burned. A flurry of emotions, none of them positive, whirled uneasily inside of me.

Exhaustion. Disappointment.

With myself. With my life. Okay, even with God.

In His omnipotence, He'd allowed everything that happened to me happen. I thought briefly of a conversation I'd had once a couple of years ago with a hurting young woman named Silver. She'd been angry, hurting, and bitter about the atrocities that she'd undergone in her childhood and young adult life. She couldn't understand why bad things had happened to her, and I'd tried to assure her that God cared. I thought of my words to her back then:

Maybe the situations that hurt us the most are the perfect situations that make us seek God the most. Sometimes things happen that force us to seek Him.

It was early morning. I had much to accomplish today; but I knew that nothing could be started or finished without me first making amends with the one who held my life and times in His hands.

Who loved me like no man on this earth ever could.

Like no man on this earth ever did.

It was time to draw close to Him, to draw from Him.

With my eyes still closed, I tried to pray, I mean, really pray. I opened my mouth, waited for words to come, waited for something, anything. But my voice felt lodged somewhere in my throat. When words did come, they felt the way I imagined a rusty door must feel when someone forces it open after years of disuse.

Loud. Squeaky. Unpleasant.

I got out only two words.

"I'm hurting."

I opened my eyes and all I could see were the pieces of my life, the shards left over from the men I'd loved and lost. Anger. Grief. These were the jagged, sharp slivers of my shattered heart.

Was I really that messed up because of men? Really? *What is wrong with you, Sienna?* I fussed at myself, debased myself.

Shame, guilt, embarrassment mixed in with the rest of the stew of feelings that simmered inside of me. With no other way of fighting what I felt, I stood, walked over to my cookbook shelf, and took off my grandmother's Bible.

I had no specific scripture in mind, no expectation that all of a sudden I would feel better just by flipping through the thin, gold-trimmed pages. I opened it where a postcard stuck out.

God is always near.
Love you,
Ernestine Jefferson

I smiled at the memory of the spry church mother from a local mega church. I'd had some dealings with her and some other members from Second Zion Tabernacle years ago when I tried to locate the whereabouts of a girl named Hope, a child nobody was certain even existed. Mother Jefferson's notes of encouragement always showed up in my mailbox just when I needed them.

I put the postcard to the side and looked at the page that it had held. Matthew 6. My grandmother must have come to this chapter often, for the crease was deep and many of the verses, written in red, were underlined.

The Lord's Prayer.

A familiar passage I'd memorized in childhood.

Our Father which art in heaven, I began reading, and I kept reading until one line jumped out at me like it never had before:

And forgive us our debts, as we forgive our debtors.

Forgiveness.

I talked about it all the time with my clients, but wasn't sure that I'd examined it truly for myself.

I wasn't, I realized, really sure how.

Zing! Zing! An alarm on my phone went off, the time that I usually set to wake up, and I knew I had to get moving if I expected to get everything on my lengthy to-do list completed for the morning.

For one, if I was truly heading back to San Diego tomorrow, I needed to book a flight, find a room, and set my plans. I'd have to let Darci know to free my schedule, though it helped that Baltimore was three hours ahead of California.

I shut the Bible and logged on to my laptop. I'd avoided planning this trip the entire week, and I knew it wasn't just because I was anxious.

The idea that I would actually see Kisu in person left me feeling numb. What would I say to him? What would he say to me? Did he know the truth and extent of RiChard's lies? Why had he sent the lion's head ring to me years ago? Why not call and talk to me? Was that his way of letting me know the truth? Was there more that I did not know, had not considered?

Once the questions started, I could not make them stop. What I did know was that Kisu had to have answers. He had to. At a minimum, I hoped that he would be able to give me an idea of where RiChard might be, that is, if RiChard was even alive.

Not that I wanted to see him. I absolutely did not! But the little bit of research I'd previously done about divorcing an absent spouse informed me that I'd have to prove that I'd done my best to look for him.

A quick check of flight information let me know that thanks to the time difference between the East and West Coasts, a nonstop flight that left midday tomorrow would get me to San Diego by the evening time. The seminar was scheduled to start at 7:30. The only nonstop flight I could find still available was out of Dulles. To get there in time, I'd probably only be able to see one or two of my early morning appointments tomorrow.

Hey Darci, I typed in an e-mail, I have to go out of town again tomorrow so I can only see my 7:30 and 8:30 appointments in the morning. Please clear my schedule for the rest of Thursday until Friday afternoon. You can offer the cancelled clients times on Saturday, if any still want to come in this week. If there are any new intakes, let Kierra know she can have them if her schedule permits. Thanks!

Kierra was the newest therapist I'd hired and she was actively building her caseload. I read through the e-mail and pressed send. Although it was only a little before six in the morning, Darci's reply was immediate.

Count it done. Have a nice trip!

She never asked questions about my life and I rarely asked questions about hers. She kept pictures of her three-year-old twins, a boy and a girl, on her desk, and occasionally updated me on her nursing studies. Outside of that, I knew little else about her, except that she was a dependable, hardworking employee whose commitment to excellence had helped my practice grow.

After booking a flight, a rental car, and a hotel room by San Diego's airport, I realized I had really nothing else I needed to do before leaving for work. My schedule was in good hands with Darci. I'd already done my morning workout. I looked at my grandmother's Bible and knew the one sentence from the Lord's Prayer would have me chewing on it for a while.

Why had I woken up so early again? The feelings I'd had about the tasks I'd just completed had made them feel like they would take longer than they did. And now I had an hour of free time.

As I put the Bible back on my cookbook rack, a folded piece of paper fluttered out. I smiled when I opened it and knew exactly what I was going to do for the next hour.

It was a recipe.

From Leon.

A no-nonsense cop, he'd gotten his tender touch with food from his own grandmother, who had raised him. During our two-year friendship that should have grown into more, but didn't because of me, we spent more time in kitchens, mine or his or my mother's, than we did dining out.

My smile widened as I ran a finger down the crease of the paper, remembering the story behind the one recipe he'd given to me.

"My grandmother made me promise not to share her secret recipes, but this one I've tweaked enough that I don't think she'd be too mad."

Mint chocolate raspberry cookie bars.

The first time we tried to make it together, the sugar spilled, the eggs splattered, and my favorite glass baking pan shattered.

"I don't think Granny is pleased." He'd chuckled, and we reworked the recipe together to make it all our own.

I realized that I had never laughed as much with anyone as I had with Leon.

I was giving Laz Tyson an answer to his marriage proposal tonight.

Fifty-three minutes, the clock on my microwave told me.

I had time.

I took out my mixing bowl, grabbed the brown sugar I kept in the pantry, bubbled with excitement once I'd confirmed that I had all the ingredients I needed.

As the bars baked in the oven and the sweet, intoxicating scent of chocolate, mint, and berry filled my nostrils, I recalled memories of other moments I'd spent with Leon: long walks around the Inner Harbor; short jogs around Lake Montebello; lively discussions with Roman around the dinner table; quiet reflection after church.

While Laz's sharp tongue and wit challenged my intellect and kept me on my toes, Leon had been like the worn comforter I kept on my bed.

Someone I could curl up with, exhale, relax, and just be.

I was giving Laz my answer tonight.

I was at a different place in my life than where I was before Leon left town to help his long-lost niece get back on her feet in Houston.

I was in a far different place than where I was when I'd left everything behind to follow RiChard blindly around the world.

Cooking the bars felt like a celebration for me, a nod to where I was now, to the decision I'd made about Laz, a decision I was determined to hold fast to. No longer would the man in my life have to wonder about my intentions or guess at my desires. No longer would I have to feel like a feather in the wind when it came to love and marriage.

My mind was made up.

I would even bring some bars to give to Laz when I saw him.

Chapter 22

"So, Ms. St. James, you're saying that I need to look real closely at my thoughts, and see what it is that I'm telling myself about my husband's infidelity."

"That's exactly what I'm saying, Shanay. However, it's not just listening to your self-talk, but examining your thoughts to see if the messages you are telling yourself are true, helpful, or logical. For example"—I looked down at the thought log journal my twenty-seven-year-old client had brought in as directed—"you wrote down that you had the following thoughts last night: 'If I were prettier, Caleb would have never cheated.' 'I deserve what happened because of all the bad choices I made when I was younger.' 'I can never trust another man again.' 'I am unlovable.'"

I looked up at my 4:30 client whose light brown eyes filled with tears. "Remember, like we talked about last time," I continued as she grabbed another tissue, "your thoughts lead directly to what you feel. If you are feeling depressed and devastated, look again at the thoughts you are having. Examine them. Challenge them. Separate truth from fiction. Change your inner dialogue to one that speaks to healing, wholeness, and moving forward. It's never about what happens to you; it's about how you respond, what you tell yourself about your circumstance. Your feelings are going to match the messages you play in your mind. You can't control what others do to you, but you can control how you respond."

She nodded and closed her eyes. "That's true," she whispered before reopening them and looking back at me. A small smile tugged on her lips. "Thank you. You have been very helpful through all of this."

I smiled back at her as she gathered her things.

"Same time, same place next week, Shanay, but not the same thoughts," I gently chided.

"I'm working on it." She laughed as she left the office.

I checked my calendar. I'd seen seven of my scheduled clients today. There had been only one no-show and one cancellation.

And no sign of Mr. Bennett, or whoever he was.

I exhaled, realizing that my body had been holding tension all day as I'd wondered constantly if he would reappear. Taking two deep breaths, I tightened and loosened the muscles in my shoulders to relax, a quick tip I offered to my stressed-out clients.

I needed to take more of my own advice, I concluded as I began packing up my things for the day. I'd said all the right things to my last client, Shanay, but how much of what I said did I really listen to myself?

"Don't you worry about a thing for tomorrow. I've already taken care of your clients and a few of them have already rescheduled for Saturday afternoon." Darci stood in the doorway, flipping through some charts.

"Thanks, Darci. I don't know what I would do without you." My things in hand, I followed her to the reception area and waiting room.

"Oh." She froze at her desk and used her free hand to run through part of her brunette hair. "Ms. St. James is done for the day. Did you have an appointment?" I heard her speak to someone just out of my view.

Him.

I inhaled and held my breath as Darci knocked over her pencil cup. "Oops." She giggled and then quickly sobered and turned around to face me. "Sienna, your client from the other day is back. I know you were about to leave. Would you like for me to give him one of your Saturday openings? The morning times are still available."

"That won't be necessary." I spoke before thinking. My heart started beating faster. "I can see him now."

I checked my watch. Laz and I had agreed to meet at a restaurant at 8:00 p.m. in Columbia, Maryland, a quasi-halfway point between Baltimore and DC, where he was still covering the terror attack. I'd been planning to go to a library to catch up on paperwork and look through some psych books and magazines until then. However, I knew there was no way I'd be able to get any work done knowing that I'd turned down an opportunity to figure out this man.

"Oh, you're leaving, Darci?" I noticed my assistant packing her bags and shutting down her computer.

"Yes. I have to pick up my . . ." She glanced over at the man, who stared back at her. "I mean"—she cleared her throat—"I have to leave a little early today to run an errand. Kierra and Soo Yun both called and said their evening clients cancelled, which is unusual, so I thought I'd take advantage of this rare free Wednesday evening to, well . . ." Her eyelids blinked rapidly as she looked from me to the man, who stared at her from his seat.

Was she trying to keep him from knowing that she had children, as if that would scare him away? I would definitely have to talk to her, the sooner the better. I knew Darci was professional enough not to cross any inappropriate lines with our clients, but just the same, I would speak to her privately the moment that I could.

"I was planning to make up this time on Saturday morning since you'll be in that day anyway." She bit her lip and I realized that my silence was discomforting to her.

"Darci, that's fine. I'm not worried about your hours. I just want you to have a nice evening."

"I'll be here Saturday." She breathed out as she scurried to the door. She pushed a lock of hair off her face and gave both the man and me a slight smile. She exited with her head down.

"Well." The Bennett man spoke for the first time. "Looks like it's just you and me."

Today he wore a brown suit with a yellow dress shirt. The shirt collar was loosened and a tie hung limply from his neck. Was he coming from work? What did he do for a living? I remembered the list of questions I had about him that I'd written down the other night.

I also remembered that I had no desire to be alone in my office with him.

"Hungry?" I gave an easy smile. "We can go back to that café and talk again like we did yesterday. Continue our conversation?"

"No." His reply was immediate and certain. "I wanted to talk to you privately today. That's why I came late to make sure that I was your last client."

Everything in me screamed, yelled, quivered, and collapsed, and yet the easy smile on my face would not leave.

"Okay, Mr. Bennett. We don't have a lot of time to talk, but I can see you for a few minutes. Come on back to my office."

What kind of fool crazy state was I in? I swallowed hard and sent up a quick prayer for continuous protection.

Chapter 23

There had only been a few clients over the years who rattled me down to my ankle bones since I'd started my social work career. Aside from a couple I'd engaged in couples counseling a few years ago who turned out to have secrets that threatened my safety, I'd been disturbed once as a graduate student intern by a late teen who confided to me vague details about being a hit man for a dangerous, well-organized gang; and another time as a newly licensed practitioner by an older, snaggletoothed woman who claimed to see the souls of the living and the dead, and kept squinting at an empty space beside me.

However, the feelings of fright and unsettledness that I'd felt on those occasions did not compare to the paralyzing anxiety I was having watching the man quietly flip through the textbooks and manuals I kept on my bookshelves.

He's not a terrorist. He is a man who needs help, and I am here to help him. My thoughts troubled me even more as I realized I still felt unsettled about what he had been doing at the airport on Saturday.

Stay logical, Sienna. I had no sound reason to continue mulling those disturbing thoughts. I also realized that I had no desire to ask him about his trip on Saturday. I did not feel prepared to hear any of his potential answers.

As had been my approach, I stayed quiet, allowing him the chance to take the lead of our conversation. After about ten minutes of walking around my office, picking up thick books and studying the various knickknacks I'd set out, he finally sat down on the leather couch farthest from my office door.

Which I'd kept open.

I felt good about doing that, just like I felt good that I'd followed some advice from Ava, my life and career mentor, about another aspect of my office layout.

"Never have personal mementos out in your office where you do therapy. Some pictures and personal artifacts clients do not need to see, for their protection, and yours." I could hear Ava's warning.

I needed to call her. Hadn't spoken to her in a while. I made a mental note to do so. This would be a good case for peer supervision.

"So." The man possibly named Bennett finally broke the silence. "You choose to practice an eclectic form of therapy. I see books from many schools of psychological thought, competing theories, even the Bible." He pointed to the small, green book I kept behind a plant on my windowsill. I was surprised he'd seen it. Most clients never noticed the pocket-sized New Testament I stored within my arm's reach for when I needed a quick boost. It had been awhile since I'd picked it up. Its sun-faded leather cover was evidence that I'd nearly forgotten it was there.

The fact that he seemed to be observing and interpreting small details of my life did not comfort me.

"Sounds like you have some thoughts about what I do, an opinion about my approach."

It was too easy of a bait, I knew. I did not expect him to take up my unhidden offer for him to further divulge his personal philosophies surrounding psychology and faith.

But I needed to try something. I needed to have some kind of understanding of this man.

It was an easy bait, and he knew it, but he took it anyway.

"Your confusion simply proves my point." He smiled, but nothing in me was warmed.

"My . . . confusion. Can you explain what you mean?" I knew that I would be annoyed by whatever answer he gave, but the trained social worker in me knew that I had to explore, explore, explore.

"Why did you become a therapist?"

I nearly did a double take. *Was he in the room when Laz asked me pretty much the same question on Sunday? Of course not. Right? Get it together, Sienna,* I chided myself. I could not let my paranoia dictate this session. I was certain that's what he wanted on some level.

The upper hand.

Why?

All the questions I'd had I'd forgotten, except one:

What is his motive for coming to see me? That was what I had to focus on. That was how I would not get derailed and end up in a land of insanity along with him.

"I find it interesting that you would want to know about my personal choices, but are not willing to disclose any basic or public information about yourself."

"Basic or public information about me?" His eyes narrowed. I had touched a nerve.

Did I press it or let it go? *Think fast!* "A name is a pretty basic fact to know about someone."

"A name." He shook his head as if he pitied me. "We're back at that frivolity again. Is that what your textbooks state? That a name is basic and necessary?"

"To get treatment, you give your name, your contact information, and you sign a form consenting to services."

"Treatment. Services," he echoed. I noticed then that he had a small balled-up sheet of paper rolled up in between his fingers. He spun it around while he spoke. "We're having a conversation. Not a therapy session."

"Why is it important to you that a difference between the two be made? Can't a conversation be therapeutic? Can you help me understand?"

"All these books on your shelf, and your Bible, too, and you ask *me* for understanding?"

"I am asking if you can share your thoughts about therapy."

The man raised an eyebrow, smiled again, crossed one leg over a knee. "Well, for one, I find it interesting that even with all your textbooks, your theories, your Bible, and all the capital letters you so proudly wear in the title behind your name, you are having trouble understanding therapy."

I swallowed down the immediate defensiveness that wanted to take over me because I was a professional, and, yes, trained to deal with people like him.

Or so I believed.

"So, there is a part of you that feels insulted when someone like me, who has degrees and textbooks purporting to understand the human mind, tries to diagnose you and claims to understand your inner psyche. Does it come off as superiority to you?" I stared at him straight in the eyes.

"I have a PhD. You have a master's degree. I am not threatened by the idea of your so-called superiority over me, or your uninformed view of therapy."

"Then what do you have against therapy?" I asked, choosing to ignore most of his statement and focus on what would move the "conversation" forward.

"Therapy by its definition implies that there is something wrong that needs to be fixed. Your Bible implies the same thing. 'All have sinned and come short of the glory of God. The heart is deceitful above all things, and desperately wicked: who can know it.' These are both verses in your Bible."

"So you don't like to hear that you can be wrong."

"Your textbooks say that the answer to everything is in changing your thoughts. Your Bible says that the answer to everything is having a change in your spirit. Which one is it? Which do you believe? On one hand, you have the power to change all that is wrong with you, which makes you all-powerful. On the other hand, only God has the power to change what is wrong with you, making Him the All-Powerful. In whose power do you believe?"

"You simplify a very complex topic," my answer. "You are comparing the tools you can use to get to an end result. An artist who creates masterpieces has different tools at his or her disposal. Pens, paper, crayons, oils, canvas, brushes. Tools are needed to get the end result, but the vision and the skill, and the capability to create, comes from a deeper place. Having both tools and the power to use them are equally important." Huh? What was I trying to say?

The man raised an eyebrow. "Why do you avoid talking about the Bible?"

"Excuse me?"

"I understand that as a secular clinician, the proper protocol is to avoid talking about specific religious beliefs unless and until the client opens the door. I have opened the door and you still avoid going in? Why is that, Ms. St. James? Are you at odds with what you believe about psychology and what you believe about God?"

"You are very interested in my thoughts."

"Only because you are interested in mine."

We paused in the "conversation," as if we had reached the halftime of an intense quarterfinal game. I picked the ball back up. "The concept of faith is important to you, although you claim to be an atheist." I absolutely refused to make the conversation about me.

"I never said I was an atheist." His voice was soft and slow, as if I needed extra time to process his words. "I said I don't believe in belief. I don't exist. Theories exist. Philosophies exist. Confusion exists. This is the nature of humans. I am outside of that capacity."

"Do you think you are God?"

"I am not anything. I do not exist."

"So then you're saying that you believe God exists?"

Silence again. Then me again:

"Why are you coming every day to talk to me, Mr. Bennett?"

His smile returned. He leaned forward in his chair. "I will tell you a secret, Ms. St. James, LCSW-C, Founder and CEO of The Whole Soul Center. I have not talked to anyone in years. I talk to you because you intrigue me. Your confusion. Your theories. Your philosophies. Your difficulty understanding and living out your own faith.

"I asked you earlier why you became a therapist, and though you chose not to answer, I think it's because you didn't have an answer. I know, you would probably answer with something that you're supposed to say, such as you became a social worker to help people. But are you really helping if you don't have the answers to your own questions, or are you just placating the part of you that wants to understand, but doesn't know how?"

It took all I had to keep my face from dropping. Who did this man think I was? I clenched my teeth to keep from saying something unprofessional as he continued.

"Like me, you are seeking to understand the truth of it all, coming to terms with what your existence, or nonexistence, means. You don't have your own answers. But that is okay, because a flawed hero is always a loved one." His hands became animated as he talked. "If you have no flaws, you'll be despised. Jesus was perfect, yet He was hated to the point of being murdered. It is human nature to embrace wrongdoers as long as they have a cause. And it is human nature to kill perfection if its actions go against what you believe. Look at the coverage of the terrorist attack."

Everything in me came to attention, chilled as he uttered those words. The itty bitty hairs on my arm even seemed to rise. He didn't seem to notice as he continued unabated.

"Every TV station has story after story about Jamal Abdul, but what do we really know about the victims, the so-called innocents? Nobody is interested in celebrating them, just focused on showcasing the suspect. I told you yesterday, Sienna, that you are a hero. You should never be a martyr, and yet there are people in the world who would make you out to be one if you died supporting a cause that the other half of the world was disgusted by. Mankind is a hypocrisy. If there truly is a God, and maybe there is one, He alone is the only one who can save us from ourselves. Otherwise we are simply evolving into despicable creatures who are slowly sinking into a mire pit of decay."

When he stopped talking, a hollow, a coldness, an emptiness filled the room that had not been there before.

"So." I thought through each word I said. "It is easier for you to say that you don't exist, than to decide whether you believe that mankind is a random, flawed accident that came into existence by evolutionary chance with no hope for redemption, or we are the purposed creation of a perfect God who is grieved by our sins and our constant rejection of him. In your eyes, both options have pain and it is easier for you not to exist than to live and feel and decide who you are. Your name is meaningless because who you are as a man, your identity, the core essence of who you are is unknown even to you."

We were at the end of the game, but there were no cheers, maybe even no winners. I was tired, and I needed him out of my office because my brain hurt, maybe even my soul, which struggled to make sense of his senselessness. He talked like he knew me, like he knew a part of me that had indeed been wrestling with my faith.

I needed him out of my office so I could quiet my own thoughts and fears and questions. I knew what I believed. I just didn't always know how to make it work for me. Or how to let God make it work for us all.

I needed the Creator's tools to make a masterpiece out of my life. Without His palette, without His initial sketch, my life would look just like it felt right now: a mess.

Jesus, fix me. Fix the picture of my life. Fix it so that when people look at me, they see an illustration of you, and not a messy, abstract, self-directed finger painting. I'm tired of feeling a mess because of my feelings, my pain, my running away from you. I need you to pick up my paintbrush again and fix this picture of me. You are the potter, I am the clay.

I needed this man out of my office. In my extended silence, I knew that he knew that he had gotten to me in a way that nobody ever had. I knew this because he was smiling, and it was a smile I had never seen on his face before.

I had no more comeback lines, only the broken picture of me and the self-assured darkness of him. *Get him out of my office, Lord!*

"Well." The man broke the silence, still smiling. "You understand now. We've officially finished our conversation. I will not be back. I'll mail your payment as promised." He stood up and started walking toward the door.

"Wait." I followed, as I even wondered what I was going to say. I needed my upper hand back. "Do you really want me to believe that you haven't shared a word to anybody in years?"

He turned around abruptly, slight irritation lining his face. "I said I haven't talked to anyone. I never said I didn't share a word."

Huh?

And then he was gone.

From the closed blinds that lined the front windows of my office suite, I watched as he bounded down the stairs of the building and headed toward the parking lot. Once there he got into a rusty green pickup truck with tags from Pennsylvania. A nasty dent was on the passenger-side front fender and a large streak of peeling blue paint ran the entire length of the driver's side. That struck me. Yesterday he'd gotten into a yellow Jeep from West Virginia. I'd written down the license plate number, I recalled, that fact giving me an idea.

I watched as he pulled away, wishing I could make out the tags on this truck, but I couldn't. He stopped at the parking lot entrance to throw a balled-up sheet of paper into the gutter and then his car disappeared down the winding road.

I exhaled.

"What just happened?" I felt sick as I sat down in one of my own waiting room chairs.

You just recommitted your life to me.

Was that God speaking? I chuckled to myself, wondering why I thought I'd heard the Lord after dealing with such a confused, obviously delusional man who was teetering on, if not already falling from, the brink of insanity.

Well, in the Old Testament book of Numbers, God did use a donkey to talk to a man too stuck and hardheaded in his own way. I shook my head as I gathered my things once again.

Yes, I did use a donkey and I can use a man who'd have no guilt about killing many to justify his own theories about evil and good, mankind and me.

I froze in my steps.

Of course I had not heard an audible voice. Years ago, during the time of my life when I'd spent my early mornings and late nights meditating on the Word of God, during the time of my life when I was not afraid to ask Him hard questions and hand him my pain, I would hear what felt like His voice in my consciousness. A clarity. An understanding that spoke so plainly to my soul, to the inner reaches of my spirit that it was impossible to deny that it was Christ Himself living, speaking, directing me from the inside out.

Making my life His public masterpiece to display.

It had been years since I'd felt and heard and knew that God was speaking to me. So long had it been that I'd questioned if it had even happened, or if I was just plumb crazy.

And yet, there was no mistaking the clear statement that had just resounded deep in me, pure and clear as a tolling bell, unmistakable as a long-lost lover's voice.

That man was a terrorist in our understanding of the word. I felt it, knew it, though I had no firm physical proof. He was a terrorist, someone who would kill to keep the masses living in fear with a purpose that made sense only to his twisted justifications. All terrorists acted out of a place of deep, dark, twisted belief.

He was a terrorist and he had a role in the attack at the airport, everything in me was convinced. His goal was to make a villain out of a hero: Jamal Abdul, a good man who the world now agreed was flawed. The media, the authorities, the masses, my father, were trying to understand why a man with commendable character would decide to kill the innocent, young, and old.

Bennett was right. The news focused not on the victims, but on the suspect. We already knew and understood death. It was part of life.

But a hero who would be a villain, and a villain of the vilest kind, was not grasped or explainable.

It destroyed the humanist belief that man could ultimately save himself. And, if we let it, it destroyed the person of faith's trust in God as we wondered how such an evil thing could permissibly happen.

When the foundations of all our beliefs are shaken, there is nothing else to do but stop having joy, to lose our peace, to settle blankly in front of our television sets, shaking and trembling in horror.

That was the aim of terror. To strip away our beliefs, to drain away the meanings we held of life, to reconfigure the wires of our inward thermostats that gave us our sense of comfort and safety. To cease to exist.

His words had unnerved me, and he had been pleased. But he had not realized that what he had meant to unsettle me had actually settled me stronger in my faith.

But where sin abounded, grace did much more abound.

It was a verse from Romans and I understood it as I never had before. Terrorists had it wrong. What they meant for destruction could actually lead to greater, more powerful acts of love, mercy, and grace as that is the essence of a perfect God from whom we can draw our response. Darkness can never overtake light.

That man was a terrorist. It was no longer a nagging feeling or a question. I was certain of it. He'd even brought the attack up himself as the epitome of explaining his point. I had no proof, wasn't sure what to do, but I was certain that he was involved.

And I was also convinced that he was not done.

Chapter 24

He'd thrown a balled-up sheet of paper into the gutter, I recalled. He'd been playing with the crumpled sheet during our talk, the small wad rolling around his fingertips the entire time of our discussion.

He hadn't meant for anyone to see what was on that paper.

With all my belongings in hand, I ran out, dropped my things in my car and then began jogging toward the entrance of the parking lot. As I neared the gutter, I slowed down. What if he was still nearby? What if he was watching me? If he hadn't wanted that paper to be found, and I got it, what would happen?

My paranoia was trying to return.

Was I just being ridiculous?

No!

I studied the surrounding streets and did not see any green pickup trucks. Still walking slowly to the gutter, my eyes zeroed in on the metal grate for any sign of the paper wad that he had intended to be washed down through the pipes that eventually led into the Chesapeake Bay.

It was there, stuck next to a crumpled soda can. I looked around me again, then casually picked up the can and paper. As I tossed the soda can into a nearby receptacle, I pushed the wad into my pocket then strolled back to my car, hoping that I looked like a concerned citizen obsessed with keeping the bay clean, and not a rejuvenated therapist determined to prove that I had somehow identified a suspect the best in Washington had overlooked.

Okay, now that I thought about it, I sounded crazy.

"God, did I really hear You? Did You really just tell me that man's a terrorist?" I threw my head back and sighed as I sat down in my car. The excitement I'd felt about having a piece of trash in my pocket began to feel like foolishness. I started the engine before I finally fished the paper back out.

It has his fingerprints. I probably should handle it with a tissue.

Way too much CSI. I shook my head at myself, and way too little spending time with God. I wished like never before that I had spent more time in His Word so that I wouldn't have any doubts that I'd truly recognized His voice. *My sheep know my voice.* There was a verse something like that in the Bible.

"I don't know what I'm thinking, remembering, hearing, or knowing right about now," I groaned as I unfolded the paper with my bare hands.

Trying to save fingerprints from a man who stated he didn't exist, what was wrong with me? That man had gotten under my skin real good for me to be acting and thinking like this. Twisted. That's what he was and that is what he had done with my brain.

Get it together, Sienna, and stop being delusional, I told myself.

The paper, once unfolded, only confirmed that I'd gone way off track.

It was a drawing, the same illustration that he'd doodled on his blank registration packet, the same drawing I'd placed in his very incomplete chart.

A cat on a windowsill. The window framed with striped curtains.

I balled the paper back up and tossed it on my car floor. It wasn't even worthy of the tiny wastebasket I hung from the rear of my passenger seat. As I drove away, I decided that I would throw it in a trash receptacle once I reached the restaurant where Laz waited for me. Fingerprints? Laz would look at me like I was sure enough crazy.

I was embarrassed at myself for thinking the man was a terrorist.

I looked back at the platter of mint chocolate raspberry cookies bars I'd baked that morning.

That task and the mindset I'd had when I baked them felt like a lifetime ago. My thoughts, my moods, my conviction seemed like breezes in the wind. What I at one second felt certain of, I doubted wholeheartedly the next minute.

What was wrong with me? When had I become such a confused being? I sighed as I turned onto the beltway, the first leg of my trip to the restaurant in Columbia where I was certain Laz was already waiting.

Certain.

I chuckled, knowing that "certain" didn't even feel like it belonged in my vocabulary.

I'd told him yesterday that I had an answer to his proposal. What was my answer? I wanted to cry as walls began feeling like they were collapsing on me.

No crying!

I told him I had an answer, and I would stick to it.

Staying true to what I had already decided felt like the right thing to do.

Even as I acknowledged that the times I'd felt most confident over the week were in those rare moments when I'd wholeheartedly believed that Bennett was a terrorist.

I only felt crazy, uncertain, and anxious when I fought against that instinct.

I-695 was clear enough for me to set my car on cruise control for a moment. After it was set, I used my right foot to slide the wad of paper I'd thrown on the far right-hand corner of the passenger floor toward me. I picked it up and placed it gently in my ashtray.

Maybe I was a little off, but something in me wanted to preserve that little piece of paper. Perhaps his fingerprints could still be salvaged. . . .

Chapter 25

Laz had chosen a fondue restaurant off of one of the main roads in Columbia. As I pulled into the parking lot, I recalled that a similar restaurant was in Towson, closer to my home, closer to my good friend Ava Diggs. I had been invited years ago by some friends at a former job to have the fondue experience once after work; I declined, never really seeming to fit in with coworkers and girlfriends the way I'd imagined most women did. Ava was ten years older than my mother and the closest I had to a "girlfriend." Not sure what that said about me.

How long had I not been aware that I was alone?

I shut the engine off, closed my eyes, and wiped a trail of sweat that suddenly streamed from my forehead.

I was about to answer a marriage proposal. The last time I had done so, the entire track of my life changed.

And not necessarily for the better.

I reached for the platter of cookie bars I'd kept wrapped up in plastic wrap and foil in my back seat, trying to remember why I'd baked them, why I'd felt the need to bring them. I reached for, then let go, then reached for again the small wad of trash that had been handled by the stranger who'd made me second-guess all I thought, all I felt, what I knew of my instincts, what I'd held on to about my faith. I stuffed the wad into my purse.

With my heart feeling like it would pop right out of my chest, I finally entered the restaurant, self-conscious that I was carrying cookies, half dreading to see Laz, to answer him.

Dread.

Why that feeling?

"There you are."

Laz appeared before the hostess could address me. Wearing a gray suit and a pink and blue striped tie, he kissed my cheek, touched my hair, winked at me, and led me to a private booth all before I could take in where I was or what I was doing.

"I think you'll like this experience, Sienna." He was all smiles as I sat down. I put the plate of wrapped cookies on the seat next to me. A pot of rich melted cheeses sat on the table along with artisan breads and fresh vegetables. I noted from a menu that more courses—salad, entrée, dessert—were to come.

All this food and I wasn't hungry.

Diamonds glittered from the face of Laz's watch and I thought about the ring he'd offered me on Sunday.

Or rather, the ring setting he'd presented for me to fill with the jewels from the lion's head ring.

"I am offering you a chance to take that past, acknowledge it, and start over, make it work for you in a layout of your choice. That is what I'm offering to you. I'm not just asking you to be my wife. I'm giving you a chance to live your life."

I smiled at him. The soft glow of candlelight that flickered across his sober face gave his features a warmth I did not usually see.

Everything is okay, Sienna, I assured myself, wondering why I even needed assurance. I thought about the wad of trash I'd stuffed into the corner of my purse, and the sick, empty feeling that had begun feeding off the bottom of my stomach increased.

"So . . ." Laz's entire attention was on me. The smile on his face told me he had no idea of the raging war of uncertainty, fear, and anxiety that was churning in me.

I've made a decision. I'm sticking to it. No second-guess-ing.

"Do we get right to it, or do we chat about our days first." I let my smile equal his, swallowing down the lump that threatened to take over my throat. *Was that man in my office a terrorist?* I could not keep my thoughts straight.

All over the place, I was.

"Well." An oblivious Laz grinned at me. "Well," an oblivious Laz grinned at me, "a good news story needs a good buildup, so I'm open to starting with the small talk. How was your day, Sienna?"

"It was . . . fine. That man came to see me today and I think we had a breakthrough." I held my breath.

"Ah." He dipped a piece of broccoli in the pot of cheese fondue. "I'm glad to hear that you're gaining ground with helping him. You're a good therapist, Sienna. Don't let the tragedies of the past few days distract you or get your thoughts and feelings off track."

"Right." I looked down, nibbled on a broccoli stalk. What was I expecting? For Laz to tell me that I needed to do all I could to prove that my suspicions weren't true? Was there anyone else on the planet who actually thought the wrong terror suspect was in custody? The even bigger question: was there anyone else on the planet who actually thought the man who said his name might be Bennett was a terrorist?

Listening to myself ask those questions in my head sealed the deal for me. I was crazy. That I even spent time thinking such things said a lot about my mental stability, or the lack thereof. And I had gone a step further and believed that God was talking to me, telling me I was on the right track with my insane suspicions.

I, Sienna St. James, had officially lost my mind. I felt embarrassed for myself, embarrassed that I'd even given space in my head to such delusions. Had that man gotten under my skin that much that I hadn't been able to think straight?

"So the blue or the green? What do you think, Sienna? I need to let the set designer know my preference soon."

How long had Laz been talking? He'd put a computer tablet on the table at some point during my mental break and was rambling about set designs, potential guests, and news topics, I gathered.

I'd missed all of it, his whole conversation. I needed to put an end to my absentmindedness immediately.

"Yes, Laz. I will marry you."

The words came out with urgency, certainty. Loudly. A woman at a nearby table looked over at us with sudden interest. A smile filled her face until she began looking back and forth between Laz and me in an effort to see "the ring." Her smile slowly faded and she turned her attention back to whatever simmered in her table's pot as Laz and I simply stared and blinked at each other.

Whatever sentence he'd been in the middle of, whatever link he'd been about to click on his screen came to a halt. His finger froze in midair.

"You . . . said yes."

We both looked surprised.

"Yes," I said again. "We still have to figure out the whole 'move to Atlanta' thing. I'm not ready to address that yet. One issue at a time," I whispered, and nodded as tears I could not explain sprung to my eyes. He reached both hands across the table and covered mine in his. Did he know an unstable shell of a woman on the verge of a complete crackup had just agreed to be his wife?

"We are going to get through this together," he whispered while rubbing the back of my thumbs.

"Are you comforting me, or congratulating us?" I asked and we both chuckled. "This is what you want, right? Us? Marriage?" I raised an eyebrow, a sudden panic settling into the other emotions that swirled around in my stomach.

"Of course, of course. I was the one who brought up the idea of marriage." He let my hands go and sat back in his seat. I noticed then that neither one of us had eaten more than a single broccoli stalk.

"Then, what is it? Are you having second thoughts?" I held my breath waiting to hear his response.

"Everything is real now, Sienna. That's all. Everything I've ever wanted: my own show, not to be alone. I . . . I'm overwhelmed. Thank you."

I saw the tears in Laz's eyes and for the first time since I'd known him, I saw the vulnerability.

Not to be alone.

The words jumped out at me. I'd just been thinking about loneliness when I'd entered the restaurant. Now I'd be leaving as a fiancée with the promise of a lifetime partner.

For better or worse.

Not to be alone.

The words haunted me.

"So I have a good jeweler friend of mine in Rockville who could help with whatever setting you want for the ring." Laz had picked up his fork and had begun stuffing his mouth with food. "And you already have the papers to get started with the divorce." He took a long swallow of whatever sparkling beverage was in his glass. "It's simple. Since nobody knows where RiChard is, you just have to show that you tried to look for him, then have the divorce decree posted in a newspaper for him to see and respond to, which won't happen, and then you'll be free to be Mrs. Tyson. Like I said before, I think the whole process should take about six months or so."

"Yeah, I know."

He spoke about divorce and RiChard so casually, I wondered if it really would be that simple. I wondered if I should tell him about my planned return trip to San Diego tomorrow. *What if I actually find out where RiChard is?*

"Unless you wanted something big, Sienna, I figured we could do a small destination wedding, just the two of us, to one of the islands. Jamaica, Bahamas. Dominican Republic. Or, maybe, we could go to Mexico. There are some interesting stories I could cover down there. Just kidding. I won't work during our wedding weekend. We could have the whole ceremony and honeymoon all in one and be done with it. Or should I say, just starting? Wow, Sienna, we're getting married." He put his fork down for a moment, blinked at me with a half smile and then went back to dipping and dripping with the cheese fondue.

Mrs. Tyson.

I forced another broccoli stalk down. "Wow," I echoed, nodded along, wondering what I was supposed to be feeling as an officially newly engaged woman.

Laz continued rambling about wedding plans and his ideas for the show and house hunting in Atlanta and dreams and plans and hopes and wishes. I nodded when he seemed to be asking me a question, smiled when his pearly whites flashed between his moustache and goatee, laughed when he chuckled.

And wondered the entire time why I felt like throwing up. I thought I'd just said I wasn't ready to talk about Atlanta. I felt irritation as he began talking about the different suburbs in the Atlanta metropolitan area. *Then where will I be if I'm not there with him?*

It was too much to think about, too much to figure out.

"I brought cookies," I interjected as the chocolate fondue course began. "I mean, I wanted to give you my cookies."

Laz's grin grew wider and he began licking his lips. But his smile dropped when I put the platter of cookie bars in front of him.

"Mint chocolate raspberry cookie bars. Special recipe. Homemade." I pulled back the plastic and foil. I inhaled and thought of Leon. My eyes sprung open and I covered the bars back up quickly.

"Really, Sienna? You tell a man you want to give him your cookies and you . . . put out a plate of cookies?"

"Of course. What were you . . . ? Oh."

An awkward silence filled the space between us as I finished tucking down the corners of the foil over the large plate.

Cookies.

Marriage would mean sharing cookies that I hadn't shared in eons with a man who seemed to be used to gobbling up crumbs from many bakeries.

Despite his many advances over the year, and the preheat button he'd occasionally ignite in me, I realized that I had not given much thought to all a marriage would entail; not just companionship, but intimacy.

With Laz.

He stared at me as I slowly uncovered the cookies again. I wondered if he, was bothered by the fact that I felt so awkward, unnerved.

"Sienna." His voice was a whisper as he reached for a bar, split it in half. "We're going to be okay. I promise."

We both took a bite out of the cookie he had broken.

But all I could taste, all I could smell, all I could feel was Leon.

"He's moved on, Ma. And you need to too."

Roman's words to me just days ago.

He was right. I needed to move on.

"Like I said, Laz, these are homemade cookies. One day, we'll have to come together to make a recipe of our own."

"That's right. We'll be cooking together." He licked some chocolate off of his fingers, never breaking his gaze from mine. "Make our own heat. And who knows? Maybe one day we'll have a lot of new creations all our own. Laz-ette. Siennafer. Sienlaz. We can get as creative as we want to be with our children's names."

Screech!

I actually heard the brakes slam down in my brain, heard the tires come to a squealing halt. Laz saw it on my face and chuckled.

"Or not. Calm down, Sienna. I was just kidding. Nobody said we are having kids. Let's just start with a wedding date. Six months from now. Then you can resume your panicking if you choose."

Sex. Babies. Panic was an understatement.

"We have a lot to talk about." *And pray about,* I realized for what felt like the first time since I'd sat down.

"And we will talk, but, as you said, we don't have to figure that out right now. Let's enjoy the moment and figure out all the other details later."

Exhale, Sienna. You are getting married. This is the right thing to do, I told myself. *Enjoy the moment.* I let my shoulders relax.

But the moment was short-lived.

Laz's cell phone started beeping. Clanging, really.

"New developments." He scrolled through his phone and began typing with a fury into his tiny keypad.

"Breaking news? About the terrorist attack?" When he didn't immediately answer, I reached for my phone to pull up CNN.

"It's not on the news yet. That was my source. I've got to go." He began packing up his things, put away his tablet, then froze and looked at me. "Sienna, when the news does air . . . don't read too much into it, okay? I don't want you worrying."

He dropped two fifties on the table and rushed toward the exit.

My cookies were still on the table.

Chapter 26

Don't read too much into it.

Breaking news about the terror attack was about to hit the airwaves, and Laz told me not to worry? Not to read too much into it? What happened? Why would he tell me that? Didn't he realize that worrying would be all I'd be able to do until I found out what he knew? What his source from Homeland Security knew?

I left the restaurant right after he did, shutting off my phone because I needed a clear mind to handle whatever else was coming down the pipes. The evening—no, the day, the entire week—had proven to be too much.

Tired, weary, and now worried, I felt fragile, like one little tap from the wrong hand would send me to pieces.

Enough!

I wanted to believe that I could just tell myself to get it together, but being this close to the edge, I knew a self-pep talk wouldn't cut it. It was after ten-thirty when I reached Baltimore's outer loop that took me to my home, but without even forming the thought, I knew I was making a stop in Towson first.

She sat on a metal chair on her porch, a closed book in her hands. Bright moonlight cast shadows on her face and a cool breeze scented by geraniums wafted in the nighttime air.

"Ava," I called out to her as I ascended the steps to the wraparound porch that graced the front of her near-century old Cape Cod. She'd nodded off, I could tell by the way her head popped up to attention at the sound of her name.

"Sienna, I haven't seen you for a while. What time is it? I must have dozed off. Here, let's go inside."

Ava Diggs. My career coach and life mentor. A legendary figure in the world of Baltimore social work who had picked me up late in my graduate school years and offered me my first job when I finished. A woman who'd helped me celebrate my son's successes and encouraged me to manage my stress. She was a former, formidable foster care agency owner who now took naps surrounded by the flowers she'd planted, sitting in chairs and lounging in old furniture she'd found and refinished.

Even in retirement, she dedicated the use of her faculties to restore, grow, and renew.

And deal with me.

"Mmm, child. I sat out there way too long. I'm going to feel that chilly air in my joints tomorrow." She shook her head as we walked into her foyer.

The inside of her house was as carefully tended as her flowerbeds that surrounded it. Artwork, throw pillows, and soothing wall colors and tones made her small bungalow grand in character, endless in warmth and charm. As we headed in silence to the kitchen, I noticed that Ava had lost even more weight since I'd last seen her a couple of months ago. Once morbidly obese, she'd changed her diet and exercise habits since leaving her agency; but the pounds that clung to her now almost seemed too loose, like a thick blanket covering frail bones.

"You eat?" she asked as she opened and began rummaging through her fridge.

"Yeah, I just came . . . from dinner." It occurred to me that I hadn't even thought to immediately tell her I was officially engaged.

What does that mean?

I swallowed hard and accepted the bowl of banana pudding she offered. We sat down at her table.

There was a time when my middle-of-the-night visits to Ava's were drenched in tears, drowned in sobs. I had not had one of those loud, sloppy sessions in years. Now our late-night talks were characterized by laughs, sighs, and silence, with the occasional single tear, patted shoulder.

How long had I been such a needy person? I wondered, as I reflected on my performance with Ava over the years. And yet, most of the people in my life who tried to meet my needs in healthy ways, I'd successfully pushed away, to distanced myself from. Run from.

Not so with Laz, I consoled myself, feeling slightly more confident that I'd made the right decision.

At some point, you have to accept what's offered to you, right?

"I made a big decision today," I announced. Ava's attention was on her plate. She picked with her pudding with her spoon, pushing the banana slices around like a toddler playing with peas.

She didn't look up, said nothing.

"And tomorrow, I'm making a trip to tie up loose ends once and for all."

"Sounds like you are having a mirror moment." She looked up at me.

I raised an eyebrow. "A mirror moment?

Ava chuckled as she finally pushed a spoonful of pudding into her mouth. "Remember many years ago when you told me that Roman was going through what you called a 'self-reflection obsession' stage? He'd be going about his business, doing whatever he was doing, but every time he passed a mirror, or even simply his reflection in a window or storefront, he'd freeze, stare at and study himself, and start primping and fixing whatever he saw wrong. Do you remember telling me about that?"

I nodded, recalling that Roman was twelve when he began noticing himself and caring about how he looked to the world. He even asked for cologne that Christmas. Where was Ava going with this?

"Sienna, life can be like that. We go about our days minding our business; then something happens to make us stop and stare and see who we really are, what we really look like, what we're really made of. Mirror moments tend to be rare, but life changing. Once we see ourselves for who we are, we have to make decisions on what to do with the image we see. Fix it, smile at it. Carry on with or without changes. We are forced to take ownership of the person we're facing in the mirror."

"I don't know if these are mirror moments or me just on the verge of losing it, Ava." I paused, absorbing her words, reflecting on my current state. "I'm second-guessing myself with everything. One moment I feel confident, the next confused. One second I feel close to the Lord, the next far away. Personally, professionally . . ." I looked up at her and she stared intently at me. "I have a new client, or whatever you want to call him, who is really throwing me for a loop, challenging everything I know about myself, what I believe, how much I can trust my gut feelings. I feel lost, Ava. And tired."

She put her spoon down. "When you look in a mirror, believe what you see in it. Believe who you see in it. We haven't talked in a while about your faith, Sienna, but I know you are one of His. That means Christ is in you, reflecting on you. Have confidence in His image in you. Doesn't the Bible say to trust in the Lord with all your heart and not lean on your own understanding? Sometimes confusion comes because we are trying so hard to make sense out of tangible facts with our minds instead of believing what the Spirit Himself is speaking to our souls."

"So, there are times when we need to go with what is screaming inside of us even if what we see doesn't make sense on an intellectual level?

"What is faith, Sienna? The substance of things hoped for and"—she leaned forward—"the evidence of things *not* seen."

We sat in silence for a while as I ate more of my pudding and Ava stared at hers. Finally, she looked up at me.

"You finished with your plate?" Ava began gathering the dishes on the table.

"I can clean these dishes for you," I offered as I stood.

"Oh hush, honey. I'm tired and all I've done is sit on my porch all day. You sound like you've been having the adventure of a lifetime so I know you are way past drained. The universe won't collapse if these plates don't get washed 'til tomorrow. Go home, Sienna. Pray, keep seeking Him, and stop fighting against your heart. Settle yourself and the confusion will go away." She let out a long yawn followed by a series of hacking coughs. I grabbed a bottle of water for her out of her refrigerator and waited for her to compose herself before I headed to the door.

A small clock that sat over top of the door frame ticked furiously ahead, as if it too wanted the day to be over.

It was nearing midnight.

"Thanks for coming to see me." Ava smiled as I stepped out on to the porch.

"I promise to get myself together so I don't keep coming by here in the middle of the night," I offered, though admittedly, my trips to Ava's home had greatly diminished over the past few years.

When I did come, she knew I was desperate.

"My home is open to you as long as you think I still have some sense left to offer you. I'm getting old, Sienna. I feel it in my bones, in my lungs, and in my head. I'm telling you to stop fighting against what your heart is telling you, and I need to do the same thing myself."

I gave her a smile and fished for my keys.

"Sienna," she called after me as I got into my car. "I want you to be happy. I want you to love your life."

"Thank you. Thank you for being a second mother to me."

We'd never talked about the nature of our relationship, only lived it out. As I started my engine and began pulling away, I looked back at her thinning figure as she disappeared in the distance.

Because of her words, her wisdom, her legacy, and her love, Ava Diggs would always be a giant in my eyes. But I knew she was also a mortal. She'd spent not just years of her time, but years of herself pouring into me to help me be a better social worker, a better mother, a better person.

I needed her to see that her investment was well spent.

I needed her to see that not only would her wishes for me come true, but that I was capable of being the full woman God had crafted me to be, and able to help reproduce that concept of wholeness and well-being in other women after me.

That is one thing my heart told me, and she'd taught me to listen to my heart. To believe it.

As I headed home, I had the makings of a plan for action to address my suspicions about the man named Bennett, who I didn't know if I'd ever see again. I also had inklings of what I had to accomplishment in what I wanted to be my last trip ever to San Diego.

My therapy skills, my civil responsibilities, my son, my family relationships . . . I had a forming vision of what to do about it all.

I'd given no thought to my wedding plans.

That felt less important than the immediate tasks I needed to complete. Besides, my heart, for the moment, remained silent on the issue, and I refused to fight against the silence.

Chapter 27

One hour, twelve minutes, and a cup of gourmet hot cocoa.

That was how long it took for me to drive home, take a shower, and enjoy a few moments of quiet reflection before I got down to business in front of my computer.

I had to do all I could to assuage the feeling that authorities were missing something with the terror case. I had to learn all I could about that man. I pulled out the license plate number I'd written down yesterday, deciding that the forty-nine dollars and ninety-nine cents charged by an online investigative company was worth the price of my peace, and possibly national security. Was getting some answers about this mysterious man really going to be as simple as paying some money for a couple of Internet searches?

A sense of urgency overtook me as I came to rest with the idea that I had to find out as much as I could about him. Why had I not felt this same urgency before? The question nagged me, because if I really believed this man was a threat to our country, wouldn't I have been doing all I could, sharing my concerns with whomever would listen? If my heart truly believed he was a terrorist, would I really have been willing to sit alone in my office with him?

But if I didn't really believe it, why was I going through the trouble of digging up info on him?

"Sometimes confusion comes because we are trying so hard to make sense out of tangible facts with our minds instead of believing what the Spirit Himself is speaking to our souls." I could hear Ava's voice, and decided to not fall into the trap of confusion that came with trying to make sense of the details. My heart was telling me to get more info and this sense of urgency had just surfaced; that's all I had to work with.

I used my credit card to pay the fee for the search and entered the license plate number I'd jotted down after seeing Bennett get into a yellow Jeep from West Virginia the other day. I wished I had the tags from the rusty green truck from Pennsylvania he'd shown up in today; or, rather, yesterday, I realized as it was now one-thirty Thursday morning. (Was it really that late?) But I was pleased that I had a beginning point.

Within minutes, the reverse license plate search yielded results.

Carlos Dean Jessup
423 Lilydale Street
Martinsburg, West Virginia 25404

I stared at the name and address listed for the plate number, wondering what it meant, what to do.

Was this "Bennett's" real name? Or a family member or friend whose car he borrowed?

I immediately did an Internet search, and the first result that came up was a Facebook page.

Carlos Dean Jessup had not set any privacy settings, it appeared. His Facebook profile was open, completely accessible, and quickly viewed by me. As I scrolled down his page and viewed his profile, I felt like I knew everything there was to know about him. The profile picture was not that of the man I'd met in the airport; indeed, Carlos had dark black hair, green eyes, and a wife named Nina who looked of Indian descent.

Carlos was a marketing professional with a major pharmaceutical company, a Pittsburgh Steelers fan, and a wannabe chef who took cooking classes every Thursday night. I looked through his wedding pictures and snapshots from fishing trips and read through his ruminations on everything from politics to his pet Pomeranian's daily mischief.

"What am I missing? What am I missing?" The question ate at me as I looked through picture after picture. I looked through his friend list, searching for blond hair, chilling blue eyes. But Carlos Dean Jessup had over 2,000 friends on his page.

Do I look through each one? Do I read through his status updates?

The questions became more complicated, more difficult as the sense of urgency I felt increased.

"God, what am I looking for?" I threw my hands up. It was now going on two in the morning. I had two sessions scheduled to start in just over five hours and I still had to pack for my return to San Diego.

And mentally and spiritually prepare.

"What am I looking for?" I asked aloud again.

And then I saw it.

It had been right in front of me the entire time.

The current status updates were comments and photos of Carlos and his wife Nina enjoying a Mediterranean cruise. The pictures began on Monday and the last update had been posted just seven minutes earlier. Updates about his vacation plans had started two weeks ago.

And he had checked in at BWI airport on Sunday evening.

It did not matter if the man who'd shown up at my office, who'd first talked to me at the airport knew Carlos. Carlos's life and schedule were posted like headline news online. Anyone who had access to Facebook would have known not only that Carlos was out of town, but also would have known where he was on the globe in real time.

And would have known that Carlos would not be missing his car.

Martinsburg, West Virginia was only an hour-and-a-half drive away from BWI. Two hours from my office in Towson. Perhaps Carlos's car had been stolen as it would be obvious that he was out of town.

I thought about my own car. Missing from the parking lot at BWI. Sitting in front of my house, most likely at the time that I would have been expected back home. I had come back a day early, though nobody but Roman and Laz would have known that my plans were changed. I realized then that I was never supposed to know that my car had been stolen. But that didn't explain why it was returned if my suspicions weren't supposed to be raised.

Unless the expectation was that my suspicions would be alerted.

Was I being set up?

I realized then that I hadn't sought more answers about my car's disappearance and subsequent reappearance for that reason. I guess some subconscious part of me wanted to dig for more information before I dug too deeply into the mysteries surrounding my car. Was there a particular response someone had expected me to make? I shook the thought from my head and focused again on the Facebook profile on my computer screen.

I was certain that Carlos's car was probably sitting in front of his home right then.

If what I was thinking was right, that man, Bennett, was a criminal of opportunity. Perhaps he used the Internet, or more specifically social media, to plan out who to target.

But I didn't post personal details about my life as openly as Carlos Dean Jessup did. And I had no way of proving that any of my conclusions were right.

My eyelids were beginning to feel like weights over my eyeballs. Sleep was unavoidable. The urgency to dig for more answers was still present, but what else could I do?

I thought about the wad of paper I'd picked up from the gutter. Even if I remembered where I'd put it, what was I supposed to do with it? Call Laz, ask him to tell his contact to investigate the piece of trash I could offer? A contact who by Laz's admission already thought I was on a fame-seeking mission?

I shut my computer down, deciding to give up my search for answers for the moment.

What else could I do?

Chapter 28

"Akiyoshi Nakamura of Tokyo had flown into BWI on a business trip. His colleagues state that he was excited about forming a new relationship with a nonprofit in Silver Spring, Maryland, which was going to partner with his marketing company in Tokyo. His childhood village in Southern Japan was to receive over fifty classroom computers through the generous deal he had initiated." The reporter spoke in a hushed voice before another news snippet played.

"This is exactly the type of thing my son would do. He was compassionate and always felt that the world was bigger than him," a pretty, senior woman named Ayuki said into a camera. "In a bittersweet blessing, the nonprofit has announced that they are doubling their gift to be one hundred computers and the school district is starting a memorial scholarship fund in my son's name." The woman wiped tears from her eyes, but gave the camera a full smile.

Continuing coverage from the terror attack aired on the television in my clinic's waiting room. Usually, I kept the news off, not wanting to upset some of the more fragile, traumatized clients who frequented my practice; but it was early in the day and I still had about fifteen minutes before my seven-thirty appointment was due. I was the only one there.

"All who knew Bart and Madison Taylor said they were inseparable. He was an entrepreneur and proud self-made multimillionaire whose high-end car collection and luxury villas have been featured in magazines and cable television networks. His wife was the PTA president at their eight-year-old son Aaron's elementary school. Other parents at the school talked about Madison's exquisite baking skills. She was known to make every-thing—bread, pies, cakes, and brownies—not only from scratch, but also with her own home-ground flour. She reportedly raised her own chickens and two cows on one of their pastoral properties to always have fresh eggs and milk on hand."

Now that's different for a cosmopolitan couple. I stud-ied the photo of the brown-haired gentleman with bushy sideburns and his blond bombshell wife who looked like a beauty pageant contestant. The boy Aaron had confident eyes and a playful smirk on his face.

"The family was headed to their vacation home on a remote Bahamian island for a quick weekend getaway. All three perished in the attack."

The camera focused in on the eight-year-old and I snapped off the television.

"Every TV station has story after story about Jamal Abdul, but what do we really know about the victims?" The words of the man who'd come to my practice daily echoed in my mind.

"Hey, Sienna!" The front door slammed open and Darci burst in.

"Hi, Darci."

Today she wore a snug black skirt that stopped a few inches shy of her knees, a low-cut black-and-white zebra print blouse, silver hoop earrings, and silver sandals. Her makeup looked like she had just left a cosmetics counter at Macy's, and she had a fresh manicure. "Don't worry about your trip today. As you requested, you just have your two clients this morning, and a couple booked for

Saturday starting at noon. I've updated your calendar, so you can check it online. I've taken care of everything, and can even handle any walk-ins of yours that might come through.

"He's not coming back, Darci."

"Huh?" She froze just as she was about to toss her purse and workbag on her desk. "Oh, I mean, Sienna, I . . . You . . ." Her hands came back to life and she resumed getting settled before turning her attention to me with a stiff smile. "What are you talking about, Sienna? Who's not coming back?"

"Darci, please. It's obvious. You've been all cheery and smiles and dressed up since that man started coming here every day. Please, Darci, don't give that man another single thought. He's not stable. Maybe even dangerous. Aside from ethical considerations, there are possible safety considerations. You are a wonderful, beautiful young woman and the right one will come along after while. Believe me, I know the struggle, but not him." *Yeah, the right one will come, but you have to not run him away,* I chided myself even as I tried to encourage and warn her.

Her eyelids, coated in thick black mascara, fluttered, and her cheeks slowly turned a deep scarlet red. "What can I say, Sienna. You've read me like a book. I'm so embarrassed. But don't worry, I wasn't going anywhere with it. It was just nice to get some attention from a man who looked so, well, good."

"Attention?"

"Yeah." She blushed again. "I ran into him last night when I was leaving the library with the twins. We chatted for just a few moments and he bought Ella and Elijah candy bars. I told him not to, but he did anyway. We thanked him and then we left. That was it. I promise." She collapsed into her desk seat with a loud sigh and looked away.

"You don't think it's odd that he just happened to run into you?"

"No. I mean, I was at the Towson library down the street. It's a public place." Her eyes zeroed in on her computer screen and she said nothing else.

I don't know what bothered me more: the bad feeling that their encounter was anything but chance, or the sad look of desperation that she was trying so hard to hide in her eyes. I searched for something else to say, but my seven-thirty appointment was walked in the door.

"Oh, I've been waiting to talk to you." My client shook her head dramatically, sending her waist-length braids in a dizzying spin. "You will not believe what my supervisor did now."

"Come on back, Ms. Johnson." I managed to smile, forcing myself to turn my complete focus to her, to her words.

But before I did, and as she settled herself onto my office couch and rambled on about the weather, her upcoming vacation, and other small talk before we got to her work-related problems that were exacerbating her depression, I discreetly pulled up my Facebook account on my phone.

Darci and I were not Facebook friends, honoring a choice I'd made to keep our employer-employee relationship purely professional. Because of that, I did not expect to be able to see her profile.

But I did.

Her profile setting was public.

Anyone who looked her up would have seen that she checked into Baltimore County's Public Library in Towson at approximately seven p.m. last night.

No, I was convinced. There was nothing coincidental about that man walking into the library the moment she walked out.

But why?

"So tell me, Ms. Johnson, how was work today?" I asked, knowing I'd have to come back to my other questions later.

Chapter 29

Sorry, we couldn't find any results for this search.

I blinked at my computer screen, wondering why I'd expected to see different results. My seven-thirty appointment had left and my eight-thirty was running a few moments late. With no other way of satisfying the continually growing urge to get answers, I'd done a search for Jamal Abdul of Northern Virginia to no avail. The odds were, I knew, that if he'd had a Facebook profile, it would most likely have been taken down; but there was no evidence that one had ever existed. No cached page. No links to screenshots. I searched by his employer name, his hometown, even his wife's name, as all had been flashing nonstop on the television coverage.

As I stared at the blinking cursor on the screen, I recalled what Laz had said in response to my question about the photos of Jamal Abdul Laz's team had been able to uncover. *"They were photos posted on different people's pages, organizational Web sites, that sort of thing. It doesn't appear that he had any social media accounts beside his professional networking ones."*

I went to the Web site of the news station where Laz worked and found the video of his story. As I watched the photo montage of Jamal again—him volunteering at senior homes, coaching little league teams, serving at soup kitchens, visiting wounded vets—I realized that he had been a hero of the purest kind. He did good deeds and never posted them himself. Others praised his efforts and he left no digital mark. With the type of job he'd had, biomedical engineering, there was no doubt that he was computer savvy. His willingness to keep his public service private said something.

He was the perfect hero to vilify if one had a twisted sense of good and evil, if one had a twisted mission to provide commentary about belief, about human nature.

Motive.

Somewhere in this confusing muddle of thought there was a motive, I was sure of it, if that man was involved.

Maybe I was wrong. Nothing about this was clear to me. I had no hard, fast facts, no explanation as to how it could have happened.

But everything in me screamed that I was somehow on the right track.

I shivered at the realization that the track had a destination, and not one I was sure of, or sure that I even wanted to go.

Or even how to get there.

I thought about the e-mails I'd gotten from Everybody Anybody. The anonymity, the randomness of the "fascinating facts," the accuracy about my life that could have easily been pulled from my tweets (my Facebook profile was private) all seemed to line up with what I had gathered about the man who may have been named Bennett.

I pulled up my Twitter account, perused through my short list of followers. How had I missed it? Someone with the twitter handle of "EverybodyAnybody_123" had recently started following me. I pulled up the profile. There was no picture, no tweets, no followers. I was the only one he or she was following.

He or she? I heard my thoughts. *He.* No question about it. I had no doubt who this was. I started to block him, but then realized this might be my sole line, my only way to contact him as he'd stated he was not coming back anymore.

That and this e-mail address. And the phone number. Dialing the number would be too risky, too blatant a first step of reconnecting.

I pulled up my e-mail account, scrolled down to the last e-mail from Everybody Anybody and hit reply.

One Fascinating Fact About You, I typed quickly, not wanting to lose my nerve or momentum, praying that I was sending the right message.

1. Your name may or may not be Bennett. ☺ Come see me again soon.

I looked at the smiley face, wondered if it was a good idea. I erased the last sentence, then retyped it. I deleted the entire e-mail, then typed it back up again. I stared at the screen.

"Jesus, please guide me. Please." I shut my eyes, opened them again, kept staring at the screen.

"Hi, Sienna. I'm so sorry I'm late!" My eight-thirty appointment stood in the doorway of my office, out of breath. "My bus was late. Darci said I could come straight back. Hope that was okay?"

"Hi, Mr. Brown, you're fine. Come in." I smiled.

As he sat down, I pressed send and exhaled.

Because Mr. Brown had been late and I had a flight to catch, we did a thirty-minute half session, addressing his grief over losing his mother and a favorite aunt within two weeks of each other. The moment our session was over, I pulled out my phone. One e-mail sat waiting in my inbox, a notification showed. I pressed it open immediately.

Undeliverable Mail: Message not delivered because this e-mail address does not exist.

What else can I do? The question haunted me. The urgency increased. But really, what else could I do? What authority would listen to me, and for what reason? My only other option, I figured, was to try to convince Laz to help me, but what could I possibly tell him to get him to feel the same urgency I felt? Plus, my plane left in a few hours. Because I'd booked my flight late, I had to fly out of Dulles Airport in Northern Virginia, an hour and a half away. Maybe the ride would help clear my mind, give me new perspective, ideas, a new starting point.

I packed my things and headed out of the office. "See you Saturday, Darci."

"Enjoy your trip." She smiled, though I did not miss the sadness in her eyes.

Here I was trying to save the whole world, and I didn't even know how to make Darci feel better.

Heroism.

Had RiChard's aim been to be a hero? A random thought. And a hero to whom? Obviously, not to his family, as he'd not only abandoned me and Roman, but also Mbali and her four children by him.

As I made the trek to Dulles, my mental attention attuned back to the purpose of my return trip to San Diego. Now that I had a wedding to plan, it was time to nail the coffin in the marriage that I'd never had with RiChard. I imagined seeing Kisu for the first time in near twenty years. Oh, the questions I had for him! What had he been up to in the time that he'd faked his death to help RiChard with his cause? Why had he sent me the lion's head ring, other than as a message to let me know RiChard was still around? Did he think I knew about RiChard's plans, that I was involved somehow? I'd never considered that; what if Kisu was angry at me for some unknown reason? Perhaps he'd be enraged at seeing me.

It was too late to have second thoughts. For better or worse, this was a trip I had to make. I needed his answers. To complete a divorce by publication, this was my proof that I'd done all I could to find RiChard's whereabouts. But then again, since RiChard had married Mbali, did that automatically nullify our union? I wished I had done more legal research. *I'm unprepared for whatever is about to happen tonight.* I swallowed hard.

Traffic from Baltimore, through DC, and to Northern Virginia was unusually light. As I thought about spending an extra forty-five minutes twiddling my thumbs waiting in the airport, my cell phone chirped. A Facebook notification. Laz had just checked in to a restaurant ten minutes from Dulles. *Hmmmm.* I'd told him nothing about my trip to San Diego, and he'd expect me to be at work back home. A smile crept on my face as I thought about surprising my fiancé.

"Fiancé," I said out loud.

The word still felt foreign to my tongue; my emotions were still a hazy cloud of uncertainty.

Yes, I needed to see him, just so I could get used to the idea that I'd be seeing him on a regular basis for the rest of my life. Even if he was there on business, I'd just nod at him from the bar area, I imagined, or send a text from a nearby booth.

Twenty minutes. That's really all I had, but I'd already talked myself into it.

I think I needed a morale boost as I prepared to make my final trip chasing down RiChard.

Chapter 30

I saw him the moment I entered the restaurant. A brightly lit establishment with a fresh, American-fare theme, it was easy to see him sitting at a pale green padded booth. He wore a sharp, three-piece beige suit, his goatee defined, his smile brighter than the tracked spotlights that cast a vibrant glow on each table. I saw him sitting there, his mouth moving nonstop as he retold some story about his news travels or broadcasting exploits, I was sure, judging from the unmistakable gleam in his eyes.

I also saw the woman sitting across from him at the table.

She had thinly arched eyebrows, a narrow, pointy nose, and shiny black hair cut in a perfect bob, similar to the one I wore before I went natural. She was the color of French vanilla ice cream. No, more of an ashy gray, I decided, getting a better look at her features as her head bounced up and down in laughter. Was she blushing?

Years ago, I'd seen Leon in a diner booth, laughing along with a beautiful woman sitting across from him. I'd been initially heartbroken, but the woman turned out to be his long-lost niece. Unbeknownst to me at the time, he had committed to helping her get back on her feet following a rough and tragic start to life.

Maybe that's why I felt numb at the moment, not wanting to read anything or feel any way about the present scene before me. There was probably a very simple, straightforward explanation as to why Laz was eating lunch with a woman who seemed to be blushing. She could be a coworker, an intern who followed him like a groupie, or even someone he was investigating for a feature story.

Or she could be his bed partner.

I hadn't shared my cookies with him. Who's to say he wasn't finding satisfaction elsewhere?

"How many in your party, ma'am?" A college-aged young woman approached me with menus in hand.

"Oh, I . . . I'm not staying." I turned to the door, wondering about my prudence at making this stop when I had a flight to catch.

"Sienna!"

My hand was on the door handle when I heard my name. I turned around and Laz was standing there. "What are you doing here?" His eyes were slightly narrowed, but a playful grin danced on his lips. The woman with whom he'd been dining had jumped to her feet and was nearly stomping toward us.

"I, uh . . ." How did I even begin to answer that question? I really didn't want Laz to know about my trip to San Diego.

Clearly I hadn't fully thought out this pit stop.

"Hi, I'm Camille." The woman was up on us. She spoke in a nasally voice and extended a manicured hand. Up close I could see that she had clear hazel eyes and a smattering of freckles. She smiled, but a challenge was not missed in her tone. Regardless, she saved me from having to explain my presence. At least for the moment.

"Camille, this is Sienna, my fiancée," Laz interjected before I could respond. A broad grin filled his face as he pulled me in for a quick hug. Her smile had instantly disappeared and from the expression that remained, I could almost hear the exclamation that ran through her mind: *He never told me he was engaged!*

"Just having a working lunch, Sienna. You are more than welcome to join us," Laz continued, nearly directing me to where the two had been sitting.

Camille had composed herself enough to keep the irritation out of her face and voice, but she wanted to make sure that I understood how important and intelligent she was. "Yes, I am a program analyst for Homeland Security, and Laz and I sometimes spar over politics and debate government policies."

She's his source! It clicked, and Laz knew it did because he gave me a subtle nod and I got the hint to keep mum.

He may have been using her for inside information to advance his career, but it was clear to me that Camille had other objectives with him in mind.

"I wish I could stay, but I can't." I politely shooed away the hostess who kept circling us with a menu. "I have somewhere I need to be in a few minutes, but I saw that Laz had checked in here on Facebook, and I thought it would be fun to surprise him with a quick, unexpected visit."

"Oh, how nice. What exactly is it that you do?" Camille was looking for an opening to disparage me.

"I'm a social worker and I provide therapy to children, teens, and adults and individual, family, and couples counseling. I have my own practice," I threw in for good measure, though I immediately regretted it. I was never the type of woman who felt the need to compete for a man's attention. I mean the man had already asked me to marry him.

"Oh, a psychotherapist." She frowned, and I could not tell if she was disappointed that she couldn't think of an instant jab, or if she'd had a bad experience with therapy in the past. With her obvious need for attention, security, and superiority, I guessed it was the latter.

"So you don't have a few moments to join us, Sienna? Maybe you can weigh in on our discussion about how much privacy from the government we're entitled to in the name of public safety." He winced as soon as he said it, realizing that he'd given me the door I'd been unknowingly waiting for in front of his source.

"Well, I really do need to go, but I must say, I keep getting bad feelings about that client I told you about. I wish the government would violate his privacy and investigate him." I gave an innocent smile.

Laz narrowed his eyes and discreetly shook his head. I knew that he was merely trying to protect his source, but shoot, I was trying to protect the whole darn country.

If I was wrong and crazy, at least my heart was in the right place.

I went for it.

"Camille, you work for Homeland Security. I was at BWI just before the explosion and I met this man who really made me feel uncomfortable. He came to my office a couple of times this week and the things he talked about only made my bad feelings about him grow."

I didn't miss her cut a look over at Laz, who had suddenly become consumed with tinkering with his watch.

"You talked about this with Laz?"

"A little."

"I think he mentioned your concerns to me." If her smile grew any bigger, it would drip right off of her face. I could imagine her thoughts again: *This woman is a nutcase. If I can prove that to Laz, then maybe he will pick me. Pick me! Pick me, please!* I was certain that was her line of thinking as she relaxed her shoulders, ready to fully engage with me.

"I've really got to go, but perhaps I can call you in a few hours after my . . . I mean, well, do you have a card?" I stumbled over my words and she looked even more pleased.

"I have a classified position and don't feel comfortable giving out my contact information, but I can take your card."

Oh, she was really feeling special about herself, wasn't she? For all I knew, this girl could be, probably was, somewhere on the bottom of the totem pole at her agency, but I didn't care. I needed somebody with the right channels to hear me.

It felt like my duty.

And the continuing sense of urgency pushed me forward, even at the expense of looking like a fool.

"Here's my card." I passed one to her, getting a flashback of the last time I'd handed out my card.

At the airport.

To that man whose name I still could not confirm.

"I don't have a name for you, but I will fill you in on what the man talked about when you call." Maybe I was over thinking. The doubt began creeping back in as I realized that neither she nor Laz seemed to be too worried about whatever else I had to say about the man I'd met.

There already was a suspect in custody, I reminded myself. I started feeling foolish as Camille stared silently at my business card.

"Oh, something else." I dug into my purse, wanting to feel like I had a smoking gun that would make them both take me seriously. I pulled out the wad of paper that the man had written on and thrown into the gutter. "He touched this, so there might be prints on it. It's kind of dirty, but I'm sure your office has the right tools to handle it." A small giggle escaped my lips as I held out the trash ball in my palm.

She was still staring at my card, her smile gone.

"Okay, I'm leaving," I mumbled, still waiting for her to take the paper out of my extended hand. When she still didn't look up, I turned once again for the door.

"Wait." She grabbed my shoulder. Reaching first for a cloth napkin from the hostess stand, she used it to pluck the wad of trash from my hand. "I will be calling you soon. Don't go far."

All remnants of her smile had disappeared, and a seriousness came through her voice that wasn't there before. She turned back to the booth, her eyes back to studying my card.

I had not a clue what she was thinking.

"Bye, Laz."

"See you soon, Sienna."

I could see the question in his eyes as I left, and I knew that I had not imagined the change in tone that had just happened with Camille.

As I got into my car, I recalled that my dinner last night with Laz had abruptly ended when he'd gotten word of breaking news. "Don't read too much into it, okay? I don't want you worrying," was all he'd said about whatever he'd learned.

I'd not heard of any new developments.

Maybe it was something insignificant that the networks had glossed over. Or maybe the development had not been released and was not public knowledge.

Either way, I had to find out what it was.

I didn't trust his "source."

Chapter 31

Changing gears.

I'd done what I could to save the world; now I had to do what was necessary to change my marital status.

Flying over the country, staring down at the fields and towns, I thought about the many trips I'd taken with RiChard during our short time together. From lush green hills in Africa to thick canopied rainforests in South America, I'd covered a lot of ground in the months when my marriage felt real. That was a blurry span of about a year and a half; no, maybe two years, my time with RiChard. I'd blocked so much out of my mind from that period of my life, it seemed a hazy fog crowded out any clear thoughts or memories.

Except the blood on his hands when he said he'd killed for Kisu.

It had not all been bad, though. Before I began questioning the goals and tactics of his personal mission to bring social justice to the world, I found myself learning, growing, awakening on my trek around the globe.

A forgotten memory surfaced in my mind of a stop we made in a rural Guatemalan community. Though we could not change the entire school system, or secure adequate educational opportunities for the entire village that we'd visited, RiChard and I were able to talk a farmer into letting his daughter go to school. The father had only sent her younger brothers to the single-grade schoolhouse that was an hour-and-a-half walk from their home, believing that his daughter should solely focus on domestic duties and had no need to expand her mind. However, after he found out I had not only gone to elementary school, but had graduated from high school with all As and Bs, he reconsidered and took out a loan for her to begin formal education. The idea of a better life for her, and not just her brothers, had never been fathomable to him.

I recalled feeling bad at the time that I could not say I'd finished college, but I rejoiced to see her off on her first day of school ever at age nine. Just before she joined the path to the schoolhouse along with her brothers, she came up to me, reached up her hands, and cupped both of them on my cheeks. We stared at each other in silence for several seconds, and I saw a fierce, independent, determined spirit in her eyes. I knew that we had just unleashed a fighter.

Yes, I'd done good with RiChard, but it was not because of or for him, contrary to Laz's belief. I was a social worker in the essence of the word long before I became one by license. I'd believed as long as I could remember that everyone deserved a fighting chance to have a quality life.

RiChard had not taught me that. He simply confirmed who I was, and I'd been living out my ideals of my own accord in the near twenty years he'd been absent.

"What would you like to drink, ma'am?" A flight attendant stood over me, her cart of beverages in the aisle. I had not even noticed that she'd passed a cup of ginger ale to the woman sitting next to me.

"Oh, I don't want anything. Thank you." I swallowed down my own saliva as my stomach twisted into knots.

What was I doing? What was going to happen?

I shut my eyes as the attendant rolled her cart to the next row of seats. I imagined walking into the café and seeing Kisu after all these years.

And why did I think he would have answers?

I opened my eyes again, as if the act would help me see, think, or understand more clearly. Kisu and RiChard had been like brothers, I recalled, remembering the camaraderie between them when Kisu joined our global adventure. RiChard had wanted him to serve as a translator for the languages he himself didn't know, especially once we'd set our eyes on rural villages in KwaZulu-Natal in South Africa, the place of Kisu's birth. We flew first to Paris to meet with him, where Kisu agreed to pause from his doctoral studies at the Sorbonne to come with us.

None of us knew that RiChard would later trick Kisu into faking his death under the premise of making him a martyr for their broad causes. We would only find out later that RiChard really just wanted Kisu out of the picture so he could take Kisu's fiancée, Mbali, as his own wife, though RiChard was still technically married to me. I was left bamboozled and in the dark for well over a decade, satisfied with his infrequent letters and packages from his continued supposed trips around the world, never suspecting a thing.

He'd lied to all of us.

I felt so hot inside that a cold soda probably would have turned into a rolling boil had I'd accepted one from the flight attendant.

Tonight, I was getting my answers, though I could not keep track of what questions I wanted to ask.

Maybe I should write some questions down, I considered, as I often did when I was in the middle of trying to make sense of a complicated clinical case.

I'd only bought a carry-on with a change of clothes and my purse, and my workbag, which was stuffed with Laz's envelopes and my folder of notes on that man from the airport.

Without having another way to contact him, holding on to his folder seemed like the only way of still keeping him close until all my doubts were dismissed.

Or confirmed.

Perhaps I should have given Camille the phone number I'd scribbled down in my notes, The one time he'd called had been from a phone number with an Ohio area code.

Maybe I'll call it when this plane lands, I considered, as I flipped anew through the folder.

One thing at a time, Sienna. I needed to focus on getting ready to meet Kisu. I shut the folder, but as I did my eyes caught notice of the blank registration form Bennett had left in the waiting room the first day he'd visited my office.

It was blank except for a hand-drawn illustration he'd made in ink in the top right corner.

I opened the folder back up and stared at the drawing of the windowsill with the cat sitting on it. It was the same picture he'd drawn on the crumpled-up piece of paper he'd thrown in the gutter and I'd retrieved and given to Camille as my only "evidence."

I guessed that woman had good reason to believe I was working on one macaroni less than a full box.

But something had changed in her demeanor in those final seconds I spent with her and Laz at the restaurant, after I'd given her my business card. I could not put my finger on it, but I recalled thinking that I needed to know what breaking news story I had somehow missed despite my continual check-ins to CNN's headlines.

Unless it was a story that had never been reported.

Reality check.

There was nothing I could do about news I didn't know about. I had no further actions to take regarding the drawing of a cat in a window from a man whose name, actions, and whereabouts were completely unknown to me.

There was nothing I could do about any of it, at least while I was on the plane.

I gave myself permission to stop thinking about it all and focused yet again on what questions I could ask Kisu.

That's why I had gone digging for notepaper, to keep my thoughts organized, I remembered.

I opened my workbag up again, forcing myself to stay on task, to come up with my questions.

Where do I have blank paper? I shook my head as I shuffled through the notes and envelopes in my bag. I pulled out one.

Laz's life résumé.

I opened it, took out the stack of awards and certificates, yearbook pages, pictures.

I smiled.

"Hey, ain't that the news man who comes on channel fifty-five?" The woman in the seat next to me stared at the images in my lap. She looked around my age, but had a slightly worn, rugged appearance to her eyes, face, and even her hands. "He is a fine somebody. If I thought I could get away with it, I would create some breaking news of my own, just to get him to cover the story. That's wrong, isn't it?"

We both chuckled.

"You know him from somewhere?" She pointed to the papers in my lap.

"Yes." I paused. "He's my fiancé."

"Really? Congratulations. You are a blessed woman. I ain't jealous." We both laughed again.

I guess I am blessed, I considered as the woman settled back into her seat and flipped through a magazine. Laz was a good catch. He was handsome, successful, and apparently into me.

Then why did I feel so unsettled?

I do feel unsettled, I acknowledged to myself. *Don't do this right now. Focus, Sienna.*

I needed to stay on task, come up with my questions for Kisu. I took a final look at some photocopied pictures of Laz in a high school letterman jacket. I hadn't known that he was a wrestler in high school, I realized as I flipped through a couple of more photos. What else would I learn about him from his pictures?

As I put the stack of papers back in the envelope, the question struck me. Pictures do tell you something about a person.

That man's drawing.

It obviously had some significance to him as he kept putting on paper the exact same illustration.

Another realization.

He was obviously obsessed with the Internet. Wasn't there a way to look up images online? I was sure of it, and decided that the moment I was able to, I would scan the picture and search to see if it showed up anywhere in the virtual universe.

The universe.

It was broad and limitless and filled to capacity with matter, but that man was somewhere in it, even if he believed he did not exist. And the odds were that something about him, even a small detail, was somewhere online. It seemed nearly unavoidable for it to be otherwise. My mind told me this, but more importantly, my mind agreed.

I had something to work with, and the thought gave me comfort.

Enough to settle down and finally pull out my pen and paper.

I had the paper. I had the pen. But no questions for Kisu came.

I decided to take a nap.

Something told me that I needed to get my rest now while I could. That sense, that knowing, did not comfort me.

Chapter 32

La Bohemia Café.

The smell of spices, mint, vanilla, and cinnamon that greeted my nostrils as I walked through the threshold awakened me. The jolt to my senses stirred my consciousness as I realized what I was doing, as I realized that I had come to a defining stop of a twenty-year journey.

What would this final destination look like? I wondered anew as my eyes adjusted to the candlelit dining space. The orange chandelier, the rustic furniture looked familiar, but the layout of the room was different. Tables had been pushed to the side and most of the seats were arranged in single file rows facing the stage where the guitarist had performed just five days earlier.

Five days.

Was that all that had passed since I'd last come this way? I thought about Ava's comments on "mirror moments" and reflected on the truths held within her observations. Yes, it had only been five days, but the hours they'd contained had been ones that were making me look at myself, at my life, at my relationships with both my family and men, with God. I was seeing, experiencing my shortcomings, my doubts, my anxieties, and my fears.

And I was growing, becoming.

I had to take this mirror moment, and make sure that my life looked its best.

I dropped my bags into an empty seat and settled into one next to it as the space began filling with intellectuals, nonconformists, and art types.

Somehow, for some reason, I felt like I belonged.

"You're back!" A woman passing out cookies squealed and rushed toward me.

Skyye, I remembered even without looking at her crocheted name badge. She put her plate of cookies down and bent down to give me a hug. Though I didn't know her, and didn't understand why she acted like we were sisters, I didn't resist, and hugged her back.

"How'd the present work out? Did the sixteen-year-old girl you were getting it for like it?"

She almost looked nervous to hear my answer. I understood. That joy bag had been a labor of love, her favorite creation; and she'd sacrificed it by giving it to a complete stranger who was going to give it to someone she would never see. She was trusting enough to believe her handiwork would serve its purpose, would be well cared for, would bring as much joy to another as it had to her in making it.

I didn't have the heart to tell her that the bag was still sitting in the back seat of my car in Baltimore and I had never even talked to the girl who it was intended for. I'd meant to mail it earlier in the week, meant to put it in my carry-on bag before I got on the plane. For some reason, the part of me that should have remembered had blocked all thoughts of it out.

"It was the perfect gift." My answer. An honest answer.

"Great!"

"How old are you?" I asked as she passed me a thick lemon sandwich cookie.

"Twenty."

"I remember twenty."

She nodded solemnly, as if she knew that I was twenty when I left RiChard in South Africa and returned stateside to really begin my life. I was twenty when I discovered after leaving him that I was carrying RiChard's child, a son who he would never hold. I was twenty when I decided I would prove my mother wrong, that I had not destroyed my life by running off "with that rebel man," dropping out of college and leaving behind a full scholarship to do so. I was twenty when I decided that I would do whatever I had to do to take care of my son first, myself second, and still manage to make an impact on the world. I decided I would go back to school, no matter how much it cost me in money and time, no matter how long it would take to finish.

I was twenty when all that happened. Now, I was turning forty next year, and I had achieved all I'd set out to do. I'd more than doubled my station in life and my salary. My son was in school. I'd gone beyond my initial dreams and had my own booming practice. I'd done all these things, achieved enough to fill Laz's envelope for me to overflowing.

And yet, I'd never felt worse.

Skyye was gone and I was left with the lemon cookie. Tart, sour, but sweet on the way down, I closed my eyes and swallowed as the crème filling melted in my mouth.

When I opened them, a man stood on the stage.

"Good evening, ladies and gentlemen. We're ready to begin."

I took another bite of the cookie, willing my heart to stop racing.

"Tonight, we are privileged to have a special guest with us all the way from Los Angeles. His research on the connections between food and the way we relate to others over meals served as the blueprint for the way we created our cozy little café here. We are especially grateful that he agreed to come at such short notice given our cancellation tonight. I am pleased to introduce to you Professor Juan D. Perez."

He gave a short clap into the microphone as I tried to understand what he'd just said.

Cancellation?
Professor Perez?
Where was Kisu?

As a tall, thin, middle-aged man wearing a brown sports jacket and blue jeans took the stage, I struggled to catch my breath. I could see his mouth moving and see the shoulders of the medium-sized crowd jerking in laughter as he spoke, but I did not hear a word he said. When he paused momentarily to take a sip of water, I gathered my things and headed toward the café's door, where Skyye stood greeting late guests.

"Another man was scheduled to be here tonight," I spoke, out of breath, although I'd only walked about ten steps to the door.

"Yes, Mr. Felokwakhe."

"Kisu."

"Yes, Kisu Felokwakhe. I'm sorry. He came by earlier today and said he was not going to be able to come tonight. We were pretty bummed about it, but Dr. Perez is renowned in his work."

"I . . . I flew all the way from the East Coast to see him, to see Kisu." I could hear the heartbreak in my own voice.

Skyye's face dropped. "Oh, I'm so sorry. That is a long way to come to not get to see him." She put a hand over her mouth, but then her smile returned. "Wait, I have an idea."

I stepped outside the café as she disappeared for a moment into the kitchen. The sun had just set over San Diego and the temperature was right around sixty. I ran my fingers over my arms where small goose bumps had begun forming. Hugging myself, standing alone, I had no idea what to do next but wait for more direction.

My heart told me it was coming.

"Here." Skyye had rejoined me. A small scrap of paper was in her hand. "I talked to one of our cooks who's been our contact with Mr. Felokwakhe. He said that Mr. Felok-wakhe runs a small library in the basement of a cathedral in Old Town. The cathedral is one of the historic sites in that area, but not one of the more popular ones among tourists, so you may be able to gain an audience with him. I've called a cab for you and they already know to bill us for the ride. I feel so bad that you came this far just for our event."

"It's okay. This trip was necessary. Thank you."

She passed me the paper in her hand. "Give the driver this address. It's only about a ten- or fifteen-minute drive from here. Raul, our cook, thinks the library closes at nine, but my understanding is that Mr. Felokwakhe actually lives in a small room behind the library, so you should be able to catch him regardless. He cancelled his lecture tonight because he said he had to finish working on a time-sensitive major project. We rescheduled him for October."

"Again, thank you."

"No problem. I've got to get back inside. Good luck." She gave me another hug and then I was alone again.

But not for long. A taxi pulled up alongside the curb and the passenger window rolled down.

"You the lady who needs a ride to Old Town?" the driver, a man with a thick accent, called out from the window.

"That's me," I replied, getting into the back seat after he clicked the doors open. I handed him the address.

"Ah, that's a little-known cathedral on the outer edges of Old Town. Not many people know about it, but *mi bis-abuela*, my mother's mother, tells me my family attended there when it was just a little mission church years and years ago. In fact, they have a sculpture garden they keep adding to on one of the newer porticos. My cousin, Cesar, designed one of the sculptures. You should check it out on your visit."

The driver continued to ramble on about the history of the church, of Old Town, of other more famous cathedrals in the area, of San Diego, of California, but my mind could not keep up with his words. By the time we pulled up to the cathedral, I was numb mentally and physically. My fingers felt like heavy weights as I dug through my purse to give him a generous tip.

"Did you want me to wait for you?" he called out of his window as I stood staring up at the edifice. Dull lights showed from just a few of the windows.

"No," I stated, giving no thought to my words or my plans as my heart raced inside of me.

"Okay," he shouted as he drove off.

He had been right, I realized, as I looked around me. I was definitely somewhere on the outer edges of the area. In the darkness, I could see crowds in the distance milling about the shops, museums, restaurants, and other attractions of Old Town; but where I stood, there was nothing except landscaping, quiet, solemnity, reflection. I looked up again at the white adobe cathedral that towered over me and glistened in the moonlight. I noted that a pathway led to a side door marked VISITOR ENTRANCE and I headed toward it.

The side door opened to a narrow staircase made of stone. I headed down it and entered a long, wide corridor. The air in here felt different. Cool. Moist.

I was in the basement of the building.

I noted a table next to the wall across from me. A series of brochures filled the surface, and I realized the church offered visitors a self-guided tour. At the moment, I was not interested in the history of the old building: its chapels, gardens, or service times.

I only wanted to find the library.

I picked up a pamphlet that served as a map of the cathedral, including an outline of the original mission building it had been built around. I noted the library's location on the illustrated directory. The library appeared to be at the end of the basement, past several rooms and corridors, beyond entrances to hallways that led to the main sanctuary, gardens, and porticos.

I began walking toward it. My footsteps sounded flat on the red stone tiled floor. Wrought-iron sconces on the wall flooded the hallway with warm light.

But the deeper I walked through the basement, the more the hallway narrowed, and the dimmer the lights became. As my footsteps became silent plods, I realized that the stone tiles had given way to an earthen floor. Obviously I was in the part of the church that had served as the original mission. The smell of clay and dirt filled my nostrils and the adobe walls looked slightly yellowed. I imagined the Spanish settlers from yesteryears walking the same narrow passage, which now began to turn and twist as it snaked around the small hillside that had been its foundation. No wonder few visitors ventured here. This place needed to be updated and renovated, starting with the lighting. Then again, I was in the basement. For all I knew, the main areas were probably pristine and inviting. It was hard to tell much about the building at night.

As I passed several doorways and stairwells that led to portico entrances, I studied my map again, wondering if I was still on the right pathway to the library. However, after one last sharp turn in the hallway, I exhaled. Tiled floors welcomed my feet again and the narrow pathway opened up into a large, well-lit space. I was at the end of the basement.

Across from me was a paneled wooden door atop three steps made of red brick. A gold nameplate was nailed to it with the word LIBRARY written on it in plain, black letters. I checked my watch. 8:33. *It should still be open.*

My heart felt like a percussion band as I ascended the steps and put a hand on the door.

It gave easily.

I opened it fully to reveal a room about the size of my entire office suite. It was lit by two stained-glass chandeliers that swung overhead and the space was filled to the brim with books, scrolls, maps, and other curious implements. There were no windows, and much to my disappointment, no persons.

Where is Kisu?

My heart slowed its pace as I struggled to fight off a sapping disappointment that threatened to overtake me. I stepped fully in and shut the door of the library behind me. I began walking down the narrow, cramped aisles fashioned from a series of wooden tables. The smell of musty papers and rotting wood clogged up my nose. Books about the Bible, history, and theology cluttered every available space. I also noted thick hardcovers addressing politics, world history, philosophy, and sociology, and recalled that one of the brochures on the visitor's table detailed the church's current focus on social issues. One corner of the room had a handmade sign that hung overhead, which read RARE BOOKS.

"Hello?" I called out and my voice seemed to fall flat on the leather-covered volumes and delicate, yellowed papers.

There was one last door, in the corner of the room. Kisu's living quarters? That had to be it, as I recalled Skyye saying he lived in a small room behind the library.

I went over to it and knocked. No answer. I tried the knob.

It opened.

Should I go in?

I'd come this far; of course I was going in. I entered the living space and pulled on a chain that hung from the center of the room. A naked bulb screwed into the ceiling flooded the space with uncomfortable white light.

A wooden chair.

A small table.

A twin-sized metal-framed bed with a thin mattress, worn blanket, and a single pillow.

If this was his living quarters, not much living was going on.

The only other items I could see in the room were a milk crate filled with a few toiletries, and a mini-fridge that hummed quietly against the back wall with a double-burner hot plate sitting on top of it.

The room smelled like tuna fish.

"Kisu?" I called out, though he obviously was not there.

I let out a loud sigh and reached to turn off the light to leave, but something else caught my eye.

A black suitcase peeked from underneath the bed. I knelt on the floor beside it and pulled it out. There was no lock, and the zipper was partially broken.

I opened it.

The inside was filled to the brim. Papers, pictures, and other documents were strewn about, in no obvious order. This was Kisu's "envelope." I smiled at the thought, taking Laz's idea that an entire life could be summed up and packaged into a stack of papers.

I sat on the bed, grabbing handfuls of the papers, and started flipping through them.

At first, nothing jumped out at me. Newspaper clippings of various stories with global interests were mixed in with recipes of international cuisine. Receipts from various stores and online purchases proved that Kisu had a hearty appetite for books. *Written words must be his company,* I reasoned, looking back through the open door where the library sat musty, quiet.

And then I got to a blue pocket folder. It was stored inside a clear plastic storage bag, tucked in a compartment almost unseen at the bottom of the suitcase. A sense of privacy loomed over it, and I wondered if it was too much of an intrusion to look through it.

I had to.

Holding my breath, I unzipped the storage bag, opened the folder, and gasped.

Chapter 33

A picture of me and Roman.

His fifth-grade graduation.

I recognized the light blue seersucker shorts suit and bowtie I made him wear, and the towering, rock-hard French roll I regrettably allowed my sister's old friend KiKi Jackson to put in my hair. Roman had a scowl on his face and I looked like I was trying to not feel self-conscious about the small mountain that sat on the top of my head.

I would have laughed at the photo at first glance, but eeriness surrounded its existence. First of all, it appeared to have been taken from a distance as Roman and I posed for my mother's camera. Who snapped this photo? And why? And why did Kisu have it?

I swallowed hard as my mind drew a blank for answers.

There were two more photos.

The next was of Mbali and her four children. This one was a professional portrait, a Christmas postcard. The photo captured an elegance, a regality, and a warmth about the large family I'd never noticed before. The back was not addressed, and again I wondered how and why Kisu had it.

The third photo was of a white woman and a toddler who looked biracial.

Who looked like RiChard.

Same nose. Same shaped eyes. Same thick black curly hair.

The two stood in front of what looked like a huge, ancient fountain. The buildings that surrounded them had an old-world European flair.

RiChard had said his mother was from Perugia, Italy. I pulled out my smart phone and did a search for "Perugia Italy fountain." The first result that displayed was for the *Fontana Maggiore,* a medieval fountain in a piazza in Perugia. The picture of the monumental fountain online was identical to the one in the photo.

Perhaps this was a picture of RiChard and his mother together when he was young. *But the clothes look too modern,* I conceded as my gut feelings agreed. I turned the picture over.

"Adriana and Luca, 1992," was written on the back.

1992. Two years before I met RiChard, who was a seasoned grad student when I was a freshman.

I turned the photo back over, studied the beautiful young woman who had soft laugh lines and long wisps of dark hair. The toddler looked to be one or two in the photo, an equally beautiful child. Perhaps the two were cousins of RiChard, maybe even a sister and his nephew. I tried to explain the similarity in features between the boy and the man I had married years ago.

But I knew in my heart I was straining to explain away the obvious.

He'd told me he was an only child, that he didn't have any family members with whom he communicated. He'd never had contact with his parents while we were together, or least no contact that I was aware of. Who knew what secrets he held, secrets hidden anywhere in the world?

As I looked again at the pictures of me, of Mbali and her children, of the woman Adriana and most likely her son, Luca, I realized what else was bothering me.

Years ago, when I'd first gotten the urn with the lion's head ring inside, I'd gone to a Portuguese class at a community college with the hopes that the teacher could help me contact the senders of the package. The urn had a return address in Almada, Portugal, though later I would learn in a letter the teacher translated for me the package had originated from Kisu.

What bothered me at the moment was that the other student in the class was named Luca. Luca Alexander, I recalled. His eyes had brightened when I'd shared some of my story, specifically when I said that my long-lost husband's mother was from Perugia. *"I'm from Perugia."* The dark-haired model wannabe had explained his sudden interest in my story. He had signed up for the class in anticipation of a trip to Rio.

It was conjecture, I knew, the thought that now nagged at me. Luca is a common Italian name, I reasoned, and the odds . . .

What was I thinking?

I put the pictures away even as unexplained tears began filling my eyes. Whatever the explanation, I knew that there were no such things as coincidences in Christ, that God's timing was perfect and purposeful.

I moved to what was next in the folder. An unaddressed, unsealed business-sized envelope. I opened it.

Photocopies of certificates.

Marriage certificates.

I took out my phone, put it on my document scanner setting. Then, smoothing each certificate down on the bed, I took a picture of each one, in order.

Adriana Salvay and Alex Santiago. Married in Perugia, Italy.

Sienna Davis and RiChard St. James. Married in Baltimore, Maryland.

Mbali Busisiwe and RiChard St. James. Married in KwaZulu Natal Province, South Africa.

Ana Clara Cardoso and Ricardo Santo Tiago. Married in Rio De Janeiro, Brazil.

What did this all mean?

The first marriage was dated about three years before mine. The last wedding happened about a year after RiChard had left Mbali.

"That bastard." I shook my head as a conclusion settled in my mind. I laughed even as hot tears streamed down my face.

Kisu had done a lot of research. His aims apparently as personal, as heartfelt, as mine. There were two more sheets of paper, folded up, placed face down in the other pocket of the folder. I shut my eyes; then, willing myself to look at them, opened my eyes again to get through it.

A faded birth certificate.

Alex Ricardo James.

Born in Chicago, Illinois in 1971.

Mother: Millicent Laquana Nelson.

Father: Martin Santiago James.

I was not a cussing woman. Indeed, I hadn't uttered one profane word since the day Shakina Monroe in second grade bet that I wouldn't say the S-word and I really wanted her candy bar. Looking at that birth certificate, however, I made up for my curse-free decades as every word I could think of spilled out my mouth.

Everything I knew about RiChard St. James, or should I say, Alex Ricardo James, was a bold, disgusting lie. His mother was from Perugia, Italy? No! His first wife was! I looked again at all the documents, stopping once again at his birth certificate. Alex Ricardo James! In my anger, I almost shredded the delicate paper up, until I remembered that I was scanning each document I'd found into my phone. I was saving the file when my senses picked up something new.

Footsteps.

Flat echoes sounded in the hallway near the library, and I knew I had just moments before I was not alone. Forget scanning. I stuffed the birth certificate into my workbag, then grabbed the last unfolded sheet of paper that was in the folder and stuffed it into my bag as well.

I'd look to see what that last paper was later. I had the information that I needed for the moment. I quickly stuffed the papers back into the suitcase and pushed it under the bed. Jumping to my feet, I checked that I had all my belongings with me: workbag, carry-on, and especially my phone! I pulled the chain to the light bulb and the room went dark. Shutting the door to the living quarters behind me, I stood frozen in a library aisle, trying to process the information I'd discovered in Kisu's suitcase, wondering what I was going to say to him, assuming that it was indeed him returning to the library.

The voices of two men sounded just outside the door where the footsteps had stopped.

"Thank you, Father. Your help with this project will ensure that many orphans in Zambia are fed. I will be depositing the money tomorrow."

"Oh, it is our pleasure, Brother Felokwakhe. Christ has called us to serve the widows and the fatherless. Thank you for doing this great work. May you be highly blessed in God's Kingdom. Good night."

Yes. Finally. Kisu.

I exhaled and relief flooded through me as the door began to open. My smile grew as an older man in a tweed suit jacket and a clerical collar turned away from the doorframe, revealing the man who had been standing by him.

The man took a step up into the doorway and our eyes met.

RiChard.

Both of us froze as I tried to make sense of why the man I knew as RiChard St. James and not Kisu was standing in front of me. He was thinner than when I'd last seen him nearly twenty years ago, his arms frail looking under the hunter green dress shirt he wore, his legs slightly bowed under his black trousers. His face, still the color of café au lait, was pockmarked and somewhat wrinkled, as if the years, and the sun, and the elements, and life itself had been harsh on him. Balding head. Slouched shoulders. Dull green eyes. I saw nothing that justified my obsession with him in our youth: no hint of his vigor; no trace of beauty; no residue of the charisma that had captivated crowds and towns, hearts and passions around the globe.

"Sienna?" His eyes widened even as mine narrowed.

"Alex Ricardo James?"

He bolted.

Before I could read the reaction on his face, or get another word out of my mouth, he had spun around and sprinted across the large hallway that led to the library door. He rushed toward an entryway opposite from the tunnel-like corridor I had come through in my journey to find the space, nearly knocking down the elder priest who looked as stunned as I did.

"Brother Felokwakhe? Is all well?" the priest called after him. "My dear sister? What is going on?"

I had no choice but to pursue RiChard/Alex down the corridor. "Wait a minute!" I yelled after him. I needed answers, and he was going to give them to me. For all I had been through, for all my son and the rest of the broken families Alex Ricardo James had left scattered around the world had endured, we all deserved an explanation, at a minimum.

"Come back here!" I struggled to keep up as he bounded up a narrow stairway. I was surprised that his legs, feeble as they looked, were able to carry him away so quickly. I scurried up the same stairs just to watch him disappear into another hallway. I followed, huffing and puffing as my carry-on and workbag bounced off my hips.

"RiChard!" I belted as he reached for the handle of a large wooden door.

Just before he opened it, he looked back at me.

And then had the nerve to smile.

My lips parted and a scream so piercing, so primal came out that, for a split second, I questioned if it had even come from me. I'd never felt the power of my own lungs like I did in that moment.

By the time I reached the door, opened it, and stepped through the threshold, I knew I would never catch him. We were outside. I stood on a covered portico, watching him disappear into the darkness. Trees and hills surrounded this side of the cathedral and cars lit up a highway in the distance.

He was not coming back.

I collapsed onto one of the stone benches that lined the walkway. The scream and the run had taken whatever fight, thought, feeling I had left in me. I let my bags fall to the ground and looked around me. I was surrounded by statues, stone figures of men and women with solemn eyes, gentle faces, Biblical scenes, stories, symbols. I looked up at the carved scene directly in front of me.

Jesus preaching on a hillside, a throng of people, some sick, some bowed, some broken crowded around him. His hands and eyes were raised, as if in prayer.

The Lord's Prayer was on a plaque next to the carving. The words I'd read in my brief quiet time earlier that week jumped out at me again.

And forgive us our debts, as we forgive our debtors.
Forgive.

It was too soon, too raw, too much to think about it, to consider.

There had not even been an apology, an explanation. I closed my eyes, seeing that last smile.

He had no remorse.

I stood, ready to run again, follow him to the trees, the highway if necessary when my eyes slid to another series of sculptures.

A cross.

An empty tomb.

The ascension.

Are you ready to stop running?

The still, small voice was like a whisper in my consciousness.

I stood still for a moment, then grabbed my carry-on and my workbag and put each on separate shoulders. I walked back into the cathedral, now on the first floor, and followed green arrow exit signs that pointed to the main front entrance. I passed by the sanctuary and a smaller chapel, my footsteps slow but steady on the red tiled floors. The place was silent, lights dimmed, visiting hours now long over. When I got to the front entrance, I sat down on the steps, and took out my phone.

"Mom?" My son answered on the first ring. "I was wondering what time your flight got here. You never told me."

"I need you to come pick me up, but I'm not at the airport."

As I waited for my son to come get me, I remembered that there had been one other piece of paper, the sheet that I had stuffed into my bag when I'd heard the footsteps coming.

I pulled it out and understood immediately why RiChard, born in Chicago as Alex Santiago James, had every reason to run.

The paper had two photocopied documents.

The first was a death certificate for RiChard St. James, in Perugia, Italy, just last year. The second was a copy of a photo ID for "Kisu Felokwakhe," but a light-skinned, pockmarked face with light eyes, and not a proud Zulu warrior, smiled at the camera.

Years ago, RiChard had claimed that Kisu was dead. Now, I had no doubt that he was, and that RiChard probably had something to do with it. It would be the only way RiChard, or whoever he was, could get away with using Kisu's identity and discard his own.

Chapter 34

"I would not be surprised if he didn't do it."

"Huh?" I looked up from where I lay amid the hotel's billowy sheets. Roman sat at the room's desk eating a whole pizza he'd picked up after getting me from the cathedral and bringing me to the room I'd booked by the airport. The television was on, broadcasting the late-night news.

"That man they arrested." Roman licked sauce off of his fingers and nodded at the TV screen. "Jamal Abdul. I wouldn't be surprised if he wasn't behind the terror attack. You sure you don't want any pizza, Ma?"

"No, no pizza," I said, sitting up, trying to make myself care when everything in me just wanted to sleep. "Why? Why do you say that? About Jamal Abdul?"

Roman had not asked me why I was in San Diego. He didn't question why he had to pick me up from a church in Old Town.

But he had not left me yet, so I knew he was waiting for me to tell him. He could sense it was something major.

"His wife. What's her name again? Keisha," he answered between munches.

"What about her?"

"The interview? Didn't you see it last night?"

"Was it breaking news?" I sat up fully now, recalling that I'd been meaning to make sure that I had not missed something about the terror attack story. *"Don't read too much into it, okay? I don't want you worrying."* Laz's words.

"No, I mean, she just seemed so broken, confused. Genuine. And the thing about his luggage."

"What about the luggage?"

Roman looked at me oddly, taking a deep swallow from a two-liter bottle of cola before answering. "She said he couldn't find his duffel bag just moments before the attack. Police are saying that he just told her that to keep his plans hidden, but she's not buying it. She thinks someone took his bag. What is it, Ma?"

I didn't realize my face was contorted. I was exhausted, overwhelmed, but I let my jaw relax. "Nothing, Roman. Just thinking how this might be one of the last Thursday nights we hang out like this. You're in school and moving up and out and away from me." I wondered if he still wanted to leave San Diego and come back to Baltimore, as he'd stated earlier in the week. I did not know how to ask. My heart pounded as I tried to sort out what I should be doing about . . . everything.

Mirror moments. Seeing who you are, what you're made of.

"Why'd you come out here, Mom? What were you doing at that church?" He avoided eye contact with me as he finally just went after the conversation we both knew had to happen.

"I found your father."

The late-night news blared on. Weather. Sports. Education report. The theme music for *The Tonight Show* came on, followed by the comedic monologue. A full thirty-seven minutes went by before another word was said between us.

"He's not the man we thought he was. He lied about everything." My words.

"I think we already knew that, Ma."

"He lied about his identity. It's worse than I'd imagined." I pulled up the images on my phone, passed my phone to him. As he looked at the scanned marriage licenses in silence, I took out the last sheets of paper, with the birth and death certificates and photocopied ID. Roman took both from me and stared at them for a few moments before looking back at me.

"He needs to be reported to the police."

I collapsed back into the bed, a loud groan escaping my lips.

"It's been a long, hard road, Ma." My son spoke gently. "You've done all you can do. You've done the best job a mom could do." He tapped the paper in front of him. "I've got this from here. I've already sent these images to my e-mail. Get some sleep."

"Leon would have known what to do." I said it before thinking.

"And Leon trained me well." Roman stood, walked to the door, then looked back at me. "I'm not mad at the man who fathered me. I pity him, and am glad that I will never have to live my life like he did. I'm just grateful for the man who helped raised me." As he stood at attention at the door, I saw the wisdom, the confidence, the gentle love, and sacrificing nurture that had been Leon. The observation both warmed me and broke a little bit more of my heart.

"Mom, we've been through a lot over the years. I don't know that I've been able to fully tell you how much I love you and appreciate all you ever did to make sure I never lacked for anything. My father may have given me my name and my DNA, but you've given me what I need to be a man of integrity. Now, I've got this, Mom. I'm taking care of this for you, for me . . ." He paused. "For all of us. You can officially cross RiChard St. James off your to-do list once and for all. Have a safe trip back home."

I saw the look on his face as he left my room, and I knew that he had a mission in mind that he would not stop at anything to complete.

I had a mission too.

After dozing off and on for another hour or so, I stood and stretched. My mind was alert, my confidence high.

If I could track down a man who'd evaded me for nearly twenty years, who deceived and lied to me and lived under all kinds of different names and aliases, surely I could figure out the identify and whereabouts of a man who was just in my office this week and who may be an unknown threat to national security.

My life, the circumstances in it, the men I loved and lost, the heartbreak, the challenges, even the work I did and the dangerous clients I tangled with in the past all had prepared me for this moment.

That is what my gut told me and nothing in me doubted it.

As I walked across the room to retrieve my phone from where Roman had left it on the hotel room's desk, I caught my reflection in the mirror that hung over the dresser.

I had bags under my eyes. My hair was matted on one side and my eyeliner was smudged.

But I was beautiful.

Not perfect, but becoming.

I reached for my cell phone. 1:32 a.m. I was certain Laz was waking up for his workday out on the East Coast. I typed in a text message and then pressed send.

I'm right about that man I met in the airport, and I'm going to prove it.

Chapter 35

I had one more picture to scan into my phone.

Sitting at the desk in the hotel room, I'd laid out everything I had or knew about the man I'd met in the airport. I'd opened the folder I started about him, organized my notes, the questions I'd had, the answers I'd never gotten.

I looked over what I had: his illustration of the cat sitting in the window; the name Bennett; the phone number with the Ohio area code; and my notes stating that he "did not exist"; that he was obsessed with the Internet and what he perceived as the evils of social media as showing mankind's tendency to be self-centered; and that he seemed fixated on identifying heroes in humanity. Oh, and then there was the license plate of the car from West Virginia. Carlos Dean Jessup. The green pickup truck with Pennsylvania tags whose plates I wasn't able to get. Also the e-mails from Everybody Anybody and the mysterious Twitter follower.

As I reviewed what I had, I remembered other details. He'd stated during our first conversation at the airport that he had attended a state university and majored in theology. He'd also asserted in one of our "sessions" that he had a PhD.

These were starting points.

I looked at what I had in front of me, knowing I had at least two actions I could take.

His phone number and the drawing.

I checked the time. 2:04 a.m., which meant it was 5:04 on the East Coast, assuming he was even there.

I used the hotel phone to slowly dial the number, not 100 percent sure what I would say or do if I got an answer, but the urgency I'd felt yesterday had returned. I had to call right then, regardless of time. A part of me suspected that the number would not work. I was right.

"We're sorry, but the number you are dialing does not exist. Please hang up and try again. Thank you."

I put a checkmark next to the phone number in my notes. It was most likely a prepaid number whose owner's whereabouts would not be able to be tracked at the moment. I took out the drawing. Using my phone's document scanning feature once more, I snapped a picture of it and then e-mailed it to myself. A brochure on the desk detailed that the hotel had a twenty-four-hour business center where three workstations were set up with Internet access and printing. I threw on some sweats and tennis shoes, comfortable work clothes for my mission, and headed down there immediately.

Another man, a young executive-looking type with tired red eyes and wearing a black suit he'd probably had on since yesterday morning, sat pecking away at one of the computer keyboards. "There's a coffee machine around the corner," he remarked as I took a seat two computers away from him. He spoke with a sharp New England accent.

"Thanks," I murmured as I logged on to the free Wi-Fi.

"Yep, there's nothing like getting the deals done before everyone else has even wiped the crust from their eyes." His eyes were glued to the monitor in front of him and his fingers moved nonstop over the keys.

He was there for business, making money, setting up deals. I was on a mission to save the world. I chuckled at myself, but for once, I did not allow any doubt to creep in.

I needed my entire attention and energy to complete the task at hand. There was no room for wavering. My flight back to Baltimore left in eight hours. I could sleep on the way back home; however, I did not want to get on the plane without having some clear direction and answers to take back to Baltimore with me.

I recalled Camille's sudden mood change at the end of our conversation, and I felt uneasy. *I'm not crazy and I don't trust her. I'm following my gut.*

I bowed my head and prayed a silent prayer: *And, Jesus, please guide my steps and efforts. Your will be done in my life. I surrender to you, even in all matters concerning RiChard.*

I opened my eyes and took a moment to exhale, to consider what I had just expressed, to mull over what I'd just asked for. I noticed the keyboard two workstations down from me had grown quiet. The businessman, for the first time, had paused from his work and stared at me. Had he never seen someone pray before?

"Morning meditation is good for the soul." His eyes darted uneasily from me back to his computer screen.

"Yes, especially when you know who you are talking to and what He's capable of doing."

He nodded uncomfortably and resumed typing. I smiled. That was the first time I'd shared anything about my faith with anyone in a long, long time.

It felt good.

I got down to business.

Image search.

I pulled up the scanned drawing of the cat on the windowsill I'd sent to my e-mail and uploaded the image to the search engine.

A gazillion results popped up onto the screen. Image after image of cats and windows and other seemingly random objects filled the monitor with what looked like an infinity of more images and Web site links to follow.

A few years back, when Roman was sixteen and had run away from home looking for his father, I'd done a search of my son's nicknames, trying to find any presence of him online. It wasn't until after I'd added a couple of extra key words that my search was narrowed and completed.

There was an option to enter a descriptive word in the search box, but what key word could I add? Bennett? No. That man seemed to not want to be tied down to a name, I concluded, thinking of how he preferred his identity to be ambiguous.

Theology. Evil. Good. Heroism. Existence.

I added all five words to the search box and then nearly fell out of my chair. Only two results displayed.

The first was a link to a Web site that served as a digital database for dissertations and theses worldwide. It was a subscriptions-only site available to universities, libraries, and other similar institutions. Beyond the link and the information posted about subscribing, there were no other hints as to how the image and key words from my search were related to it.

The second result led me to disturbing information.

It was a link to a YouTube video that had since been taken down, I discovered. The only thing that remained was a screenshot from the video and the short description underneath.

Read this book. My life is changed forever. Here's my review.

The creator of the video was named E.P., and the young white male in the screenshot holding up the book was not the man I was searching for. This young man looked to be about twenty-one or twenty-two years old with sandy hair that drooped over his eyes and touched the tip of his nose. He had babyish features and black wire eyeglasses, giving him a look of innocence.

I zoomed in to get a better look at the book he'd held up for his Webcam. It was bound in a blue hardcover and the title, in small gold letters, was blurred in the image.

What I found disturbing were the search results I got when I tried to find out more information about the young man. Using the screenshot for an image search and entering E.P. as keywords, the first result was a news article detailing his death. His name was Ephraim Peterson and he'd been found dead in his car at the bottom of a lake just three weeks ago. He was only twenty-two. Police believed the Ohio native had swerved off a bridge in the nighttime hours while driving home after working at a neighbor's farm. There were no witnesses to the crash, no continuing investigation, the whole thing deemed a terrible tragedy.

He'd died two days after he'd posted his video.

I tried to find more information about him, but there was nothing else to be found. No Facebook profile, no Twitter feed, not even a white pages listing for an address or phone number. If not for the YouTube video and the article about his death, there would have been no record of his existence, at least on the Internet. The only other fact I discovered from my search was that the town he was from was in the same area code where the phone of the man from the airport had been registered.

That could not be a coincidence.

There's so much more to this story. I know it. I feel it. I shook my head, straining to think of what else I could do.

I tried again in vain to see if the video would play, but it had been removed, or maybe even corrupted somehow. There had been only two views, and I was a current viewer.

"Excuse me," I called over to my fellow night owl worker, "do you know how to enlarge an image?"

The businessman rolled his seat next to mine and clicked a few buttons, making the screenshot of Ephraim Peterson holding up the book even larger, before rolling back to his workstation without a word.

"Thanks," I murmured as I tried to make out the title of the book. The words were still blurred and the title looked ridiculously long, but I could make out a few of the letters and piece together some of the words:

Deconstructing. Theological. Moral. Finite.

There was no author listed, but the publisher's imprint was at the far bottom of the front cover. I was certain that the words "Window" and "Press" made up part of the publisher's name. Or maybe that's just what I wanted to see as I was determined to find answers, and somehow connect that man to all that was currently wrong in the world.

One last Web search yielded nothing of significance with the words from the title or imprint. If this book existed, and clearly it did because it was in poor Ephraim Peterson's hands, its author, and publisher, had kept it well hidden.

Self-published. Had to be. I could not imagine that the man worked along with anyone else, especially if, as he'd asserted, he had not talked to anyone in years.

I was making a lot of assumptions I realized; but every conclusion I came to made perfect sense to me. I just did not know how to explain it to anyone else.

I logged off the computer, shut it down.

"Take care of yourself. Don't work too hard." I smiled over at the man whose fingers had to be tired and cramped as he had not stopped moving them across the keyboard.

"No such thing as working too hard."

There was no humor to his voice. No light to his eyes. No life in his shoulders. He had on a designer suit, designer shoes. Even the briefcase that sat on a chair next to him had a brand name. I imagined everything in his life was high end and he would keep working until he had that car, that house, that jet, that position, that whatever it was that would never be enough.

Yes, I was in the right field. I'd made the perfect career choice for my gifts, talents, and interests. My focus in life, though often confused and flawed, ultimately was to help others be the best they could be. That's where my heart was as I searched for answers to help, to heal, to listen to and encourage those I served.

For what shall it profit a man, if he shall gain the whole world, and lose his own soul?

The Bible verse crossed my mind as I closed the door to the business room behind me.

The Whole Soul Center.

This was my purpose, my God-given calling, and it was already up, running, and growing.

I'd have to talk to Laz more about the proposed move to Atlanta.

For now, I had another call to make.

Chapter 36

"You're still up?" Roman sounded as surprised as I did when he answered my phone call on the second ring.

"What are you doing up? You sound like it's three o'clock in the afternoon and not three in the morning." I raised an eyebrow as I talked to him on my way back to my room.

"My brother and I are working on something together."

"Oh? Oh."

"I told you. I have this, Mom."

"You need to be getting your rest to deal with your classes tomorrow."

"I told you. I have this, Mom," he repeated.

There would be no changing his mind or stopping whatever ball he'd started rolling, and it was clear that he would not be elaborating on whatever actions he, and his brother, were taking. Though I had not said it, I wasn't worried. My son took after me in some ways. Once he had a mission in mind, he would see it through to the end with determination and integrity.

At least that's how I envisioned my efforts at problem solving.

It occurred to me that the same pang of pain that usually shot through me at the mention of RiChard's other family did not surface just now; at least, not to the degree it usually did.

Maybe that's what the beginning of forgiveness felt like. Not experiencing the pain again at the same level.

"What's up, Ma?"

I'd been quiet too long. *Focus, Sienna.* "Roman, is your school's library still open?"

"Twenty-four hours a day. Why?"

"I need you to log me into a database they should have on their computer system."

"O . . . kay." He paused. "Mom, I told you I'm taking care of everything."

"Roman, this has nothing to do with your father. I've moved on."

He paused again. I heard a long sigh and then he said something to his brother. Was someone else besides Croix with him? I wondered, as what sounded like a female's voice sounded in the background. Did Roman have some girl in his dorm room and was he trying to play it off like it was his brother? *Focus, Sienna!* I could feel myself about to have conniptions. I was on a mission. I had to stay the course. Save the world.

Maybe I just needed to get some sleep; my thoughts were getting delusional.

"Mom." Roman finally got back on the phone. "I'll be there in twenty minutes, but I'm bringing you back to my room. I can access the library's database collection from my computer."

"Mmm, hmm," I managed to get out as we both disconnected. Exhaustion seeped into me. I had twenty minutes to take a quick nap.

The urgency now raging inside of me told me I needed as clear a head as possible.

Between waiting for Roman and driving back to his dorm room, I managed to get in nearly fifty minutes of Zs. As I stepped into his corner suite, I realized I'd forgotten how spacious it was. And I had no idea it was so technologically advanced.

With computers, game systems, stereo speakers, and gadgets I didn't recognize, I wondered if I was stepping into his dorm room or the twenty-second century.

"Do you study here, sleep here, or play here?" I asked as I stepped into his room for the first time since I'd helped him move in last August.

"A little bit of all three." He chuckled. "Let me get you set up." He guided me to his workstation as I stepped over mounds of clothes and looked at both loft beds that were in the room. One was unmade, the other barely touched.

"You said you were with your brother. Is he staying here again?"

Roman shrugged, but gave me a half smile. "We'll be okay. It helps when you have a common purpose to work on together." He pointed to the monitor. "I've got you logged in. What database do you need?"

"One that that will let me search for dissertations and theses from around the country."

He clicked on an icon and within seconds I was entering the key words I'd pulled from what I'd made out of the title of the book from the YouTube screenshot: Deconstructing. Theological. Moral. Finite. I pressed search. A couple of seconds later, a title popped onto the screen.

"Whoa, that's a mouthful." Roman studied the screen from his bean bag chair behind me. "What's that about, Mom?"

"Nothing." How did I even begin to explain?

"It's something. Can't imagine why you'd have an urgent desire to read *The Secrets to Deconstructing Heroism and a Critique of the Philosophical and Theological Views of Moral Evolution in the Finite Universe* at four o'clock in the morning. That's some pretty heavy information to start out your day." He chuckled and moved closer to the screen. "By J.B. Infinity? Is this some kind of joke?"

"No. It's not a joke."

"What's going on, Ma?" Roman sobered again as he could see the seriousness in my eyes, the growing panic on my face.

"This is the dissertation of a terrorist."

"Huh?"

"I think this is the man who is responsible for the bombing at BWI. No. I am certain of it. I feel it. They have the wrong man in custody."

I looked up at my son, who stood beside me, staring at the screen. Then he looked at me. "Okay, Mom. I know I expressed my doubts earlier, but that's taking it to a whole other level." He clicked the Web site off.

"Wait! What are you doing?" I grabbed his hand as he maneuvered his mouse to shut down the system. "Roman, I need to print that out. I need to at least write down the title. Don't turn it off. I need to—"

"Ma, you need to get some sleep. I'm used to pulling all-nighters, but this staying up until four in the morning is not for you."

"Roman, I know what I'm doing. I know what I'm talking about. Pull the site back up. Now."

"You're in my kingdom, Ma. We're playing by my rules. You've had a tough week. You've got jet lag two times over. You saw RiChard for the first time in twenty years. You just missed a terrorist attack by a flight last Saturday. Get some sleep, and I'll make sure I get you to the airport before my eleven o'clock class. Your flight leaves at ten, right?"

I narrowed my eyes at my nineteen-year-old son. "Um, I don't care how old you are, or which side of the country we're on. Understand that I am *always* the queen. You will *always* be a subject in *my* court." I gave him The Eye, the look I used to use to flash him back into immediate compliance in the church pews when he was eight, at PTA meetings when he was twelve.

He sighed, rolled his eyes, sucked his teeth. But he turned the computer back on. "I don't believe this," he muttered, shaking his head. "I will print out the title and the abstract for you, Ma, but please promise me that you won't do anything drastic. Actually, please don't do anything at all until you've had at least eight hours of sleep."

I would have told him that I could not promise him anything, but my eyelids were betraying me. I had officially and suddenly met my limit of consciousness for the day. "Go ahead and print it out. I'm going to sleep." I headed to the futon under his loft bed. "Don't let me oversleep."

It wasn't until the next morning that he broke the news to me. After driving me to the hotel to check out, he turned his car towards the airport. I struggled to stay awake in the passenger seat.

"You have the abstract?" My words slurred together as I tried to remember why I had been in San Diego and why I was on my way to an airport yet again. "What is today?"

"It's Friday. It's eight o'clock in the morning. You are on your way back home to Baltimore, and, no, I do not have the abstract."

"What?" I immediately came to attention as the events of the past twelve hours came back to mind.

"The article apparently had been removed from the database. There was no other information except what was up on that screen you saw last night. Just the title and the author's name. I did print that out for you and put it in your workbag." We were at the departures terminal. "Mom, please don't do anything until you've had some sleep."

I gave him a smile and kissed his cheek as I got out of the car.

I didn't think either one of us was reassured.

Chapter 37

The Secrets to Deconstructing Heroism and a Critique of the Philosophical and Theological Views of Moral Evolution in the Finite Universe.

By J.B. Infinity no less.

This had to be him. The title, even the author's name had all the hallmarks of that man's convoluted, confusing reasoning.

B. Maybe for Bennett?

My questions only increased as the plane approached DC. In my exhaustion, I'd forgotten that I had flown in and out of the DC. area, and not Baltimore; but with four hours of in-flight uninterrupted sleep, I felt ready to tackle whatever was next. I wanted to catch up with Laz and show him my research.

But this only proves that his mind may be a little off, I imagined Laz saying. *What does his dissertation have to do with the terrorist attack, if you can even prove that this is even his work?*

There are too many coincidences, I'd respond. *The man happened to call me from a number that was in the same area as a now-dead young man who took to the Internet to discuss the dissertation-turned-book.*

Explain the book. Who published it? Where does it exist? Laz would question next.

Before we go there, I imagined myself responding to him, *let's consider that he also coincidentally was at the airport just before the attack, with verbal plans to go to the same destination that the suspect in custody happened to be going to with his family. Why not look up his itinerary and see if that was indeed his planned destination and if he was in line to board the plane?*

Okay, what's his name? I imagined Laz asking. *Let's start with that and then we can move on.*

His name? I would reply. *Uh . . .*

Even in my imagination, Laz, the fact-finding, investigative reporter, won. I needed more proof. Though my gut told me I was on the right track, I still needed that definitive piece of evidence, that undeniable fact of correlation before I talked to anyone about my suspicions.

My car.

Even the officials at the airport had acknowledged that it wasn't there when I went to pick it up; but when it showed up inexplicably in front of my house, the police officer who responded to my 911 call refused to even take a report. My guess was that the yellow Jeep from West Virginia was being safely driven by its owner with nobody but me even aware that it may have been stolen.

No matter how I looked at it, I was still at square one. No name. No clear connecting point. No irrefutable evidence to turn over and be taken seriously. *Maybe I should skip trying to catch up with Laz just yet.*

"Ladies and gentlemen, we have been cleared for landing. We will be at our gate in ten minutes." The pilot's voice was scratchy on the overhead speaker.

My conclusions, though they felt right, were scratchy at best. What could I present to anyone? I thought about Camille and shuddered. I had to have something more tangible to offer. She said she would be in touch with me soon.

Though I'd left California in the morning hours, the time difference on the East Coast meant my nonstop flight was arriving just after six-thirty p.m. Not far from DC, Dulles Airport was in Northern Virginia, near Jamal Abdul's hometown. I had an idea.

It was a risky idea, and it would involve Laz, but I had to take action. What other options did I have?

As soon as I landed, I dialed him.

He answered on the first ring and spoke before I could get out one word.

"Meet me at the same restaurant from yesterday in thirty minutes." He hung up.

I dialed right back.

"Hey—"

"Thirty minutes!" He hung up again.

What was wrong with him? What was going on?

I started to call back. I started to simply get in my car and drive home; but his pointedness and urgency told me that I needed to get in my car and meet him at the restaurant, no questions asked.

I got there nearly fifty minutes later and saw him as soon as I turned into the parking lot. I could not miss him as he was parked in the first space by the entrance. Oddly, he sat slouched in the driver's seat, his face almost out of view. He waved a hand at me and pointed to an empty parking space next to the black Range Rover he was in. Did he get a new vehicle? I wondered as I pulled into the space and cut the engine. I'd never seen him in this SUV before.

"Quick," he called out to me from his slightly opened window. His hand waved in a frenzied gesture.

"What?" I wrinkled my face as he hurried me even more as I got out of my car. I heard him unlock the door.

"Get in, quick." He pointed to the passenger seat. "Wait. Leave your phone in your car."

"Laz, what are you—"

"Sienna, please. I don't have time to explain, but I will. Please leave your phone in your car, and hurry up and get in mine."

My phone was my life line, but the look on his face told me I needed to do as he said.

"Is this a new car or something?" I asked as I stepped into the Range Rover.

"What took you so long?" He completely disregarded my question and glared over at me. "I told you to be here in thirty minutes. It took you almost an hour."

"Um, traffic?" And getting out of the airport and getting to my car. I didn't tell him all that as I recalled that I had never told him about my plans to fly out to the West Coast; though he didn't seem to have any questions about my whereabouts and he somehow knew that I was near the restaurant.

He groaned as he put the car in reverse, then backed up and braced himself like he was about to shoot out of a chicane on a Grand Prix racetrack. After several loud screeches, he pulled out of the lot and a few turns later we joined the bumper-to-bumper traffic on Dulles Toll Road. He swerved and changed lanes three times, all to a loud chorus of beeps and honks.

"Okay, Laz. I'm here. I left my phone in my car for some reason and you are driving like you're about to have a baby. You're scaring me. What is going on and why the new truck?"

"Had to change things up for a moment."

"What is going on, Laz" I asked again. He sped deeper into Northern Virginia, signs for DC pointing the other way. "Where are we going?" The car bumped and jostled along.

"How was your trip?"

"Excuse me?" I looked at the side of his face and noticed his clenched jaw.

"Your trip to San Diego? How was it?" He cut me a look and my mouth fell open. "Well," he continued, "aren't you going to ask me how I know that you're just coming back from San Diego?" He glared at me.

"Why should I ask you anything seeing that you haven't answered a single one of my questions yet?" I kept a sharp edge in my tone, though something in my confidence suddenly felt disabled. How did he know where I had been?

"They're following you."

"What?" I looked over at him like he was crazy. His eyes were on the road. I still didn't know where we were going, but wherever it was we were getting there in a hurry. "Who is 'they?'"

"Homeland Security."

"As in the whole department? Or just Camille."

"Yeah, her. I mean, I don't know what's going on. She just told me that your phone is being tracked and your whereabouts are being monitored."

"So she thinks there is something to my concerns about that man?"

"No, Sienna, she thinks you're crazy."

"That's what she's telling you?"

"No, actually she's not telling me anything, but I don't know why else she would have such a sudden interest in having your constant whereabouts monitored." He stared intensely at his rearview mirror and changed lanes.

"And you call me the paranoid one," I joked, but my heart began beating faster. What was going on? And why was Camille interested in the details of my life? I had my suspicions. Was she that intent on making me look like a fool to Laz? "I'm surprised you're getting involved." I studied him as his jaw clenched tighter. "Why did you pick me up and whisk me away? Are you sure my phone's really being tracked, or is she just pulling your leg?"

"This isn't a joke, Sienna. Your phone and everything you've done and accessed on it are now at full disclosure for the government to see. You're my fiancée and you have my best source at Homeland Security sniffing your tail for unknown reasons. I just got offered a national news show—to host, not to be the headline story. This is not the way I'm trying start my new job."

"Huh? Oh." His scooping me up and away had nothing to do with me, I realized. This was about him, his reputation. I wasn't sure how I felt about that; how to interpret that. "Well, do you even want to know why I was in San Diego?"

"I'm sure you have your reasons." He rushed through his words. "Is my home number on your phone? Of course it is," he muttered.

"Laz?" My lips, my heart tried to form a question. "Where are we going?" My voice shook as I whispered the only question I could ask out loud.

"There's a place I stay not too far away from here when I need an escape. It's nice, private. Away from it all. I need you to stay there until I smooth everything out. And I will. We don't need all this attention on you. I can't afford to have any confusion at this point in my career."

"Of course. That wouldn't be good for you." I resisted rolling my eyes.

"For us." He gave me a half smile and patted my hand, then stared intently at the highway in front of him. I looked out of the window, trying to remember what it was I'd wanted Laz to help me with, what it was I'd wanted to say.

"Can you get an interview with the wife?"

"What?"

"Jamal Abdul's wife, Keisha. Can you interview her? Doesn't she live here in Northern Virginia? I have some questions I need her to answer."

"Sienna, did you hear anything I said just now? Are you paying attention to what is going on? I'm trying to get you off grid and out of the attention of authorities, but you seem determined to keep playing detective. Leave it alone, please, Sienna. It's not cute anymore."

"Cute? You think I'm aiming for cute?"

He let out an exasperated sigh. "That's not what I meant. Poor word choice. Heroism. That's what you're aiming for. You have a hero complex. You need to feel like you are saving somebody. It's a lovely quality, but right now it's getting in the way of your common sense. They have a suspect in custody. There is nobody else you can save from the terror attack."

"Hero complex?" Heroism. The word struck me. "Are you serious? Does this go back to your whole belief that I made the wrong career choice?"

"We're not getting into that right now."

"Oh, I'm sorry. I forgot. We're only focused on your job and your dreams. I'm just a lost woman who got sidetracked onto a career path—a successful career path, mind you—all because I chased some man around the world. And the answer to that mistake is now to drop everything I've worked for and achieved and chase another man all the way down to Atlanta."

"You are completely taking my words out of context."

"Well, I don't know how else to take them."

"We're not talking about this right now."

"So, you not only decide what I'm going to do with my own life, you even decide when I can talk about it."

"Sienna, there is a lot going on. This is not the time."

"Then I guess it's not the time to tell you that I saw RiChard."

"Nope, this isn't the time. We will talk about your trip to San Diego later. We're here now." He screeched to a stop in front of a small ranch house that sat back on about a half acre of land.

"Did you even hear what I said? I saw RiChard."

"And we'll talk about it later. Let's go." He got out of the car and then opened my car door. Without waiting for me, he headed down a crumbling cement walkway to the front door of the home.

Was this man serious? I wanted to scream, holler, protest, tell Laz a thing or two; but instead I got out of the truck behind him.

Dated and worn, the small ranch house looked to be a far cry from the usual glitz and glamour that defined everything Laz bothered with. I was in a state of numb shock as I neared the home, but my emotions did not keep me from noticing the peeling green paint on the doorway and shutters, the rust around the porch's red mailbox, the scuff marks on the metal screen door.

"I thought you said you were bringing me to a nice place."

"It's nice enough," he murmured as he took out a key and opened the door. He checked to make sure the shades were drawn before he clicked on some lights.

The house was warm and stuffy but clean. Formal floral furniture filled the living room and the tiny kitchen had a chrome table and red vinyl chairs.

"And where exactly are we?" I looked at the walls covered with decorative plates. The end tables were covered with doilies. I searched for photos, portraits, but there were none.

"This is my family's house. It was my grandmother's, then my mother's. Now I own the deed."

"So this is where you came from?" I ran my hand over the dusty keys of an upright piano that sat in the dining room, looked at a framed quilt that hung on the foyer wall. "Let me find out that the urbane, professional Laz Tyson is really just a country boy from rural Virginia at heart. You've never talked much about your family. I know you spent your teen years in Baltimore with your father. What's the story behind this house, your grandmother, your mother? Where are they? Who are they?"

The anger I'd felt moments ago seemed to have disappeared from my emotion bank and landed on Laz's face. "We are not here to talk about my past, your past, my mother, my sisters, RiChard, or anything or anyone else," he boomed. "I am all about the future right now, and I've got to fix the present distraction you've caused before it gets too out of control."

"I'm not a child, Laz. You don't have to talk to me like one. And why are you so insistent on blocking out the past? I've never seen you like this." Curiosity bested me as I studied his scowling face.

"No. No psychoanalyzing. That is not why I am with you." He turned toward the door.

"Then why are you with me, Laz? I am a therapist. I am a woman who is recovering from her past, and, to hear you tell it, I am currently messing with your future, though all I am doing is following my instincts, instincts you've said in the past you respected. What are we doing here? What is this, what are we doing, Laz?"

"We're moving forward." He opened the door, stepped out on the porch. He paused for a moment and looked back at me. "The TV works, but there's no cable. There should be a box of lasagna in the freezer. The microwave doesn't work right, so just use the oven to heat it up. And if you need to get in touch with me, there's a phone in the back bedroom. Only call me if there is an urgent emergency. Otherwise, I'll be back in the morning. By then everything will be back to normal."

Normal. I didn't even know what that was anymore. I was too tired, too frustrated, and too frazzled to fight against him.

"Funny, Laz, you gave me 'you in an envelope' so that I could know more about you, but all you really had to do was bring me to this house. I've discovered more about you just looking around these rooms for the past five minutes than I have in any of our conversations. I had no idea your roots were so basic and, well, humble—the complete opposite of how you portray yourself. You've piqued my interest, Lazarus Tyson."

"This house does not define me." His words came out in a sharp whisper, a borderline low growl. He turned and left.

Standing alone in a foreign house in a town I'd never heard of, I listened as the wheels of the Range Rover screeched away into the distance.

What is his problem? I shook my head, rubbed my eyes with both hands. Sat down.

Chapter 38

I'd been running and going and thinking and stressing all week. For the first time since last Saturday, I was by myself with no agenda, no expectations, and no phone.

And no clear understanding of why I was in this house.

Large velvet pillows filled the flowery green sofa on which I sat. As I sank down into the cushy pillows, I felt everything inside of me begin sinking too. The realities of the past week came into focus.

Adrenaline had been keeping me afloat, but now deflation took over.

I'd seen RiChard.

And the moment went nothing like I'd imagined all these years. Sure, I'd pictured seeing him again, and the daydream alternated between a heart-stirring reunion and me telling him off and then getting an apology.

Neither version happened.

I actually ran after him. I recoiled at the thought, recalling how I'd tried to chase him down for answers. As if there could be any explanation for doing women and children so wrong. As if anything he could have said would have somehow made things, made me, feel better.

I had wasted the best years of my life waiting, loving, missing him.

And for what?

A deep bitterness filled every limb, every blood vessel within me. I could taste it. My body shook under its weight, the grief and anger so great, I could not think nor feel anything else.

"I can't live like this." My voice echoed in the small house. I was in a place beyond tears. "I can't function like this."

I had important tasks to do, a mission to complete. Bitterness would only immobilize me. I had to shake it. I fought to shake it, but I could not break free of the chokehold that had suddenly clamped around my neck. I felt it squeezing out the last bit of joy, the last bit of peace I had in me.

I realized my eyes were closed and I opened them. There was a family Bible on the coffee table in front of me, a thick, maroon, leather-bound volume that looked to be a foot and a half tall, maybe five pounds heavy. I wrestled against the pillows and moved to the edge of the couch, reaching out a hand to open the Bible.

A family tree filled the first few pages. Different-colored ink, different handwriting on the blanks of Laz's family history gave testament to the many generations who'd handled it.

I stared at the names, the birth and death dates, the marriage dates, and all I could think about were those multiple marriage licenses in RiChard/Alex's suitcase.

The bitterness increased into a physical suffocation.

I turned the pages.

Genesis 1:1.

In the beginning God created the heaven and the earth.

I thought about it, thought about the "conversation" I'd had with that man, Bennett, his views on the universe, on evolving, on existence.

Whatever you believed about the origin of life would determine what you believed about life's value and purpose, I realized. If we were here by a random act of chance, then morality and virtue and how they were defined had no real meaning as everything that exists would just be the result of a universe-sized accident.

But if you believed, as I did believe, that there was a Creator who fashioned the world with purposed intent, then life itself had purpose and intent just by nature of being created.

I looked at the first verse of the Bible again, recognizing that I had to be strong in the basic elements of my faith if I was to have any hope at successfully wrestling with the complex issue that now faced me.

Forgiveness.

Forgiveness was about as complex an issue as it got.

Forgiveness was at the heart of many therapy sessions I'd facilitated. The matter of forgiveness surrounded crimes of passion and court cases, was at the root of issues exposed on talk shows and in ongoing drama on Facebook posts. The lack of forgiveness changes our countenance, our decisions, our moods, our motivations, and our actions.

Forgiveness was why Jesus died and rose again.

I knew all of this on a mental level; but my heart level was a different story. The pain was oppressive. My feelings completely justified.

But I needed to be able to live my life apart from the pain.

Forgiveness was not about RiChard or whether he deserved it.

Forgiveness was about me.

I shut the Bible, but then opened it again. The gold-trimmed pages were heavy on my fingertips, but not heavier than the weight that felt like it was taking me under in waves. Sitting in that house, at that moment, I was fighting for my life. That Bible felt like the only life preserver I had. I opened up to a random page. My eyes fell on a single verse. Psalms 27:6.

And now shall mine head be lifted up above mine enemies round about me: therefore will I offer in his tabernacle sacrifices of joy; I will sing, yea, I will sing praises unto the Lord.

I could not get my eyes off of the verse as I absorbed its meaning.

David the psalmist acknowledged having enemies, but his head was lifted up above them so he could offer sacrifices of joy.

A sacrifice cost something.

Surrendering often brought discomfort as a possession, a mentality, a lifestyle, a right to hold on to something was decisively let go.

I'd never thought of joy as being a sacrifice, but in that moment I understood. To offer sacrifices of joy meant giving up the right to be sad, to feel hurt, angry, and disappointed.

I recalled another Psalm of David I'd read years ago.

Thou wilt shew me the path of life: in thy presence is fulness of joy; at thy right hand there are pleasures for evermore.

If I was going to stay in God's presence (and I needed to in order for my spirit, soul, and body to survive,) if I had any chance of knowing the right path to take at this moment in life, or what decisions to make about marriage, my family, or my mission to find that man from the airport, if I was going to ensure that my gut instincts were being directed by the Holy One on High and not just my own broken heart and thinking, I had to offer up sacrifices of joy.

I had to surrender my right to be unsettled, upset, and sorrowed by RiChard's unjust actions, and accept that joy was God's expectation of me in His presence.

And forgiveness was the dagger to kill my soul's deep sorrow.

It hurt, it was hard, it pained me, but I was determined to make joy my sacrifice. I needed God's presence; I needed clarity for what path to take for everything going on in every area of my life.

And it wasn't just *a* sacrifice of joy that I needed to give. The verse said "sacrifices." That meant a continual act of surrender was required, a multiple offering of my will, my thoughts, and my emotions to see Him, to see the way clearly.

I took out a sheet of paper. I didn't know if I would ever see RiChard again, but just as Jesus told His disciples to commemorate His sacrifice on the cross by taking Communion, I felt the need to commemorate this moment of me deciding to let go of bitterness and surrender to joy.

"I forgive you, RiChard." I wrote it down and said it out loud as tears filled my eyes, the numbness in my body dissipating. I could feel again. "I forgive you, RiChard," I said again, and I realized that a small smile had taken over my face; a lightness had begun filling my spirit. Joy filled the room. "I forgive you!" My voice was almost at shout level.

I took the paper, folded it up, wondered where I could put it as my feet suddenly felt like moving, my heart suddenly felt like praising. Songs of worship whose words I'd forgotten for years began flowing from my mouth as a sense of peace that I could not explain or understand washed over me.

I was in the presence of God, the one who had pleasures in His right hand evermore, the lifter of heads, the forgiver of those who also forgive. The line from the

Lord's Prayer did not bother me anymore. *Forgive us our debts, as we forgive our debtors.*

I. Was. Free.

I felt like dancing, swirling, singing, laughing, crying all at once.

I was free. Even the air felt different as I breathed it in, exhaled it out. Pure, fresh, sparkling clean, renewed. Me and Jesus, the Sacrificial Lamb who'd made forgiveness possible, we were just all right. On good terms. First-name basis.

I looked again at the folded up paper in my hands. I knew where I wanted to put it. The joy bag, the crocheted purse Skyye had fashioned and I'd bought to give to Roman's sister, would be the perfect place.

The words of forgiveness belonged there. Not the note I'd just written, per se, but a card, a letter, something that spoke to the freedom, the forgiveness I had in my heart, the freedom I now felt to pursue a relationship with RiChard's other family.

It did not hurt now to think about them. A revolution had happened in my soul and my mind was now open to new possibilities.

"Lord, let me be a vessel of healing."

And I was trained to be one. I smiled. Yes, I was a worker for social justice, a servant for the public good. I was destined and prepared to help bring hope and healing, restore relationships, and encourage inner peace through my work as a therapist, my calling as a social worker. The message I had for my corner of the world was powerful and radical: there is freedom in forgiveness, the fullness of joy in God's presence, and it's worth sacrificing our right to be angry and upset to experience it all.

I know not everyone believes in the same God I worship. Saying anything about Christ and his sacrificial death is not "PC" but I didn't need words to get out the truths I was experiencing. My "mirror moment," as Ava termed it, was showing me that allowing Christ to reflect off of me would be enough for the world to see His glory, and I would look fabulously good doing so.

I knew exactly what I needed to do next; no doubts, no second-guessing, no questions about it.

Clarity came with freedom. And so did courage for the next leg of the journey. Clear vision and strength were byproducts of joy.

Chapter 39

I had to get to my car.

The joy bag was in the back seat and my phone was in the glove compartment. Plus, my workbag containing my folder and notes about the man from the airport was in the passenger seat. I kicked myself for not bringing that and my carry-on bag with me, but Laz had rushed me, and I'd had no idea where we were going or what we were doing.

I looked for the sole phone in the house and shook my head when I found it in what looked like the master bedroom. Wood paneling covered the walls of the tiny room and a comforter decorated with bright apples and cherries covered the queen-sized bed. The phone was on a nightstand next to the bed. It was a rotary phone, bright red and looking like it had seen better days.

"I hope this really does work." I picked up the handset and relief flooded through me. A dial tone never sounded so good. There was no point in calling Laz. I needed a cab. Thankfully, there was an old department store catalog on the nightstand next to the phone. It was addressed to a Lozella Tyson and had the full address of the home; otherwise, I would not have known where to tell the cab company to come.

Within thirty minutes, I was en route to the restaurant lot where my car was parked."Wait," I called out to the cab driver as we passed a strip mall not far from Laz's secret family house. "I need to stop at that ATM so I can have money to pay you." I pointed to a bank.

"I take credit cards, ma'am."

"That's good, but I, uh, still want to stop at the machine." I needed cash. One benefit of hanging out so much with an investigative reporter was that you picked up tips and hints for staying low-key. Avoiding a paper trail became my aim.

"Thanks." I smiled politely as he let me out in front of a bank I'd never heard of. Hopefully the bank was obscure enough that any transactions I completed at its ATM would not be posted until the next business day, Monday, three whole days away.

I hope I'm not still dealing with all this next week. I refuse to be. I was determined that the weekend would not end without me getting complete answers about that man from the airport. I had peace about what I was doing, but the urgency had not left. Now that my thoughts were clearer, the urgency had, in fact, quadrupled.

A quiet rain had started falling by the time we pulled up to the restaurant parking lot about forty minutes later. "Ma'am, we're here." The cabbie pointed to the fare on the meter. "It was a long drive so it's not going to be cheap." He raised an eyebrow at the horror I was sure he saw on my face.

Except my sudden alarm had nothing to do with the cost of the trip.

My eyes had scanned the parking lot as we'd pulled up in front of the restaurant doors.

My car was not there.

"Um, here's your money, but do you mind waiting for a moment? I need to see if my party is here."

"Lady, it's raining and it's Friday night in DC. I can get a lot of business right now."

"I promise that I'll be right back out. Just give me five minutes, please."

"Five minutes, no more." The cab driver grunted as he counted the twenties I'd handed him.

"Thank you." I used my purse to cover my head and hair from the growing rain shower as I stepped out of the cab. I headed immediately into the restaurant.

My car had gone missing from the airport, I recalled, but it had happened when I wasn't expected to be in town.

This felt different.

"Welcome, how many in your party?" A different hostess from yesterday greeted me with a couple of menus.

"I need to use your phone. I . . . I'm not sure that my party is here, and I, well, I left my phone in my car."

"Sure, you can use the one right here." She passed me a handset from her stand and walked to a group of seven who'd entered behind me. I quickly dialed Laz's number. His phone rang for a while before he picked it up.

"Hello, who's this?"

"It's me, Laz."

"Si . . . I mean, uh, where are you calling from?" His voice dropped to a near whisper. He also sounded more formal than usual.

"Someone stole my car."

"What? No. That did not happen."

"I'm back at the restaurant right now. My car is not here. That man stole it. I didn't tell you how it was missing on Sunday when I went to get it from BWI, but then it was in front of my house Monday morning. I'm telling you that man from the airport is somehow involved with the bombing and he's stalking me."

"Don't be ridiculous. And why are you not . . . where I last saw you? It's not missing. Something came up. Wait, hold on, please." It sounded like he put his hand over his phone, but I could still hear his words as he spoke to someone near him. "I'll be right back. I have to take this call in private." I could hear his footsteps and a door slam shut. When he got back on the call his whisper was as potent as a full-blown yell.

"Sienna, what are you doing? I took you to that house for a reason. You were to stay until I came to get you tomorrow morning! I told you I'm working to make everything okay. You're screwing it all up!"

I had a lot I wanted to say to that, but I lost my train of thought watching the cab pull away from the front of the restaurant. Had five minutes passed already? I turned my attention back to my conversation with Laz.

"How are you going to tell me that my car is not missing? I'm here looking at the empty space where it should be. And who were you just talking to? Are you with her? Camille?"

"No, Sienna, I am not with her, but, like I said, something came up. Right now, she is just independently investigating some things. She was going to take whatever information she thought she had to a higher level, but I begged and pleaded with her to not do so. She wanted to follow your phone, check out your car, and that's all that was supposed to happen; but after she checked it out, she started making other calls and apparently had it taken away. I don't know what is going on, and she has stopped giving me information. I wish you had just listened to me and stayed where you were."

"Wait a minute. You knew that woman wanted to look at my car? You were working with her against me?"

"No! I mean, yes, I knew she wanted a closer look at your car, but I didn't realize she'd have it towed away. I just told her where your car would be and when. She doesn't know that I picked you up or hid you. I was doing that for both of us, keeping you out of the spotlight until she leaves you alone. Now, I don't know what I'm going to do." He sighed.

"So, she thinks I had something to do with what happened at the airport?" I wasn't worried. There was absolutely nothing that could tie me to such a ludicrous claim.

"Sienna, did you hear what I said? She has stopped talking to me about anything related to the case. I don't know what is going on right now. I don't know why she has your car or what she is doing with it. I'm trying to get another source right now, and I need to get off this phone so I can finish talking to an FBI agent who seems willing to talk to me."

"Laz, come get me, take me to her, or whoever, and I'll set everything straight. If they have my car, they'll see the notes I've taken. I can tell them all of my concerns. Everything will be okay. Calm down."

"How dare you tell me calm down, Sienna? Do you think the network offering me a nightly news show will still want me if my fiancée was at one time a person of interest in a terrorist attack? Why did you have to insist that you knew something about anything, Sienna? They already had someone in custody and you've only complicated matters."

"Oh, ma'am, you're still on the phone?" The hostess had returned from seating several parties. "We need that line for reservations." She smiled, but I saw the slight irritation in her eyes. I gave her a gracious nod.

"I'm almost finished, thank you. Laz, I've got to go. Can you come get me?"

"No, I can't do anything until I know what's going on," he spoke quickly. "I gotta go. I'm losing the FBI agent. It looks like someone from CBS is talking to him." The phone went dead. I handed it back to the hostess.

"Did you still need a table?" She looked at me sympathetically. "Is your party coming?"

"I need a moment," I replied, because I did.

"Sure. You can have a seat at the bar while you wait."

"That's not necessary. I will just . . ." I froze as I looked over at the bar. Several television screens hung over it airing different networks. One screen had the words CBS

BREAKING NEWS running across it. "I will sit down for a moment."

I was glad that the bartender was busy taking orders from a party of five on the other side of the long bar area. I stared up at the muted television, which had captions running across the bottom of the screen.

An anchor sat somberly at the desk.

"We have breaking news into our news room," the caption read. "Authorities have confirmed that there is a possibility that the suspect being held in custody for the bombing at BWI may not have acted alone. We are hearing reports that additional evidence has been recovered from the mechanism used to set off the explosion. Though authorities have not officially disclosed any details of the bomb, what type it is, or how it was able to evade airport security personnel, sources are telling us that some type of scrap of paper collected at the scene is being investigated. The source tells us that it appears to be the remnants of a business card that may have been inadvertently left behind."

I'd given my business card out twice over the past week. Once to the man at the airport. Secondly to Camille. This latest news development could not be a coincidence. Or maybe it was. I swallowed hard, trying to understand what this meant, what I was supposed to do.

I got off the barstool, wondering if I could talk the hostess into letting me use the phone again. I needed Laz to come get me.

As I walked to the window, I noticed flashing lights in the distance. Were police cruisers coming this way? Laz knew I was at the restaurant. Had he told Camille or anyone else? Was his phone tapped? My imagination started going wild.

Person of interest. Laz had used those words. Me? Was there actually someone somewhere thinking I had something to do with what happened?

It was ridiculous, ludicrous! And yet, if Jamal Abdul had nothing to do with the attack and was still identified as a suspect, anything was possible. I swallowed hard again, watching as the flashing lights that had looked far away mere seconds ago seemed to be not so distant anymore.

I'd wanted to talk to authorities all along about my suspicions. Actually, I had talked to someone, but now I was uncertain about what had resulted from my talking. No, I knew what the result of that conversation was. My car was towed and Laz tried to hide me and now wanted nothing to do with me. There couldn't be any warrants or anything out for me or I know Laz would not have helped me in the small way he had.

Helped me? Let me correct my thoughts. Helped himself.

The lights were getting closer.

They could be going to an accident nearby, or they could be ambulances and fire trucks rushing to a hospital or fire. Shoot, it could be a presidential motorcade; I was right by DC after all. *I'm being paranoid,* I told myself.

Paranoid or not, I didn't want to take any chances. I did not want to talk to Homeland Security, the FBI, NSA, traffic cops, or mall security guards until I had something definite that could tie that man to the bombing.

It was no longer just a matter of national security.

I had my own behind to cover.

I headed back toward the bar area, away from the front windows. Following the signs to the restrooms, I was glad to see the kitchen entrance was nearby. A waiter exited, balancing a tray of plates, and I stepped behind him into the clanging, yelling commotion of a Friday late-night dinner rush at a popular restaurant. Cooks and other staff were engrossed in their stations, but I did not wait to see if I'd be noticed as I rushed toward a back entrance.

Within seconds, I stood outside on a truck loading dock. I jumped down and headed toward a line of trees that bordered the restaurant's parking lot.

As nervous as I had been walking through that church basement just last night, nothing compared to the nerves that overtook me now. Last night I had a map in hand, a destination in mind, though I would have never pictured the outcome.

Tonight I had no direction, no place to go, and plenty of outcomes were playing on my brain's movie projector. I wanted a new script for this scenario.

With no car, no phone, and no clue as to what to do next, I cut across the treed lot and headed toward a main thoroughfare. I could rent a car, I considered, but quickly shot that idea down. I'd have to use my credit card and I was avoiding a paper trail. Call my mom? My sister? *Lord, what do I do?*

I was not too far from Dulles Airport so several hotels were nearby. I decided to get a room, watch the news, figure out what was going on.

Figure out what to do next.

I stopped at the closest one to me, a three-star establishment. Not too big, but not too intimate, quiet, but still near the main roads. The rotating marquee outside the entrance advertised a business center with free Internet access and a daily continental breakfast.

Perfect.

"Do you have a reservation?" A young girl with long braids smiled as I stopped at the front desk.

"No. I just need one night."

"Name?"

"Josephine Davis." My middle and maiden names.

I paid in cash and was given a key and a standard room with views of the parking lot. I would not miss any approaching police cars or any other potential authority figures trying to find me. Yes, my imagination had gone wild, envisioning all manner of frightening scenarios. I used my money to buy a change of clothes—another t-shirt and an additional pair of sweatpants—from the gift shop, along with a baseball cap and sunglasses in case I needed to play down my appearance tomorrow. My intention was to shower, then flip through all the news stations to soak in every detail about the attack and current developments.

I got as far as the bed and crashed.

As my eyes closed in sleep, I meditated on the meaning of joy, and the determination I had not to let anything steal it from me.

The joy of the Lord is your strength, another verse echoed within me as I offered up another sacrifice, exchanging my fear for his peace. *The joy of the Lord is your strength.* I set my mind on those words, knowing that I was going to need all the strength I could get for tomorrow. Tomorrow, I was putting this whole business behind me. I was determined that the sun would not set without me having all the answers I needed for myself, my safety, and my sanity.

Tomorrow was reckoning day and I was determined to get a full account from all interest-bearing parties.

Chapter 40

4:27 a.m.

My eyes opened before the sun had even decided to get the day started. At least one of us had some sense. I got out of bed, struggling to remember why I was waking up in a hotel near DC and why I had nothing on me but my purse, some cash, and a bag of new tourist-looking clothes from the hotel gift shop. As my memory woke up, I began to plan out my morning. First on my list was to get more information about that man so I could find his whereabouts to direct the attention of authorities to him and off of me. My next task was figuring out how to get home.

I'd been wearing the same clothes for nearly twenty-four hours, so it felt good changing into the ensemble I'd bought from the gift shop. I put my sneakers back on, grabbed all my things and headed to the hotel's computer room. Though I no longer had my notes or the paper that Roman had printed out for me, I had what I needed.

The name J.B. Infinity. I Googled it. No result.

Roman had told me that his school's library was open twenty-four hours a day. I looked up its phone number online and called it on the courtesy phone that sat in the business center.

"I'm trying to find more information about an article I attempted to read on one of your databases yesterday," I informed the journals specialist to whom I was transferred.

"Sure, what's the name of the article and what information did you need?"

"I don't have the name, just the author. I don't even remember what journal it came from."

"Okay, give me a second and I'll get onto my master database to see what I can find to help you."

I held my breath as I heard the librarian's fingertips clicking on a keyboard. After a few moments, she got back on the line. "Okay, what's the name you have?"

"J.B. Infinity."

The woman chuckled. "Now that's funny. I had a student in here late yesterday looking for more information about that same author. He said he was helping his mother with a research project."

Roman!

I let out a light laugh. "Ha, ha, ha, that is funny. Uh, were you able to find any information?"

"As a matter of fact, we did. I called the database company to find out if there was another way to access the article, and was informed that they removed it following a revelation of fraud."

"Fraud?"

"It's an unusual story, really. The database only publishes theses and dissertations from master's and doctoral students, and this person pulled a fast one over them. He submitted it as his dissertation when in reality he was not enrolled in any real program."

"What school did he attend?" I held my breath.

"That's the thing. I guess an intern or somebody had been the one to upload and accept the paper, because the school the author listed was simply 'Life Lessons State University.' The author tried to argue that he or she was getting a PhD. in a self-created program of study based on life experience, and that an accredited institution was not necessary to validate a person's understanding of the world, specifically philosophy and religion."

That explanation sounded consistent with everything I knew about the man known as J.B. Infinity. He didn't want to be categorized, challenged, or validated by an outside structure. He set and met his own standards of conduct.

"If he didn't want to have an institution validate him, why throw 'State' in his self-created university?" His reasoning made no sense as I thought out loud.

"Apparently the author stated that he or she was living off of government benefits and that's how his life lessons were being funded."

"You keep saying 'he or she.' Did the database company not have any other identifying information?"

"No. All their correspondence with the author was by e-mail. That is what I was told."

"So no other name, no address?"

"No, nothing. The person I spoke to said that the author gave a city and state of his or her supposed university, but when they looked it up it was in the middle of nowhere. Literally. Like farmland in the middle of Amish country, miles away from anything. That was their first clue that something was awry with the submission. Wait, hold on, please."

I heard another voice asking the specialist for help finding an article on DNA sequencing, and I knew that my phone call was about to come to an end.

"Ma'am, I'm sorry, but I do have to go," the woman said when she returned to the line.

"Thank you. You've been very helpful. I'm surprised you remembered all of this."

"Well, a story that unusual would be difficult to forget. Really, you should thank your son. He did the legwork for you on this one."

"Huh? Oh," I replied and we both laughed. "I guess it was too obvious."

"It would have been too much of a coincidence otherwise, and there's not that many coincidences in one day."

"You got that right." I thanked her again and the call disconnected.

Roman thought I had been overreaching, but he must have trusted my judgment enough to try to search for answers.

Then again, knowing him, he may have thought it had something to do with his father. I had no idea what he planned to do with the information I'd given him about RiChard, but it occurred to me that since he said he was taking care of it, I truly felt like I was finally free of my search for answers.

I trusted my son and he trusted me.

I guess, despite my shortcomings, fears, and failures, I'd done a good job with him after all. I would thank him later. If he'd been calling my phone, I did not know. And I didn't want to call any of my loved ones until I had the current situation resolved. My mother and sister would just panic, my father would grunt loudly and pass the phone back to my mother, and Laz . . . Well, he would just tell me, as he already did in so many words, that I was completely on my own.

Leon would have known what to do.

I stared at the phone I'd just hung up.

In the unlikely event that authorities were tracking my loved ones' phones waiting for me to call, Leon would not be on that radar. I had not talked to him in nearly three years.

Dare I?

I knew his cell phone number by heart. I'd dialed it in my dreams, mumbled it in my waking hours, whispered it in my prayers.

Dare I?

I picked up the phone and dialed before I gave it another thought.

"Hi, you've reached Sam and Sandra Ellison," a chipper female voice greeted me. "We can't take your call right now, but leave a message and we'll call you when we can."

Someone else had his number.

Leon was gone. There was no way to reach him. For three years, I'd held on to that number: my last life line, my final resort.

And he was not there.

I was on my own. I was officially, unequivocally, completely alone.

I am with you always, even unto the end of the world: Jesus' last words to his disciples before he ascended to heaven. For some reason, that's just where I felt like Jesus and I were going. To the end of the world.

Chapter 41

I took the Metro to Union Station. Caught a train to Baltimore. Transferred to the light rail and then boarded a bus to Liberty Heights. I got off in front of a dollar store, the destination my only plan to address my lack of wheels.

The store had just opened and I saw her clearing out seasonal merchandise on a shelf by the front door.

"Yvette," I called out to my younger sister and she turned around.

It was her first real job since she'd become a mother at age sixteen. That was twenty years ago. She'd had a couple of other gigs over the years that my mom or dad managed to get her, but she always seemed to lose them or quit after only a few weeks. This job at the dollar store had held out for over two years. She'd started as a part-time cashier and had now worked her way up to a full-time assistant manager.

It was not easy work for her, and not just because of the heavy lifting and crazy hours. She had to learn to watch her tongue, and dealing with the general public and moody management had not been an easy teacher.

I was proud of her.

We never talked about it.

Her oldest son Skee-Gee's arrest and subsequent imprisonment for armed robbery and assault just last year seemed to have changed her, aged her, settled her down once and for all. He had seven years left to serve and she had four other children to raise differently.

"Hey, Sienna," she called back at me over her shoulder, as if it was normal for me to be walking into her store 8:30 on a Saturday morning. I walked over to her, helped her pack some pink stuffed Easter bunnies into a large cardboard box. One let out a loud plastic squeak as she threw heavy bags of jelly beans on top of it.

"You look tired." I helped her seal up the box.

"Yeah."

"Everything okay?"

"Mm-hmm." She turned to another aisle. I followed.

"Wedding plans going well?"

Her face brightened slightly and a small smile took over her lips for a quick second. "Yup." She took out a box cutter and opened up a package filled with wind chimes. They tingled and clanged in the otherwise quiet store. "What you need, Sienna?" she finally asked, pausing for a moment, two chimes dangling in her hand.

"I need to use your car." I swallowed and felt my throat bob up and down.

She stared at me a second, then looked back at her work. "My keys are under that first register."

"Thank you. I'll bring it back before you get off."

"No worries. I can get Demari to pick me up when I'm done."

"Thank you," I said again, grateful that she hadn't asked me any questions. I turned to leave. "Oh." I turned back to her. "By any chance, did you move my car from BWI's parking lot last weekend and drive it to my home Sunday night?"

"Now why would I do that?" She glared.

"Nothing." *Let me get out of here.* "Thanks, sis," I called out to her as I grabbed the keys to her '99 Buick Century. The air conditioning didn't work and it stalled on occasion, but I was glad to have a way to get around for the moment.

I had more plans.

"Oh, one more thing." I walked back over to her. "Do you have another box cutter and do you know where I can get a prepaid phone?"

Yvette didn't even raise an eyebrow. "Here, just use mine." She folded up the box cutter she'd been using and put it in my hand and then grabbed a cheap cell phone out of her apron pocket.

I didn't want to tell her that I wanted a phone with no ties to anyone, but I'd never known my sister to share anything with me without a fight. I accepted both. Her keys jingled in my hand as I walked toward the front door.

"Sienna," she called after me. I looked back and she looked away. "Be careful out there."

I would have said thank you one more time, but she had already disappeared down another aisle.

"Love you, sis," I whispered and shut the door behind me.

Chapter 42

Rare books.

One thing that jumped out at me from the night I saw RiChard in that old church library was that there had been a section in it for rare books. The idea that a forgotten library could house books that were seldom seen by the masses appealed to me. I hoped that this appeal was my gut guiding me to the next step on my journey. J.B. Infinity's hardcover volume did not show up on any Internet search, except for the cached frame of a young man—a now-dead young man—holding it up for a Webcam. If this book wasn't considered rare, I didn't know what would be.

Of course that did not mean any bookstore or library had it; heck, even the college database had deleted the dissertation it was based on from its listings. And, if for some crazy reason that young man's death was somehow related to that book, I was certain it would not be simply sitting on a shelf for purchase.

But if I was willing to come to such a drastic conclusion, that the young man's unfortunate accident had something to do with that book, then it would not be such a stretch for me to believe that I could find that book by following my latest hunch about rare book stores.

I'd done an Internet search of rare book stores in Baltimore before I left the hotel and I had the printed list with directions in my purse. I took the list out and planned my stops. Most of the bookstores were either in or near downtown.

"Sorry, I doubt that we carry that book you're describing." A man in gold wire frames looked down at me from the elevated platform where his antiquated cash register sat. "Just because a book is not commonly known, that does not make it rare in the pure sense of the word. It has to have some type of intrinsic value. A self-published work on religion and philosophy would not be here just because it's not at Barnes & Noble."

"J.B. Infinity? Nah, haven't heard of that." A young woman with fiery red hair and facial tattoos shook her head apologetically at the next rare book store. "That name isn't showing up in our catalogue either."

"Ma'am, this is a comic book shop."

"Oops. Sorry." I left the third shop wondering if I needed to come up with another plan.

The fourth shop had not yet opened for the day and the fifth and sixth shops were boarded up, vacant.

"Should I even bother?" I mumbled to myself as I pulled up to bookstore number seven. This one was in Charles Village, an area of the city known for its large, Victorian-style row homes, many of which had brightly colored porches and pillars and ornate architectural details. The bookstore I entered was in the basement of such a row house.

A burly white man with a gray bushy beard was just opening the front door as I descended the steps. "You're up early looking for books." He smiled at me as the door swung open with a loud thud.

"I'm looking for a specific one. I don't think the author's name is on it and I barely remember the very long title; but I can recall some key words from it." I smiled back as I followed the man. Both he and the shop smelled of tobacco. I had to blink several times to adjust to the dimness of the small room. As my eyes did adjust, my heart sank. There would be no success here, I surmised. The place had only a few bookshelves with even fewer books.

How is this even a store? I kept the smile on my face despite my disappointment.

"All right, what words from the title do you have for me? I'll see if it sounds familiar." He went through great motions, straining and stretching, to flick on several light switches. Even then the room still felt dark.

"Deconstructing heroism. Theological. Philosophical. Finite universe."

"Finite universe, heroism." The man repeated after me, scratching his balding hairline as he looked up at a teardrop chandelier that had only one working light bulb. "Was it a little blue book with gold letters on the front?"

"Yes." My heart quickened its pace.

"I may still have it. Not what I usually keep in my stock, but I might not have gotten rid of it yet."

"Not what you usually keep in stock? You might have gotten rid of it?" I repeated, trying to keep up.

"Yeah. I saw it at a flea market a few months back and would have thought nothing of it, except the print inside looked like it was made from an old-fashioned printing press. Do you know how rare that is nowadays?"

"No, I—"

"I mean, it looked like it was made with one of those presses where you do one page at a time. Have you ever seen one of those before?" The man spoke faster, became more excited as he explained the rarity, all the while fumbling with stacks of books that were out of my view behind a long counter. "You gotta place each letter line by line on one side, on the frame; and then you gotta blot the letters with ink using big pads. Then you press out each page one at a time, like I said. They used to do that in the olden days. Do you know how long that would take?"

"No, I—"

"You have to go through that process for each page, letter by letter, and there were a lot of pages in that book.

I can't imagine there being more than a few copies. I don't know if I have one here anymore."

"Was there a reason you would not have kept it?" I was relieved to finally get out a full sentence, but concerned about what his answer would be.

"Oh, there was a reason, and a good one, too." The man stopped fumbling through the piles and frowned up at me. "That book was crazy, if you ask me. I was fascinated by the print, but when I actually sat down and started reading what it said, I knew that I didn't want that book anywhere nearby. It was talking about good and evil, heroes and villains and how—in the author's opinion I must stress—the two were backward. Honestly, I felt like I was reading a recipe for how a madman could cook up some trouble, hurt people, kill people, set other people up."

"You mean like framing others for a crime?"

"Yeah, but it was about more than framing someone for a crime just for crime's sake. It was about proving a point that good and evil can flip on each other and the world would know no different. I'm sorry, miss." The man shook his head, giving his shelves one final look through. "I'm pretty sure I got rid of it, 'cause it made me too uncomfortable."

"Thanks for your time. You've been helpful." I was disappointed that I didn't have the book, but if that man thought its pages read like a crime manifesto, maybe even a terror plot, then maybe the authorities would be able to get a copy of the deleted dissertation from that database of graduate school papers.

It made sense to me. He wanted his story out, but the database didn't accept it. I'd have been willing to bet that he printed the book by hand himself as a way of keeping it in print. *But why not make it public? And why would a young man who had access to it suddenly be dead? And where the heck do you get a printing press from?*

As I headed back to my car, I realized that for as many answers as I thought I'd just gotten from the shop owner, I had nothing but more questions.

I started my engine but a loud shout caught my attention.

"Wait, miss," the store owner called after me, a sheet of paper dangling from his hands.

I rolled down my window.

"I don't know if this will help." Coffee cake crumbs spilled down his beard and were matted into his moustache. "But I remembered that I did make a copy of one page from that book, just so I could better analyze the print one day. I copied the least creepy page, the title page. There was nothing crazy about that page; well, unless you count that ridiculously long title." He guffawed. "Here, you can keep it. I made another copy." He passed me the single sheet through my window and turned back toward his shop.

I looked at the sheet, read it from top to bottom, then called after him just before he disappeared down the stairwell.

"Excuse me, sir. You said you found the book at a flea market. Where was this?"

"Oh, not too far from this little town called Lasker up in central Pennsylvania. My old lady likes buying Amish crafts and such and makes me drive her up there every now and then. I don't mind much, 'cause if we pass a flea market or a yard sale, I always find a book or two to bring back, you know?" He looked down to his basement entrance door. "I got to go, miss. My phone is ringing."

Amish country.

Old-fashioned printing press.

Life Lessons State University on farmland "miles away from anything."

An obsession with religion and philosophy, heroes and villains.

Was J.B. Infinity an outcast from one of those peaceful Amish communities? *"I have not talked to anyone in years,"* he'd told me. Or was he simply hiding among them, shielded from discovery since they did not use modern technology like computers and televisions, smart phones. The Internet.

Lasker, Pennsylvania.

I looked at the sheet of paper in my hands again.

The Secrets to Deconstructing Heroism and a Critique of the Philosophical and Theological Views of Moral Evolution in the Finite Universe.

There was no author listed, but the publisher's name was printed clearly at the bottom of the page. *Through the Window Press.*

And underneath was a familiar hand-drawn illustration of a window framed with striped curtains, a cat sitting on its sill.

Chapter 43

I needed to get online. I needed to do some research. Where was Lasker? What was in Lasker? Wherever it was, whatever was there, I felt like it held answers.

It had to.

I had nothing else to go on.

My sister's prepaid phone was as basic as it got. It made phone calls, accepted texts, but there was no Internet access, no World Wide Web feature.

I left Charles Village and drove to Hampden, where I remembered from Roman's middle school science project days that there was a small electronics store off the beaten road. I parked at a meter and entered the tiny showroom. A shrill chime announced my entrance and I headed to an aisle of computer tablets before any salespersons could capture me.

Lasker, Pennsyvlania.

I typed the name of the town into a search engine box on the first floor sample I saw.

It was in south central PA, population 903, mostly Amish. I pulled up images that resulted from the search. Idyllic country sides, farmland, and isolated houses, barns, and bridges made up the bulk of the search results.

What am I looking for?

I didn't have an answer to my own question. I shut my eyes, exasperated.

Stuck.

"That right there is a power-packed machine that can be both a tablet and a laptop, making it all you need to buy. It's got both Wi-Fi and 4G. I've been watching you tinker with it for a while. Tell me what you think of it." The saleswoman had bright orange eyeglasses and a fake smile.

She was interrupting me.

"I'm not getting anything right now. Just looking."

How far away was this Lasker place from Baltimore? I wondered. Couldn't be too far for that man to be coming back and forth from there.

I was making too many assumptions and I knew it.

He'd called me from a phone with an Ohio area code and had driven a Jeep from West Virginia. Though the rusted green pickup truck I'd seen him in last had Pennsylvania tags, PA was huge state. He could have driven the truck from anywhere, assuming it was even his.

I doubted that it was.

Two hours and twenty-three minutes.

A map feature on the tablet/laptop combo showed a complicated route, one I was sure was filled with small two-lane highways, cows, maybe even dirt roads.

No, it couldn't be that rural, I analyzed the map, trying to find something familiar. I'd gone to college initially near that part of Pennsylvania. My pre-RiChard days.

I smiled. Thinking about his name didn't prick as much as before.

I truly was free of him.

"I see that smile. I knew you'd be impressed."

The saleswoman had never left, I realized. She stood near my left shoulder, smiling as she peeked at the screen in front of me.

"There are so many apps that you can get for maps and driving directions. Like I said, that beauty is more than a laptop. It's a tablet when you need it."

"I'm not getting anything," I repeated as I slid my fingers across the touch screen to exit the map application. The woman still stood there, smiling. A clipboard and pen were in her hands. I turned to leave, but then had an idea. "Actually, ma'am, do you sell any GPS units?"

Ten minutes later I had a brand new, top-of-the-line GPS unit sitting on the dashboard of Yvette's old Buick. I hadn't planned to spend that much of my cash, but it seemed to be the only way to get that saleswoman out of my way.

Lasker, Pennsylvania. I programmed the unit to that area.

Street address?

I had no idea. What was I doing? I needed more information before I started driving to a place where J.B. Infinity may not even have ties.

But my gut had me on this path and I wasn't fighting against it.

I started up the car. It stalled then thought better of it before roaring to life. Darci said she'd run into him at the library the other night. Perhaps he'd said something in passing that would illuminate the way for me to go looking for him. I didn't want to call or e-mail her for fear that authorities were tapping into everyone who was in my absent phone's address book. She'd said that she planned to come to the office early Saturday morning before I was even scheduled to see clients.

This would be a good time to check in, I decided. Plus I could get her to handle my scheduled afternoon appointments.

There was no way I could lead a therapy session right now. I was too close to answers, and too close to being held for questioning myself.

I felt it.

I wanted to go to authorities only after I had a smoking gun, or something close to it.

Chapter 44

I drove past the parking lot of my office building twice. Call me paranoid, but the idea that police or some other authority figure could bring me in for questioning before I had answers frightened me. There were no unusual cars on the lot, no suspect-looking people.

I need to calm it down, bring it back down a level, I chided myself.

Darci's bright yellow Beetle was parked in her usual spot, three spaces down from the stairwell that led to my office suite. I realized that my shoulders had relaxed at that observation. I was confident that I would get some more answers, direction as to where to go.

I bounded up the steps, unlocked the front door myself instead of waiting for her to buzz me in.

"Darci!" I was out of breath from the run. "I have a question for you. Darci?"

Her purse was on her desk chair, but she was not in the waiting room.

"Darci?" I called down the lit hallway, opened and closed each of the four office doors in the suite. *Where is she?*

I walked back to the waiting room. Her purse was definitely there. So were her keys. I moved the mouse of her computer and the screen came to life. She had logged on. Looked like she was updating some billing statements, I noted.

"Darci?" I called out again though it was obvious there was nobody but me in the suite. I heard a vibrating noise. Her cell phone clattered on the corner of her desk. Call from Mom darted across the screen.

"That's odd," I said aloud. Darci never went anywhere without her cell phone. Even when she went to the bathroom she had her phone in hand. I used to joke with her about it until I became the same way.

Call from Mom darted across the screen again as it buzzed anew. *Should I answer it?*

"Darci?" I called out again as the caller disconnected and her screen turned back to her screensaver, a picture of her three-year-old twins, Ella and Elijah, eating ice cream cones at a fair.

If the phone rings again, I'll answer it, I decided, picking it up, suddenly aware of the growing discomfort in my stomach.

"Maybe she's at the café," I mumbled, staring at the phone, waiting for it to ring again. It was not unusual for Darci to jog down the steps to the café downstairs to grab a coffee, a muffin, a piece of fruit, or a salad. I put the phone back down and stepped out of the office, locking the door behind me. Yeah, she was probably down there, getting a late-morning treat. She's probably also freaking out that she doesn't have her phone on her. *I'll tell her where it is when I see her, share a laugh when I tell her that I was worried that . . .* Worried that what? I couldn't finish my own sentence. Clearly I was over thinking everything right now.

The café had just a few patrons. Breakfast was nearly over and the cooks and servers were preparing for the lunch rush.

Darci was not there.

I scanned the small dining room, glanced at each booth, checked over the couple of people standing at the counter.

"Excuse me." I stepped up to the cashier. "Did the young lady I work with come through here today?"

"Who, Darci?" The cashier smiled and I nodded. "Yeah, she was here a little while ago. We talked for a minute and then she ordered a coffee to go. She headed out the opposite way from your office so I don't know if she was going straight back."

"Okay, thanks!" Yes, I clearly was over thinking. There was a dry cleaner's and a postal store on the back side of the office building. Darci frequented both. I smiled and nodded and turned to leave. There was no reason for me to stay.

As I put my hand on the glass door to open it, I saw a police cruiser turn into the parking lot. My heart quickened a beat as I grabbed a newspaper from a stand just inside the doorway and plopped down at an empty table nearby. *This is ridiculous, Sienna,* I chided myself again as the police cruiser circled the lot and turned out of it in the opposite direction. *He just wanted to turn around, it looks like.* I shook my head at myself as I slowly eased the paper away from my face. I folded it up and laid it on the table.

DASHED DREAMS, the main headline read. My eyes caught notice of both the headline and the rows of photos of the terror attack victims underneath it.

"The college lacrosse team that could have been champions," one picture's caption read. Several on the team had been killed; most were injured. "A retiree who'd just opened a restaurant." I recalled the interview of this woman's grandson that had aired the day of the attack.

It was all a shame. No reason, no sense for it all, and no time to waste trying to find that man, his real name, his location, his story. Who else would be looking for him?

I stood up to leave, but I could not pull my eyes away from the last photo. The little eight-year-old boy and his parents, the businessman and the PTA president. FROM WHEAT CROPS TO CASH HARVESTING: THE FARMER WHO BECAME A FINANCIER.

I froze at the headline beneath the photo of the wealthy family of three. He'd been a farmer? I decided to skim through the rest of the article, but I only made it through the first two sentences.

He started life toiling the fields of Lasker, Pennsylvania and she was a high school beauty queen in her hometown near Amish country Ohio.

This is not a coincidence. I stared at sentences again.

"Ma'am, are you okay?" A busboy looked at me with concern as I held on to the table. "Yes," I whispered though the room swirled around me and I felt like I was going to throw up.

I had to go. I had to start driving. I didn't know exactly where in Lasker I was headed, but I knew from looking at a map that it was not that big of an area.

Somebody had to be walking around there. Somebody had to know something.

"God, guide my steps," I prayed as I left a dollar on the table for the paper and headed once again for the door. I started to go back up to the office, but when a second police cruiser passed by the lot, I decided to head directly to my car. I had on a baseball cap, shades, and sweats, my sister's keys in my hand.

"I look and feel a mess," I conceded as Yvette's Buick roared to life, "but I'm on the right track."

It felt good knowing I trusted my instincts again.

"Merge onto North 83." The monotone voice of the GPS system was my only company as I started the two-and-a-half-hour drive to Lasker. I'd done a point of interest search on the GPS for the sake of having an address to input and was en route to a service station. The way Yvette's car groaned and wheezed up 83, a car service station seemed to be just the place I needed to be headed.

"Please don't let this car break down." I pushed down the thought as I drove through Northern Baltimore County and then crossed over into the York area of Pennsylvania.

"In 2.5 miles, exit left." My GPS guide took me off the highway. Forty minutes past the PA state line, I was driving on narrow, winding roads, passing rusted silos and farmlands being prepped for seeding.

As I drove through the Pennsylvania countryside, I reflected on the journey I'd taken to get to this moment. From doubting myself and feeling overwhelmed by confusion, bitterness, and pain, to being willing to travel to an uncertain destination with confidence and peace despite the still many unanswered questions, I knew that I had grown into a more complete woman. As the roads wound around herds of cows and slow-moving tractors, passed bubbling streams and open fields, I thought about my family and the relationships I had with each member: Roman, and his quiet insistence on making things right; my parents, their hopes and criticisms, their love; Yvette, and our inability to ever really define our sisterhood. I recalled conversations, memories, heartbreak I'd had with the men I'd loved or at the very least tolerated, starlit nights in foreign lands, rousing laughter over kitchen tables, playful arguments at art galleries and lectures.

There were still decisions to be made. Discussions that had to happen.

I was prepared.

I reflected on the victims of the terror attacks: their stories, the tragedy, the senselessness, Jamal Abdul, and his possible innocence. The randomness of it all. My determination to address it.

Maybe I was a little zany, a little too stubborn in my drive to set things right and get to the bottom of a matter. If my son had been a little too reckless over the years with his resolve to get answers, I could agree that he'd gotten that trait honestly. As did I. I chuckled, thinking about my mother and the daughters she'd accidentally raised to be opposite sides of the same coin.

Our family's stubbornness came at a cost.

All of us struggled with saying what needed to be said in relationships. I thought again of Leon and smiled. It hurt. I missed him. I messed up what we had. And now I was left with Laz.

The stench of manure brought me back to the moment, to the urgency of my mission.

To the realization that my GPS guide had grown silent on me.

"Uh-oh," I mumbled as I looked at the now-gray screen that sat on the dashboard.

Reception lost, it read.

"Don't do this to me," I spoke to it flatly, knowing that it had already been done. I truly was in the middle of nowhere because even the satellite system that fed the GPS didn't know where I was.

There was nothing around me but fields ripe for plant-ing and forest vegetation that rustled in the quiet breeze.

As the road dipped up and down over small hills and passed clusters of tall trees and wild shrubbery, the signal followed suit, fading in and out of reception. The voice of direction would chime in with a hint of where to go next and then fall silent, as if testing my ability to stay the course.

Nearly three hours after I'd started this leg of my jour-ney, I reached a sign that read, Lasker City Limits. I stayed straight on the two-lane highway on which I travelled, looking, waiting for another sign to give me direction on what to do next.

I didn't have to search far. A small service station came into view and I recognized the name as the one I'd used as a destination address. It could not have come at a better time, I acknowledged, as Yvette's old car sputtered and squealed and cried out for some gas and attention.

My sister was going to kill me when she found out how far I'd driven her wheels.

The station had a single pump, a vintage—that is, ancient-looking—contraption with large numbers on a mechanical dial, complete with chrome, and bright red paint. I pulled up to it and my heart sank as I noticed the thick rust that lined the nozzle, the $0.00 on the dial.

"That pump doesn't work, miss." A man came out of a small wooden shack, shouting the obvious. He had a warm smile and wore a long sleeve shirt, pants, and a straw hat.

I could feel my eyebrow raise, my inward panic button about to go off. Yvette's car couldn't go much farther without some TLC, especially gas. I looked up at the sign that hung over the shack. SAUL'S SERVICE SHOP. What exactly was he servicing if it wasn't cars?

As if reading my mind, he pointed to a pile of wood, wheels, and metal parts that sat on the other side of the shack. "Carriages and buggies. That's the business I do around these parts." A horse harness was draped over a nearby wooden fence.

"Oh, you're Amish?" I didn't know how else to ask.

"Uh, not really. I mean, I respect their way of life, the simplicity of it, and they tolerate me setting up shop here. Actually folks around here think I'm aiming to be one of them. I keep saying that one day I'm going to get baptized into one of the local communities around here, but they want to see that you can handle living without all the perks of the Western world, like television, phone service, electricity. I've cut back on a lot of that stuff, but we'll see."

"Just cut back on it, not fully eliminated it." I smiled and pointed to a cell phone that peeked out of his pants pocket.

He let out a nervous chuckle and pushed the phone out of view. "Yeah, it's a process. By all appearances to most eyes around here, I've done away with all the luxuries of the world."

"You actually get a signal out here?" I was genuinely curious. Yvette's prepaid phone had given out miles ago.

"I, uh, have a satellite dish that keeps me connected to the rest of the world. I guess you could say I'm straddling the fence as far as letting go of the world and its comforts."

"You're not from around here are you?" I looked at him slyly.

"Born south of Cleveland." He chuckled. "Left in my early twenties, been living here ever since. That was over thirty years ago." He swung his head to the side, looked up and down the street. "Look, I do have a gallon of gas you can have if you want it. Follow me."

I hesitated because I didn't know this man, but really, what choice did I have? I needed gas and I needed answers; he had at least one of those things.

"Do I follow you by car?" I called after him from the driver's seat as his footsteps crunched away on the gravel lot.

"You can park there"—he pointed to a space next to the shack he'd emerged from—"and come with me to that barn."

I followed his pointing finger to see that the gravel lot gave way to an elbow turn, after which sat the entrance of a large green barn. The wooden building had been obscured by both the shack out front and several tall, leafy trees.

"Um." I swallowed hard. "Okay." I pulled into the space, shut down the motor, and grabbed the box cutter I'd stored under the passenger seat. I studied the industrial-strength blade for a moment, wondering if I'd have the fortitude to put it to action if it became necessary. I pushed it deep into one of the pockets of the sweatpants I wore.

This man could have something other than gas waiting for me in that barn.

Am I crazy? I asked myself as I caught up to the man, who was rounding the corner. The barn came into full view. It was huge. I wondered how he'd been so successful at keeping it out of view of passersby. Was it intentionally hidden? If so, why?

My imagination was active again.

"I keep some canisters of gasoline on hand. There's a couple of non-Amish farmers around here who use motorized equipment. Sometimes I find use for gas too." He winked, but I didn't know why.

Until he unchained and slid the massive door open.

The early afternoon sunlight exposed the interior of his barn and I gasped.

A rusty dark green pickup truck with a dented fender and a streak of blue peeling paint, identical to the one I'd seen "J.B. Infinity" driving on Wednesday, was parked inside.

Chapter 45

The man looked a little puzzled by the blatant shock on my face. "Yeah, I guess it does look bad that I have a truck if I'm supposed to be aiming to be Amish."

"Does . . . does anyone know you . . . you have this?" I studied the Pennsylvania license tags, wishing I'd been able to see the ones on the truck that man had driven.

But I had no question that this was the same one. The dent, the peeling paint were telling.

"It's not public knowledge, if that's what you mean. I rarely use it." He walked to the side of the barn where several steel red cans of gasoline were stored.

Several rifles hung along the wall.

"Oh, I hunt sometimes." He chuckled as he followed my eyes to the wall. "You city folk always seem to get nervous around hunting rifles."

"Why did you leave the Cleveland area?" I asked, more out of nervousness than curiosity. I wanted to keep walking, keep talking. Get out of there.

"I'm embarrassed to say." He shrugged. "But I guess confession is good for the soul. I got caught up with some foolishness of my older brother. We weren't Amish, but my family comes from a strong religious tradition. My brother, Ezekiel, kind of went a whole different way with it. He started his own church, made up his own doctrine, and a bunch of us followed along. I guess you could say he, well, started a cult. He had us sell all we had and come out here to live simple lives among the Amish. We weren't Amish, though. I don't know what we were. I think, in retrospect, he just moved us out here to keep us in isolation. We gave all the money we made from selling our possessions to him, for the benefit of his church, no questions asked." The man picked up one of the gas containers and started walking back toward my car. I followed.

"Ezekiel seemed like a good man and we trusted him," the man continued, "and then the rumors started and that was the end of that. I hope unleaded is okay." He uncapped the gas tank, poured a couple of gallons in. "That should hold you until you get to the next town where a full service gas station is."

"Thanks, um . . ." I looked back at the service station sign, "Mr. Saul?" I smiled, trying to absorb his story and figure out where I was supposed to go next all at the same time.

"Oh, Saul was the name of the man who owned this place years ago. My name is Mordecai. Mordecai Bennett."

Bennett.

A chill went through me as the man recapped the tank. "Do you need anything else, miss? I sell maps of the area if you're having problems with your GPS. Losing signals is easy around here."

"Yes, I will take a map." I followed him toward the shack, trying to figure out what questions I was supposed to ask, what information I needed to know. "Rumors. You said something about rumors and your brother?"

"Yeah." The man shook his head. "When his wife Judith died about fifteen years ago, things started falling apart. That's when the rumors started, if I had to pinpoint everything. Turns out my brother was just taking our money and using it for himself. While we were here using oil lamps and horses and plows, he was investing

our money and building a beach house for himself in the
Caribbean. Even his wife wasn't exempt. She died from
cancer. He claimed not to have enough money for her to
have treatment. It hurts to know that she probably didn't
even have to die, you know?"

"Wow, that is . . ."

"Terrible. Unholy. Embarrassing that we were all
duped like that." Mordecai opened the door of the shack.
Despite its rugged exterior, the inside was clean and tidy
with a small store area up front. A door toward the rear
was open, exposing what looked like a small living space
in the back. I thought of RiChard living in the back of the
church basement library. He'd spent a lifetime deceiving
others and was more or less forced to live out his days
in a self-made prison. This man, Mordecai, had been on
the receiving end of deceit, and found himself equally
imprisoned by a shame and confusion that kept him
stuck in that shack.

The fact that he was "straddling on the fence" about
who he wanted to be spoke to the chokehold his brother's
deceit had on him, had on his life. He knew his brother
was wrong, but he wasn't sure what or who was right.

"What happened to your brother?"

Mordecai shook his head, grabbed a stack of maps off
of a counter. "He up and disappeared about nine or ten
years ago. Nobody knows what happened or where he
went."

"And you don't know what happened with all the
money either, huh?"

"Oh, we know. His son took it. Made a life for himself.
Picked up where his father left off and made millions."
The man looked off into space and tapped the stack of
maps on the counter.

"So, you and the rest of the congregation went after
him, right?"

"There is no congregation anymore. Most of us either absorbed into the Amish communities up here or went back to the lives we'd come from. We were a peaceful community. Whether it was due to forgiveness or just moving on, nobody has ever gone after Ezekiel's son, Bartholomew. He got married to a pretty girl whose parents, Johnnie and Beverly Taylor, had followed us here from Ohio. Bart and Madison left about a month after Ezekiel disappeared, and the two of them have never looked back."

Bart and Madison? Why did those names sound familiar?

"You wouldn't believe it if I told you," the man continued, now looking me straight in the eyes, "but you know that terrorist attack that just happened down at the airport in Baltimore? Bart and Madison and their little boy . . ." He shook his head. "Tragic. Wrong place, wrong time, the randomness of it all."

Or was it random? The thought chilled me even more. What if the terror attack was a smokescreen to hide a premeditated murder? If Bart or his wife were active on social media, a determined killer could have easily been tracing their steps, staying up with their whereabouts.

Anything felt possible right now.

"And you are certain that all the members of the church moved on? Nobody seemed particularly bent on vengeance?"

"Naw, none of us were that kind of people. I've kept in touch with everyone over the years. We've all moved on in our own peaceful ways."

Bennett.

The name perplexed me.

"Did, um, you have any other family members beside your brother, his wife, and their son?"

"No. Well, my brother Ezekiel did have another son, a younger son, but he's been out of the picture for years."

"How so?" I cocked my head, every sense in me heightened.

"Like I said, after Judith died, unnecessarily if you ask me, that's when all the rumors started. And most of the rumors seemed to originate from the little brother. He was going around telling everybody what Ezekiel had done with our money. Ezekiel was furious, and we didn't know about his deception yet. He kicked my little nephew out of the church. Excommunicated him. Isn't that the word? We weren't allowed to say his name, talk about him, or even acknowledge that he'd ever been born. Funny, that was ingrained so deeply in us, I haven't thought about him in years or even wondered how he's doing. *Nicht existierend,*" he whispered, looking down. "That's what Ezekiel renamed his youngest son, Bart's little brother. *Nicht existierend.* It's German for 'nonexistent.'"

The Non-Exister. I could hear his voice. See those dull blue eyes.

"What was this nephew's name?"

"Jebidiah. Jebidiah Bennett." The man looked me in the eyes. "Funny, he tried to tell us the truth about his father. He sounded the alarm about his mother's needless death, warned us about the misuse of our money, and yet he was the only one who was punished. Jebidiah, in retrospect, was the hero, but we all made him out to be the bad guy."

I thought my heart would beat right out of my chest. "Where is he now?"

The man shook his head. "I haven't seen J.B. since he was excommunicated over a decade ago. That was a year or two after Judith died; then my brother disappeared a year later. My nephew Bartholomew moved on not long after that. The house where they all lived is in ruins now. Vacant, rotting. Nobody goes near there."

"Where is it?"

"Oh, that old house? It's on the other side of the trees behind my barn, in the middle of the old cornfields. Some members of the community used to keep up those fields for a while, but nobody harvested the fields last fall. Those old stalks are now sitting there rotting away. It will be just a matter of time before those fields are nothing but dust." The man stopped talking for a moment. "I'm sorry. I'm holding you up. You didn't stop here for all of this. Thanks for listening, though. It's good to get my story out. Freeing." He turned toward the door and I followed him.

I wondered at his sudden rush to end the conversation, but the clip-clop and squeal of an approaching horse and buggy explained.

"Mordecai, dear friend, there you are." A man with a long beard and straw hat came out of the carriage. "I came by earlier this week and you weren't here." He spoke with an accent I did not recognize.

"I was gone for a couple of days. I had business to take care of a few towns over. It was a long walk." Mordecai suddenly spoke with the same accent.

I smiled and waved them both good-bye before getting into Yvette's car and starting the engine.

If Mordecai had been away earlier that week, as I'd just heard him say, he probably had no idea that his pickup truck had gone missing.

Chapter 46

Jebidiah Bennett.

I had a name and the makings of a possible motive. Murder by way of terrorist attack. He'd been cast out by his community, by his own father, betrayed by his brother, and had spent years in silent isolation with nothing more than his twisted thoughts. He was looking to do more than prove his misdirected points about heroism and theology; he was on a mission of revenge.

There was only one major question that remained: *Where is he?* That was not a question I needed to answer, I decided, finally taking out Yvette's phone from my purse. I wanted to call Laz. Tell him where I was. Get him to mediate a conversation between me and Camille so that I could clear everything up.

No signal.

I looked back at Mordecai, who was engrossed in conversation with the man from the buggy. I didn't want to interrupt, especially if, as I'd noted on my way there, I could pick up a signal just by driving around.

I pulled off the lot and turned back onto the road. Trees surrounded me for a bit and then I reached a clearing. I pulled to the side of the road next to a cluster of tall grasses and shrubbery. Just beyond were acres of dried and dying cornstalks, for as far as my eye could see.

I had a signal.

Laz's voice mail came on immediately. "Laz! His name is Jebidiah Bennett and I am one hundred percent certain he is the actual bomber. One of the victims is his brother. There is a personal edge to this story that brings it all together. I'm currently in L . . ." The call dropped. "No!" I groaned. I got out of my car and started walking around it, holding the phone in various positions, trying in vain to get another signal.

I walked farther away from the car, stood next to the line of stalks that towered over my head. Surprisingly, my efforts paid off.

A signal came through.

And so did a phone call.

It was Darci's extension at the office. She probably had been trying to reach me for a while, I realized, wondering why I was not at the clinic seeing clients. I had not left any kind of message that I wouldn't be in. *But how did she get Yvette's prepaid cell phone number?*

"I am so sorry, Darci." I couldn't waste words, not even with a hello. I didn't know how long my signal would last.

"Sienna!" Yvette's voice caught me off-guard. What was she doing at Darci's desk? I wanted to ask her but she had her own questions. "Where are you and what are you doing?"

"I—"

"Your receptionist's mother called *my* job looking for you," Yvette interrupted, "because she's looking for her. Apparently your worker is not answering any of her calls, and the mom is concerned because she's watching her kids for her and she says her daughter always answers when she has them. Then she went to your office and saw that nobody was there, but your worker's car was parked out front. Now, I don't understand why you have my work number as an emergency contact for you, because I don't have time to get involved in your employee's affairs. I have my own employees to manage."

"So, nobody knows where Darci is?" My mind tried to catch up with what I'd just heard.

"Do you really need me to start over?"

"No. Wait, how did you get in my office?" She'd called from Darci's extension, I remembered.

"Police was here, girl."

"Looking for me?"

"Did you hear a word I said? They're looking for your girl, Darci. Everything is not always about you! But just so you know, I didn't tell them you have my car or a box cutter. I didn't ask any questions, and I don't want to know."

"Wait, are you suggesting that I have something to do with Darci's disappearance?"

"Of course not, but if I told the police that you came to my job early this morning asking to use my car and borrow a box cutter, it don't take a fool to figure out that they would start looking at you differently, especially since her car is parked out in front of your office and she ain't nowhere to be found."

"This isn't good," I mumbled.

"You think?"

The call dropped.

"Oh, God, help me." I realized I was pulling my hair out from underneath my baseball cap. No. I was not going to fall apart.

Darci.

Where could she have gone?

Jebidiah Bennett had been stalking her online. I remembered her bump-in with him at the library. Somehow, some kind of way, he was involved in her disappearance.

But why?

And what could I do about it? I turned toward my car, the fields behind me; then I checked my phone. Still no signal.

"Jesus!" I threw my head back toward the heavens, saw the fringes of dried, decaying cornstalks instead.

Old cornfields.

Mordecai had said something about the home of his brother and nephews being vacant, rotting in old cornfields in the trees behind his barn. I ran to my car, stood on the hood, looked out over the cornstalks that towered like skimpy dried giants for what looked like hundreds of acres. In the distance, I saw it.

A house. Dilapidated. Some windows boarded.

Mordecai had a cell phone in his pocket, a satellite signal he depended on. I could go back and get his help to call the authorities.

Then tell them what?

I needed more answers. That house, as old as it was, had to have some.

I ran to the car and jumped in and started the motor all in one motion. The tires skidded as I got back on the road. I zoomed down the two-lane highway looking for a path, a driveway, a clearing, something, anything that would take me to that house.

Three minutes down the road I found it. An old, long driveway. I nearly missed it from the street as it was overgrown with weeds. Thick, tangled grasses hid the decaying mailbox and towering, rotting cornstalks surrounded the dirt driveway on either side. The house looked to be about a mile away up the drive, barely viewable in the midst of the overgrowth.

"Let's go." I narrowed my eyes and slammed my foot on the accelerator as I turned onto the neglected driveway. The dirt and weeds were bumpy under my wheels and I jostled about in the seat, my head and elbows getting bruised in the process.

This driveway is going to kill Yvette's car.

The car must have heard my thoughts because after going over two more hard bumps, the engine stalled. I shut it off, turned it back on again. It cooperated.

For four more feet.

Then it died completely.

"Forget it." I jumped out and started running toward the house, grateful that I had on my tennis shoes and that I had been working on getting my body back in shape. I was only slightly out of breath when I reached the vacant home.

It was a two-story farmhouse, made of white-painted wood and decaying into black rot. The front door had a large piece of untreated lumber nailed over it; the wraparound porch had planks missing in key spots.

The front entrance was not an option.

I ran around to the back. The back door was up high, as if there had been steps that once led up to it. Indeed, I could see crumbling concrete where the steps had once stood. I jumped up and down a couple of times, but there was no reaching the door. The one solid step disintegrated when I put one foot atop of it. I ran to the side of the house.

Windows and more windows. All boarded shut.

I ran to the other side of the house and stopped.

There was one window open.

I walked up to it slowly, preparing myself for what I knew I would see.

Striped curtains hung just inside of it. The curtains billowed in the afternoon breeze. A porcelain cat sat guard on the sill. My heart raced as the open window beckoned me.

I came out of my frozen state and grabbed three cinderblocks that were scattered on the ground around me.

What am I doing? I didn't stop to answer my own question as I piled the cinderblocks on top of each other and used them to hoist myself up to the wide open window frame. I sat down on the sill and brought my legs inside.

I was in the kitchen of the home.

Everything was dusty. Cobwebs covered the kitchen table and chairs and rodents scurried underneath the floorboards.

What am I doing? What am I doing? Now, I was out of breath, and I knew the lack of oxygen was affecting my common sense. *I need to get out of here!* But then do what?

I looked around the kitchen that had been finished in all white. White walls, white chair, white dishes arranged perfectly in white wooden cupboards with frosted glass doors.

The white made the ink stand out. A large stain of black ink was on the floorboards of the kitchen on the way to the home's formal dining room. I stepped slowly across the floor to study the ink, but my eyes caught notice of something else instead.

The dining room had a large table and a large, unusual contraption next to it. I scrunched up my face, trying to make sense of the tiny metal letters that were spread across the table, the large white paddle-looking things that had black ink smeared all over them. I looked back at the wooden contraption that was about half the size of the dining table it stood next to.

An antique printing press. I remembered the explanation given by the rare bookstore owner about the printing process, and was convinced that was what I was looking at.

And then I saw the book.

A blue bound hardcover lay on the floor. I didn't need to see the title to know what it was.

I would have studied the contents of the dining room some more, but the living room got my attention.

The walls of the front room were covered with crosses, crescents, stars of David, ankhs, every kind of religious symbol the world over. I was staring at the mind of someone in spiritual confusion, and it made sense. The spiritual leader in his life had been deceptive. Spiritual deception was all Jebidiah knew.

I am the Way, the Truth, and the Life: no man cometh unto the Father, but by me.

Jesus' words were simple, plain, and straightforward, and yet most of the world didn't hear them, receive them. How much more difficult would it be to hear if you purposely covered your ears, deliberately closed your heart?

Jebidiah was lost, but didn't want to be found.

I turned back toward the kitchen, but stopped in the dining room to pick up the book.

This was all I'd have to give to authorities. I stared at the title: *The Secrets to Deconstructing Heroism and a Critique of the Philosophical and Theological Views of Moral Evolution in the Finite Universe.* I flipped through the first few pages and immediately understood why the bookstore owner wouldn't want to keep it in his possession. Though presented as a philosophical argument, it was clear that each chapter detailed specific plots of death and destruction. There were more than just plans to bomb an airport. I shivered as I flipped through the pages, seeing the terrifying thoughts and illustrations of a madman, the ruminations of someone preparing to commit unimaginable horrors.

Though his name was nowhere on the cover or the title page, he'd made notes throughout the pages, specifying dates, places, and concrete steps of action, including a detailed outline to carry out a bombing at BWI.

This was his personal copy.

I turned back toward the kitchen and retraced my steps to the open window *to get out of there!*

But a sound caught my ear.

It was slight, but enough to make me turn back around.

Was that door cracked open before? The kitchen pantry door was ajar. I didn't recall it being open. I heard the sound again and wondered if I was just seeing things, imagining things, and mistaking the loud thuds of my heartbeat as a sound outside my body.

But I heard it again.

A muffled whimper.

Was an animal in there? My feet were stuck to the floor as fear suddenly consumed me. I couldn't move. I forgot how to breathe. I couldn't think, scream, or even tremble.

I heard the muffled whimper again, and this time the pantry door slowly creaked open.

Darci.

She sat tied to a chair, her mouth gagged with a rag. She wriggled her head against the back of the chair, her eyes wide, her whimpers louder.

"Darci!" I came back to life and ran to her, first undoing the rag from her mouth.

"Sienna, run!" she yelled immediately.

"What?"

The pantry door slammed shut behind me and the small room fell into darkness, enclosing me and her in its bowels. I could hear my own heavy breathing and Darci's whimpers.

And, I realized in horror, a third set of inhalations, exhalations sounded right over my shoulder.

He was in the closet with us.

Chapter 47

He began to clap, slowly at first, and then into a full round of applause.

I could taste my own sweat and realized that every pore in my face was open and dripping.

"I knew you were a hero." His words cut through the darkness. "I knew that you would look for her, that you would find her, because you care. You care about people and don't seek recognition for yourself. That's why you are Sienna St. James, LCSW-C, CEO and founder of The Whole Soul Center. The hero always comes to save the day."

The flick of a match, the smell of sulfur.

A candle lit the room.

He set it down on a shelf next to a dust-covered white canister labeled FLOUR. "One day people are praising your name. The next day they want to burn you alive at the stake. It's human nature. It's been proven over and over again throughout history. Look what they did to Jamal Abdul. One day he is an American hero. The next a heathen terrorist. And he did nothing wrong."

"You don't . . . you don't have to hurt us." I heard the pointlessness in my own voice. This man had already been responsible for the deaths of many, including his own brother and eight-year-old nephew. We meant nothing to him, nothing more than pawns to prove his twisted points.

"Oh, I wasn't going to hurt anyone." He smiled, his blue eyes twinkling. "You are. Or rather, you have a choice to make, Sienna. First, give me my book."

I looked at the blue volume I'd tucked tightly under my arm.

"Give it to me now, please," he commanded. I had no choice but to pass it to him. That book was the one solid thing I had to prove who he was and what he'd done.

And he knew it.

"Good girl. Now, this is what you need to decide." He pointed to a small device attached to the ropes that bound Darci to her seat. Her whimpers grew louder. "That's a detonator attached to those ropes. It's very sensitive. It's counting down now. It started the moment you came through my window. If it gets to zero, boom." He widened his arms in an exaggerated motion. "If she doesn't get untied in the next, let's see . . ." He checked a watch. "Forty-seven minutes now, she's dead, and everything points to you. I set it up that way, and I'm good at what I do. Before you doubt my skills, consider this: I've committed what some view as a terrorist attack on American soil, and the government doesn't even know I exist. They're not looking for me. They've got a suspect in custody." He turned toward the door, pulled on the handle, then stopped.

"Oh, I said you had a choice." He turned back toward me. "See, I know you'll be tempted to simply get this poor mother of two free from the ropes, but I should point out that the ropes are attached to another detonator." He pointed to several taut strings the width of dental floss that went from the ropes to another unfamiliar device. "If you undo the ropes to free her, that other detonator will go off and trigger a remote I've got set to your cell phone. If you untie her and allow the other detonator to go off, when your phone rings and someone answers, a much bigger, stronger bomb will go off somewhere in this great country of ours that will make the bomb I left at BWI seem like a firecracker in comparison.

"The choice is yours. No matter which option, you still come out the bad guy. The good news is that you get to decide if you stand here and watch this nice lady you know die, or if you both go home and watch the news coverage of the slaughter of hundreds that you directly caused. It's hard doing the right thing, the choices you have to make."

Every limb on my body shook in fear. My mouth opened and I waited to hear what words would come out of it. Despite my temporary paralysis, my voice came out solid and strong. "You didn't have to choose to become this bitter against those who hurt you. Look what your anger has done to you. I know your story, Jebidiah."

"Well, fancy that. You know my story, and I didn't even post it on Facebook. Good luck, Ms. St. James." He opened the door and left. I watched as he hopped out the window and then I ran over to Darci's side.

"Darci, I am so sorry. I'm sorry." I grabbed the box cutter from my pocket, looked at the complicated web of ropes that bound her body.

"Sienna, you have to go!" Darci screamed as I hesitated. "There is no way I could live with myself if I went home and learned about hundreds of people dying. Don't waste any more time on me. Sienna, please! Go! Please! He told me before you came that the other detonator will go off regardless of what you do. You've got to stop it. Don't worry about me."

I stared at the ropes, trying to make sense of her words, the strings, our predicament. My brain had turned to mud and every thought that tried to form in it was stuck.

"Sienna, you have time to get help. I beg of you, go! Now!" Her scream jolted me to action. I ran to the window of the kitchen. Forty-five minutes. I set the timer on Yvette's phone.

Didn't need a signal for that function.

"I'm going to get help. Everything will be okay." I did my best to reassure both her and me.

"Just kiss my babies for me. Tell them Mommy always loves them."

I paused at her words, but only for a second.

Forty-four minutes.

Clouds had gathered during the moments I'd been in the home. Yvette's car was done and dead nearly half a mile away down the driveway. Dry cornstalks, which reached upward of six feet tall, blocked my view of anything beyond that cursed house and the road that led to it. I wasn't even sure which direction Mordecai's service shop was from my vantage point.

And Jebidiah Bennett was somewhere nearby.

I wanted to drop to the ground, curl up in a ball, wait for it all to end; but I knew that wasn't an option. I ran around the house toward the driveway, but immediately turned around.

Jebidiah was in view, fiddling with Yvette's car in the distance. The hood was up. He was going to get it started, I was sure.

The driveway was not an option.

I ran back to the rear of the house. I closed my eyes, tried to imagine standing on top of my car to see where the house was in relation to the trees that bordered Mordecai's service station.

I couldn't remember. My nerves were too shook up.

Forty-three minutes.

"I'm making this harder than I need to and I don't have that kind of time." I ran to the side again and jumped through the window.

"Sienna, you're still here?"

I could hear the panic in Darci's voice.

"I have a plan." Didn't know if it was a good one, but it was the only one I had at the moment.

I ran up the stairs, nearly falling through them on a couple of loose steps. I ran to a bedroom and looked out a window. Jebidiah was in the car, driving. *Is he coming back to the house?* My heart skipped a beat as the car rolled toward us, but then stopped. He hopped out and popped the hood again.

I had to get out of there for both of our sakes, or there would be no hope for either of us or for the people in the zone of his planted bomb.

I ran to another bedroom and looked out the window. Mordecai's green barn showed through a row of trees about two miles away.

Rows and rows of dead cornstalks were between here and there.

I dashed down the steps, jumping over the open holes left from my previous ascent.

"Okay, I'm getting help!"

I dashed out the window and picked up one of the cinderblocks and ran toward the fields. I started out in the direction of the trees, but quickly saw why cornstalks help create good mazes.

Even in their deteriorating states, I was lost within three minutes of entering the fields. I looked up at the sky and saw clear blue. At least the clouds had left, I considered, as challenges worse than rain entered my mind.

What if I'm still in these fields when it gets dark? Are there any wild animals or snakes I need to watch out for? How will I ever get out of here?

I realized that these were the scenarios that had played through Jebidiah's mind. He didn't kill me because he probably thought I'd never make it out of the maze of his family's old cornfields.

Don't panic, don't panic, don't panic. I took a deep breath, slowed down my heart rate.

I'd brought the cinderblock for a reason, I remembered. I set it on the ground and then, fighting through the overgrown stalks, I ran and sprung up from off the top of it. For that quick second of my jump, I saw treetops in the distance. Landing back on my feet hurt as the dried plants smacked me in the face. Some of the leaves and ears crumbled at contact.

Yes, this could work!

And so I ran through the old cornfields, pushing the crumbling stalks out of my way, gagging on the pungent smell; coughing, tripping, jumping, falling, and getting up and going at it all again.

It took me almost twenty minutes to get in view of the line of trees that bordered the property.

That's when I heard the rustling, the footsteps.

I froze.

Nothing.

Maybe it's all in my mind, I decided, looking at the timer. I didn't have time to stand there and figure it out.

"Jesus, help!" I prayed aloud.

It was a deer at the edge of the field, I realized as I stepped into a small clearing. I watched as the deer darted off and I saw green wood peeking through the trees.

The barn.

I ran like I never had before, praying that all would end well.

Mordecai was not in the lot.

Nobody appeared to be around.

I burst into the shabby building and looked around for a phone. There was no sight of either a phone or Mordecai.

"That's right, he's keeping a front of having no technology." My heart sank, but then I remembered the back room. He said he had a satellite dish to keep him connected. A phone, a computer, something to communicate with the world had to be in there. I rammed into the closed door with the cinderblock, nearly knocking the wood door off its hinges.

"Help!" I screamed.

I heard Laz's voice.

"Laz?" I stumbled through the tiny room, trying to make sense of it all. "Laz, are you here?"

A television.

A small flat-screen television sat inside an open dresser drawer, its cord dangling and plugged into what looked like a small portable generator that had about seven other cords pressed into it.

This man had all kinds of fire hazards on his property.

Laz was on TV.

"Authorities have confirmed that they are looking for the owner of a black Honda Accord as new security footage shows the car being driven on the Delaware Turnpike at the time the driver was purporting to be on the West Coast the day of the BWI bombing. Officials have not released any names, but are actively seeking this new person of interest as other key evidence potentially ties this person to the scene of the bombing. This person may now be driving an older model Buick Century and is believed to be somewhere in Pennsylvania. That is all we are being told. This is Laz Tyson reporting live in DC. Back to you in the studio, Ray."

"And that is the coverage we have from one of our local affiliates," a newscaster on CNN somberly stated. A still shot of a black Accord, my car, going through a toll on the turnpike filled the screen, followed by a stock photo of an older-model Buick Century.

My car was seen on the Delaware Turnpike last weekend while I was with Roman in San Diego? So I wasn't crazy. It had been stolen.

When would the nightmare end?

I heard a click behind me and knew that it would not be anytime soon. I turned around slowly. The barrel of a long hunting rifle pointed directly at me and Mordecai Bennett was the triggerman.

"Who are you and why are you here?" he asked as I raised my hands in the air. He looked from the television screen to me and back, the rifle steady though his hands appeared to be shaking.

"Please, don't shoot. I've been tracking down your nephew Jebidiah and he's been behind everything. He's got blond hair, blue eyes, and deep dimples when he smiles. Think about it, how else would I know what he looks like if I haven't seen him myself?"

Mordecai's hands shook even more as I saw the battle in his eyes, him trying to decide if he believed me. I kept talking.

"There's a woman attached to two bombs in that old house in the fields. It's going to go off in twenty minutes and many people will get hurt. Killed. That's what your nephew said. Please call the police and tell them to get here quickly."

He studied me for a few more seconds and then slowly lowered the gun. "I already called the police. They're on their way."

Chapter 48

They caught him in my sister's car. The sputtering vehicle had died once again only three miles down the road, and authorities were specifically looking for a Buick Century.

His book, which served as a detailed outline for carrying out his plots, was in his hands. The bombing at BWI had been a starting point for him, to "wipe the slate clean of any and all of his past existence." The bomb he planned to detonate from my phone would have wiped out the community where his sister-in-law's parents lived. A plan for Mordecai's demise was in a plot detailed in chapter five. Every plan he had not only caused death and destruction to many random, innocent people, but each plot included a regular haunt of a member of the church that had excommunicated him.

Nobody would have seen the connection, and, after all was said and done, he would have lived life truly as a nonexistent because the people who knew he'd even been born would be buried in their graves, all around the country.

His father's remains would later be dug up from the cornfields that surrounded the old house. A fractured skull pointed to homicide and Jebidiah Bennett was the only suspect in the case.

"A lot of vicious crimes are a result of relationships gone wrong. The pain and bitterness that can result can lead to extremes. Granted, most of the time, those extremes don't involve taking another's life, but extremes in mood, like depression, extremes in emotions, like rage, can be just as debilitating emotionally as a physical loss. If you are dealing with deep-seated pain and bitterness from broken relationships, seek help, be whole. Get your freedom."

I looked a little chunky on TV, I decided as I again watched my interview on CNN. I'd been exhausted and I looked rough in my sweats and running shoes, remnants of rotting cornstalks still in my hair. SOCIAL WORKER SIENNA ST. JAMES, THE THERAPIST WHO TRACKED DOWN THE TERRORIST was the caption underneath. The young woman who'd interviewed me live in front of the abandoned farm house in Pennsylvania was from a local station and was obviously new at covering breaking national news. She didn't have the poise or presence that Laz would have had during such an important interview with the woman who'd led authorities to the correct perpetrator of a terrorist attack.

That I was that woman still felt surreal.

But it felt good.

I'd trusted my instincts, I'd dug for the truth, and I didn't let fear hold me back, even when it justifiably should have.

Once the authorities arrived following Mordecai's call, the end of the nightmare came quickly. Special ATF agents were able to remotely disable the detonator tied to my cell phone number, allowing Darci to be freed from the ropes just in the nick of time.

There were no more casualties and Jamal Abdul was free to go home to his wife and two kids.

"Do you, um, like consider yourself, um, to be, like, a hero, Ms. St. James?"

It had been painful watching the news reporter struggle during our live interview. Seeing how challenging it was for her to stay confident under a national spotlight gave me a new appreciation for Laz's journalistic ability, and, well, his cockiness. He deserved to have that new job in Atlanta. That station was getting a natural anchorman.

"No. I don't consider myself a hero. I consider myself to be someone who tries really, really hard to do the right thing, whenever I can, however I can do it." I'd looked directly into the camera as I continued. "Heroes are people who are superhuman, who stand out for having supernatural strength and powers. I'm just a mom, a sister, a daughter, a friend who has flaws and failures and occasional triumphs. Any strength or power I have has come from learning the supremacy of love, the necessity of courage, the freedom in forgiveness, and the joy and clarity that comes from surrendering to the God of it all. No, I'm not a hero. I'm a fighter with more victories than defeats because the people and challenges in my life have developed my muscles and fine-tuned my aim."

The video ended. I turned off the CNN app that had played it and considered turning off my phone completely; but a text message was waiting.

Roman.

So proud of you, Mom. You're the strongest woman I know. The police know about RiChard. Ms. Mbali reported him for fraud and found out there are warrants out for him under different names all over the world. Croix and I are working together to make sure justice is served. Things aren't perfect, but we will all be okay. Thank you for finding my father. He's not the man I expected him to be, but I will always be the man you raised me to be.

I stared at his message, reread it several times, thought about that picture of him at his fifth-grade graduation. That light blue seersucker shorts suit and bowtie.

I smiled.

I love you and I'm proud of you, I texted back. Tell Mbali to be on the lookout for a package, a belated birthday present for her daughter, your sister. Yes, we will all be okay.

I pressed send and walked back into the building where I had been waiting for nearly thirty minutes. I found an empty bench and sat down.

"There you are!"

I heard his voice and smelled his cologne, even before I saw his face.

Laz.

"I'm so sorry I'm late, Sienna. I had a last-minute change to a story I'm working on and it threw my whole day off. It's chilly for April, isn't it?" He blew into his hands, wiped his nose with a tissue. Barely looked my way.

We had agreed to meet at the Walters Art Museum, in downtown Baltimore. It was late Sunday afternoon, the first day of a new week, a new chance, a new everything.

I still had on my church clothes from the morning. My stomach was full from my mother's Sunday dinner. Chicken and dumplings.

"Yeah, I'm glad I got your message when I did." He sat down next to me. "I drove straight from taping in DC to try to get here on time." Our bench faced a painting in shades of yellow and orange. SUNBURST, the sign underneath read. I thought of my own artwork, my portraits and collages. Maybe I could find a local gallery willing to display my work.

A passing thought.

"Sienna, you did good, girl. Your interview. Your determination. I'm in awe of the woman you are." He glanced over at me. I still hadn't said anything. "Look, Sienna, I know we have a lot to talk about, but I need you to know that I have done nothing but support you, on a personal level, throughout this whole ordeal. Professionally, I have to do my job. I am required to report stories as they are given to me, and it is my duty to protect my reputation to ensure the integrity of my news reports. I owe it to the station. My actions and on-air reports over the past couple of days were not an attack against you. I'm sure you know that. I have a tough career, Sienna. I do what I have to do."

"I know, Laz. I can respect that, just like I'm sure you will respect that I have to do what I have to do right now." Our eyes met. I took out the small gift bag I'd hidden in my purse and passed it to him. "A going-away present for you."

He didn't say anything as he opened it. "You're . . . giving me the lion's head ring." He held up the massive jewel. Its rare gems danced in the sunlight of the open foyer.

"You told me I could do what I wanted with the jewels on this ring, that I could take it and reset it as a way of starting over." I shook my head. "I don't want to reset it. I want it to stay as is. And I want to give it to you."

"This thing is worth—"

"Nothing to me."

Laz raised his eyebrow, cocked his head to one side.

"RiChard was a complete fraud. That wasn't even his name. Our marriage was a sham. I don't even need a divorce. I believe I can just get our vows annulled as we married under false conditions, plus he had multiple wives before and after me."

"Your marriage was a sham, huh?"

"Yes, just like a marriage between us would be."

"Ouch." Laz looked away, blew out a loud sigh. "That was a punch below the belt, Ms. Fighter."

"But it's true and you know it. You don't need a wife. You need a worshipper and I can't worship you the way you want me to."

A large mass of people came in, looked like a tour group from another country. The foyer became an echo-filled cavern of foreign dialects, loud footsteps, and laughter. The commotion continued until the group filed into another corridor and then silence filled our space.

"I . . . I can't keep the ring though, Sienna." Laz's voice was barely over a whisper.

"Laz, you told me that you were offering me a chance to take my past, acknowledge it, and start over, and make it work for me in a layout of my choice. That's what you've done. You really have offered me that, and that's what I'm doing. I'm moving on. I'm leaving my past behind me. I'm leaving it with you. Take good care of it." I smiled.

He was quiet for a moment; then he nodded slowly. He smiled back at me, the ring dancing on the tips of his fingers.

"It was going to be good for us in Atlanta, Ms. St. James. Dinner parties. Private receptions. I was going to get you a white Benz to match mine for your wedding present."

"No, it will be good for *you* in Atlanta. I'm a social worker. Here, in Baltimore. I'm a social worker and a whole woman."

"That you are, Sienna, that you are." He bit his lip, nodded again. "Well, you take care of yourself, and if you go chasing down any more terrorists or come across any other newsworthy stories, you got my number." We both chuckled.

He grabbed my hand and I squeezed his.

Then we both let go.

***

The air in Downtown Baltimore *was* chilly for April, I realized as I left the Walters, but the sun was out and not one cloud hung in the sky. For the first time in, hmmm, my entire adult life, maybe, I felt completely whole, completely free, and completely loved and loveable.

With nowhere to go, no plans for the rest of the day, and no fear of the future, I walked all the way down Charles Street to Fayette then Light Street and ended at the Inner Harbor. Colorful boats filled the murky waters and a crowd stood watching a street performer juggle flaming torches while riding a unicycle. I laughed along at his cheesy jokes and then I entered a nearby bakery on Pratt Street.

All that walking and thinking and feeling so free, I believed I'd earned a brownie or two.

It was a new shop and a group of high school-aged boys and girls who were supposed to be working were instead standing around giggling, joking, and playing. Nice that someone had given them a chance. I shook my head and chuckled as they suddenly sobered and ran to their positions around the small, bright dining area that smelled of chocolate, berries, and lemonade.

"The boss is back," they whispered among themselves, quickly grabbing gloves and aprons, scrubbing tables and straightening chairs.

The door to the kitchen swung open and the owner stepped out. Our eyes met as he set out a tray of fresh-from-the-oven chocolate chip cookies.

Leon.

Reading Group Guide

1. Throughout the novel, Sienna struggles with whether to trust her instincts. What exactly are instincts or gut feelings? What purpose do they serve? Should we trust them? Why or why not?

2. Sienna unexpectedly receives a marriage proposal from Laz. Do you think she should marry him? Why or why not? How does her relationship with Laz compare to the initial relationship she had with RiChard? How does it compare to her previous relationship with Leon? What factors should Sienna consider regarding marriage? What issues, if any, would need to be addressed with Laz before a potential wedding, and how?

3. The man Sienna suspects is a terrorist challenges her to examine what she believes. When looking at the basic elements of her faith, Sienna makes this observation: "Whatever you believe about the origin of life will determine what you believe about life's value and purpose." What does this mean? What are your thoughts about her assertion?

4. Laz questions Sienna's choice to become a social worker. What are your thoughts about his belief that her career choice was somehow related to RiChard? Do you think she is in the right occupation? Why or why not? What factors have influenced your own career choices?

5. Who is your favorite character and why? What about the character's life, words, or actions speak to you?

6. Consider the character of Sienna St. James. What are her motivations? Her intentions? What are her successes and her failures? In what ways does she grow throughout the novel? What areas of her life need further growth?

7. How would you describe Sienna's relationship with the Lord? What about her sister Yvette's walk with Him? Can you relate to where either one of them are spiritually, and if so, how?

8. Sienna acknowledges that there are multigenerational themes of stubbornness and problems with communication and relationships in her family. Reflect on your own family tree and all of its members. Do you notice any common themes, concerns, or issues across the generations? If so, how can these themes best be addressed and by whom?

9. Sienna's office assistant, Darci, a single mom of twins, appears to take great interest in the man who shows up at the office. What advice would you offer Darci about relationships and men, especially as a single mother?

10. Ava Diggs, Sienna's mentor, introduces the idea of "mirror moments." She says, "We go about our days minding our business, then something happens to make us stop and stare and see who we really are, what we really look like, what we're really made of. Mirror moments tend to be rare, but life changing. Once we see ourselves for who we are, we have to make decisions on what to do with the image we see. Fix it, smile at it. Carry on with or without changes. We are forced to take ownership of the person we're facing in the mirror." What are your thoughts about mirror moments? Have you had such moments in your life? What were the outcomes?

Author Bio

Leslie J. Sherrod, the recipient of the SORMAG Readers Choice Award for Christian Author of the Year (2012), has a master's in social work and has worked as a therapist, just like her current protagonist, Sienna St. James. Her novels, *Without Faith, Losing Hope, Secret Place,* and *Like Sheep Gone Astray* have been featured in Baltimore's Enoch Pratt Free Library *Writers LIVE!* series, as well as local CBS and NBC affiliates, and on AOL's Black Voices. She has received a starred review from Booklist and is a contributor to the bestselling *A Cup of Comfort* devotional series. Leslie lives in Baltimore, Maryland with her husband and three children.

What We Believe:

—We believe that Jesus is the Christ, Son of the Living God.

—We believe the Bible is the true, living Word of God.

—We believe all Urban Christian authors should use their God-given writing abilities to honor God and share the message of the written word God has given to each of them uniquely.

—We believe in supporting Urban Christian authors in their literary endeavors by reading, purchasing, and sharing their titles with our online community.

—We believe that in everything we do in our literary arena should be done in a manner that will lead to God being glorified and honored.

We look forward to the online fellowship with you. Please visit us often at www.uchisglorybookclub.net.

Many Blessing to You!

Sheila E. Lipsey,
President, UC His Glory Book Club

UC HIS GLORY BOOK CLUB!

www.uchisglorybookclub.net

UC His Glory Book Club is the Spirit-inspired brain-child of JoyLynn Ross, Author and Acquisitions Editor of Urban Christian, and Kendra Norman-Bellamy, Author for Urban Christian. This is an online book club that hosts authors of Urban Christian. We welcome as members all men and women who have a passion for reading Christian-based fiction.

UC His Glory Book Club pledges our commitment to provide support, positive feedback, encouragement, and a forum whereby members can openly discuss and review the literary works of Urban Christian authors.

There is no membership fee associated with UC His Glory Book Club; however, we do ask that you support the authors through purchasing, encouraging, providing book reviews, and of course, your prayers. We also ask that you respect our beliefs and follow the guidelines of the book club. We hope to receive your valuable input, opinions, and reviews that build up, rather than tear down our authors.